Devil-Devil

Graeme Kent

Copyright © 2011 by Graeme Kent

All rights reserved.

Published in Great Britain in 2011 by Robinson,
an imprint of Constable & Robinson Ltd.

Published in the United States in 2011 by
Soho Press, Inc.
853 Broadway
New York, NY 10003

Library of Congress Cataloging-in-Publication Data

Kent, Graeme.
Devil-devil / Graeme Kent.
p. cm.
HC ISBN 978-1-56947-873-8
PB ISBN 978-1-61695-060-6
eISBN 978-1-56947-874-5
1. Murder—Investigation—Fiction. 2. Solomon Islands—Fiction.
I. Title.
PR6061.E635D48 2011
823'.914—dc22
2010032520

Printed in the United States of America

10 9 8 7 6 5 4 3 2 1

ACKNOWLEDGEMENTS

I would like to thank Peter Noel Orudiana and Timothy Lopiga of the artificial island of Asimae in the Lau Lagoon of Malaita, guides and friends. I owe more than I can possibly say to my dedicated agent Isabel White, for her indomitable inspiration and determination. Thanks are also due to the charming and gifted editorial team at Constable & Robinson: Krystyna Green, Jo Stansall and Imogen Olsen, plus the sales, marketing and publicity departments, and all the team. I also owe a considerable debt of gratitude to everyone at my US publishers, SohoConstable, who have turned long-distance encouragement almost into an art form!

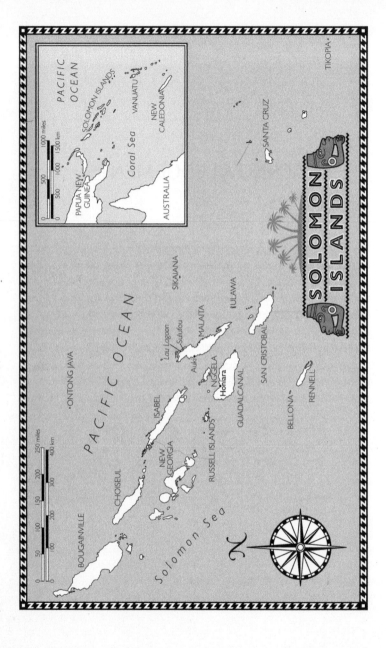

1

THE GLORY SHELL

Sister Conchita clung to the sides of the small dugout canoe as the waves pounded over the frail vessel, soaking its two occupants. In front of her the Malaitan scooped his paddle into the water, trying to keep the craft on an even balance. Sister Conchita could see the coastal village a hundred yards away. The beach was crowded with islanders. She wondered whether it had been worth the perilous sea journey just to see the shark-calling ceremony when all she wanted was a shower and a meal. Of course it was, she told herself severely. If she intended serving God in the Solomons then she had to get to know everything about the islands.

The half-naked islander in front of her suddenly gave a scream of terror. Turning, he thrust the paddle into the sister's hands and dived over the side of the canoe, disappearing into the frothing white foam. Sister Conchita sat rigid with apprehension, the pitted wooden blade clutched loosely in her hands. Bereft of the islander's control, the canoe started pitching and swinging wildly.

For a moment all that Sister Conchita wanted to do was to cower helplessly in the bucking wooden frame. Then her customary resourcefulness took over. Snap out of it, she thought grimly. You got yourself into this hole, better get out of it the same way, girl. Muttering a fervent prayer, she tightened her grip on the paddle and thrust it with all her force into the water.

For the next five minutes the wiry young sister fought the sea. The momentum of the current was sending her at breakneck speed in the direction of the beach and the watching islanders, but the waves were crashing over the canoe at an angle, buffeting it from side to side. Several times the entire tree shell was submerged beneath the surface, but on each occasion it surfaced sufficiently for the sodden nun, coughing and gasping, to resume her paddling.

Doggedly she kept the prow of the canoe pointing at the beach. After an apparent eternity of choking, muscle-aching effort the shore actually seemed to be getting closer. One final shock of a wave descended on the canoe and hurled it sprawling up into the shallows off the beach.

Half a dozen brawny, cheering Melanesian men in skimpy loincloths splashed into the water and laughingly hauled the canoe up on to the sand. The crowd of assembled islanders broke into delighted applause. Dazedly Sister Conchita stood up and limped out of the beached craft.

Gradually her vision cleared. She blinked hard. Standing in front of her, joining vigorously in the acclamation among the large crowd, was the islander who had discarded his paddle and left her to fight the sea alone. Struggling for breath, Sister Conchita fought for the words adequately to express her opinion of him.

'They've just been pulling your leg, sister,' drawled a contemptuous voice from behind her. 'They wanted to see what you were made of. You didn't do so bad. Most sheilas just stay in the boat screaming bloody murder.'

The nun turned to see John Deacon, unshaven and clad in khaki shorts and shirt, regarding her coolly from the edge of the crowd.

'Mr Deacon,' said Sister Conchita, trying to keep her balance. Deacon was an Australian who managed a local copra plantation. She did not like him, suspecting him of ill-treating his labourers. However, she always tried, she suspected in vain, to conceal her feelings.

'Local custom,' explained the stocky, broad-shouldered Australian laconically. 'Any stranger approaching the beach, the guide jumps overboard. Actually the current is bound to bring the canoe up on to the shore, but if you don't know that, it can be a mite disconcerting.'

'You can say that again,' said Sister Conchita.

'At least you had a go,' acknowledged the plantation manager. 'The natives like guts.'

'Have you come for the ceremony?' asked Sister Conchita politely, trying to change the subject. She did not wish to be reminded too much of her undignified arrival.

The Australian snorted with derision. 'I don't believe in superstition,' he told her. His eyes scanned her tattered, once-white habit. '*Any* superstition,' he told her with emphasis. 'I'm here to pick up a cargo.'

Suddenly Deacon was swept aside by a phalanx of island women, offering the nun rough blankets with which to dry herself, together with a husk of coconut milk. In a chattering group they conducted her to a site at the water's edge and waited eagerly with her. An artificial lagoon about twenty yards in diameter had been constructed there with piles of stones marking its edges, and an aperture on the seaward side to allow fish to swim in and out.

As the nun watched, an old man in tattered shorts and singlet emerged from one of the huts and walked down towards the stones. A profusion of ancient bone charms rattled on a string around his neck. A naked small boy of about ten years of age accompanied him.

'*Fa'atabu*,' muttered an awed woman. She translated for the nun's benefit. 'This one is the shark-caller,' she said, indicating the old man.

Four islanders splashed out into the shallow waters of the shark area. They were carrying large flat stones, which they banged together under the water. Simultaneously the shark-caller started chanting in a high, tuneless voice. The crowd, which had swollen in numbers to several hundred, looked on in expectant silence.

For several minutes nothing happened. Then a reverent murmur went round the crowd. The fins of half a dozen sharks could be seen entering the enclosure.

The men, still clashing the stones together, fled from the water. Women picked up a few baskets of raw pork and placed them at the water's edge before withdrawing hastily. Completely unperturbed, the boy hoisted one of the baskets up on to his shoulder and staggered out with it into the water, to a depth of several feet. To the accompaniment of screams and shouts from the crowd on the shore the sharks began to swim steadily towards the boy.

Sister Conchita found herself clenching her fists at the sight. The boy stood still for a moment. Then he reached up into the basket and started feeding the sharks lumps of raw meat, dropping these into the water just in front of him. As the sharks approached, accepting the food, the boy began to caress them. Throughout, the shark-caller continued his keening.

Sister Conchita looked on, fascinated by the sight. Out of the corner of her eye she became aware of Deacon and two Melanesians carrying a bulky sack along the ramshackle wooden jetty protruding into the sea. A dinghy was tethered there, bobbing in the water. Farther out to sea she could see the Australian's trading vessel at anchor.

The sister did not want to leave the ceremony but she thought that it would only be courteous to say goodbye to the brusque plantation manager. Reluctantly she slipped through the crowd and made her way along the wharf. Deacon and his helpers were trying to load the sack into the heaving dinghy. The islanders were struggling to lower the sack to Deacon, waiting impatiently below. As she approached, one of the Melanesians dropped his end of the bulging sack. It burst open, disgorging a cascade of seashells.

Sister Conchita increased her pace to see if she could help. Some of the shells rolled across the wooden platform and nestled at her feet. The nun stooped to pick them up.

'Leave that; we'll sort it!' ordered Deacon, scrambling up from the dinghy.

Sister Conchita ignored him. She had cradled three shells in her hands and was examining them with increasing excitement and anxiety. She would have recognized them anywhere. Before she had left Chicago she had attended a museum display of South Pacific seashells. The ones in her hands were a delicate golden brown in colour, with a round base tapering exquisitely to a point.

'Are you deaf? I said I'll take those!' shouted Deacon, lumbering towards her.

Sister Conchita was intimidated by the Australian's looming presence but stubbornly she clutched the beautiful shells to her.

'I think not, Mr Deacon,' she said, refusing to take a pace backwards, although every instinct warned her to get away from the plantation manager. 'I believe these are glory shells,' she went on. 'You have no right to be taking them off the island. They're a part of the culture of the Solomons.'

The *Conus gloriamaris*, or Glory of the Seas, was the rarest of all seashells to be found in the Solomons, sought after in vain by almost every islander. It fetched over a thousand dollars among collectors. Its export was expressly forbidden by the government.

'Mind your own business!' grunted Deacon. 'Or . . .'

'Or what, Mr Deacon?' asked Sister Conchita, still standing her ground, although she was conscious that she was trembling. It had been a long time since she had been exposed to an example of such apparently uncontrollable wrath. With relief she realized that a group of village men, attracted by the altercation between the two expatriates, had abandoned the shark-calling ceremony temporarily and were hurrying along the jetty behind them.

'This is a Catholic village, Mr Deacon,' said Sister Conchita clearly. 'I don't think its inhabitants would take kindly to seeing a sister being manhandled.'

Deacon looked at the dozen or so men getting closer. With an impressive display of strength he hurled the sack into the bottom of the dinghy, scattering its consignment of shells.

'I won't forget this,' he promised vehemently, glaring up as he cast off. 'I'm not having some bit of a kid who hasn't been in the islands five minutes telling me what to do.'

'And another thing,' the nun called after him. 'Just in case you have any more illegal shells in that sack, I shall be asking the Customs Department in the capital to examine it when you get there.'

Deacon was already rowing the dinghy with vicious strokes back towards his small trading vessel. Sister Conchita turned with a grateful and rather tremulous smile to face the approaching islanders. She realized that, as usual, she had just insisted on having the last word. It was a failing she was well aware of and would have to take to confession yet again.

2

THE GHOST-CALLER

Sergeant Kella sat on the earthen floor of the *beu*, the men's meeting-house, patiently waiting for the ghost-caller to bring back the dead.

Most of the men of the coastal village had managed to cram into the long, thatched building with its smoke-blackened bamboo walls. According to custom, a small wooden gong had been struck with a thick length of creeper to summon the assembly.

Kella could hear the women and children of the remote saltwater hamlet talking excitedly outside as they waited for news of the proceedings to filter from the hut. Most of the men were eyeing him with suspicion as he sat impassively among them. A touring police officer would not normally have been allowed inside the hut, but he was present in his capacity of *aofia*, the hereditary peacemaker of the Lau people.

Kella hoped that Chief Superintendent Grice would not hear about the detour he had made to this village. Back in Honiara his superior had been explicit in his instructions.

'You're going to Malaita for one reason only,' he had told Kella. 'You are to make inquiries about Dr Mallory, nothing else. After your last little episode over there, I said I'd never send you back. But you speak the language. I take it that you can ask a few simple questions and come back with the answers?'

Hurriedly Kella had assured the police chief that he could. After six months sitting behind a desk in the capital he would have promised almost anything to get out on tour again. Now here he was, only two days into his journey, and already he was disobeying instructions.

The village headman entered the hut. He was a plump, self-satisfied man clad in new shorts and singlet and exuding the confidence of someone who owned good land. With a few exceptions, the Lau area chieftains were not hereditary but were chosen for their conspicuous distribution of wealth. This man would have achieved his position for the number of feasts he had hosted, not for any fighting prowess.

The headman cleared his throat. 'We are here to find out who killed Senda Iabuli,' he muttered grudgingly in the local dialect. Plainly he had not wanted the meeting to take place. 'To do this we have sent for the ghost-caller, the *ngwane inala*. He will tell us who the killer is.'

The ghost-caller was sitting with his back to the wall, facing the other men. He was in his sixties, small and emaciated, his meagre frame racked periodically with hacking coughs. He wore only a brief thong about his loins. His face and body were criss-crossed with gaudy and intricate patterns painted on with the magic lime. Barely visible beneath the decorations on his face were a number of vertical scars, slashed there long ago when he first set out to learn the calling incantations. Laid out on the ground before him were two stringed hunting bows, some leaves of the red dracaena plant, a few coconuts and a carved wooden bowl containing trochus shells.

According to the gossip Kella had managed to pick up since his arrival at the village, the ghost-caller had been summoned to investigate the sudden death of Senda Iabuli, a perfectly undistinguished villager, an elderly widower with no surviving children.

Iabuli's first and only claim to notoriety had occurred a month before. Early one morning he had been on his way to work in his garden on the side of a mountain just outside the village. He had, as always, crossed a ravine by way of a narrow swing bridge consisting of creepers and logs lashed together. As he had made his precarious way to the far side, a sudden gust of wind had caught the old man and sent him toppling helplessly hundreds of feet down into the valley below.

The event had been witnessed by a group of men hunting wild pigs. It had taken them most of the morning to descend the tree-covered slope into the ravine to recover the body of the old villager. To their amazement, they had discovered Senda Iabuli alive and well, if considerably shaken and winded. His fall had been broken by the leafy tops of the trees, from which he had slithered down to end up dazed and bruised on a pile of moss at the foot of a casuarina tree.

The old man had been helped back to the village, confused and shaking, but apparently none the worse for his experience. For several weeks he had resumed his customary innocuous existence. Then one morning he had been found dead in his hut.

Normally that would have been the end of the matter, but for some unfathomable reason a relative of Iabuli had demanded an investigation into his death. This was the family's right by custom and had caused the headman to send for the ghost-caller. Kella had heard of the events and had invited himself to the ceremony.

The ghost-caller picked up one of the red dracaena leaves and split it down the middle. He wrapped one half around the other to strengthen it. Then he placed the reinforced leaf in the carved bowl. Next, he shuffled the two stringed bows on the ground before him. Each was a little less than full size, fashioned of palm wood, with strings of twisted red and yellow vegetable fibres. The bows represented two Lau ghosts, the spirits of men who had once walked the earth. The ghost-caller threw back his head and started to chant an incantation in a high-pitched, keening tone.

The calling went on for more than an hour as the caller begged the right spirits to enter the *beu*. They had a long way to come, for the souls of the dead resided on the island of Momulo, far away. Suddenly the chanting ended. The caller stiffened, his back rigid and his eyes closed.

'The ghosts ride,' murmured the headman, nodding sagely, as if these events were all his doing. Some of the elders nodded obsequious agreement. The custom man before them was now possessed of the spirits of the departed *agalo*.

'Who comes?' demanded the ghost-caller. Spasms racked his body. Voices began to emerge from his mouth. There were two of them, speaking in different pitches. Kella had been expecting them both. The ghost-caller had taken no chances, adhering to the main ancestral ghosts of the region, ones everyone present would know. He had selected Takilu, the war god, and Sina Kwao of the red hair, who had once killed the giant lizard which had threatened to devour all of Malaita. Only a ghost-caller was allowed to address these spirits by their names.

As each ghost spoke, the relevant bow quivered on the ground. The caller was good, thought Kella. The police sergeant had been watching the emaciated man closely, and was sure that there were no threads connecting the weapons to the ghost-caller, which could be twitched surreptitiously to make them flutter. He could only assume that the custom man was drumming on the ground with his iron-hard heels to set up the necessary vibrations.

'Oh Takilu, can you tell us anything about the passing of Senda Iabuli?' quavered the ghost-caller.

Neither bow moved. An audible sigh of relief went round the room. If the war god was not involved it probably meant that the old man's death had been due to natural causes. Now there should be no internecine blood quarrels to divide the village.

'Sina Kwao,' resumed the ghost-caller in reverent tones, 'can you tell us what happened to Senda Iabuli?'

The bow on the right quivered fiercely. A gasp went up from the assembled villagers. The ghost-caller pounced.

'How did Senda Iabuli die?' he asked. 'Was he killed by a devil?'

The bow trembled once, a sign of assent. Awed and frightened cries filled the men's house. Kella relaxed. All in all it was quite a good performance, he thought. The headman must have briefed the ghost-caller cleverly. By attributing the death to a devil, the relatives of Senda Iabuli would be mollified.

But the ghost-caller had not finished. His weary eyes flicked lizard-like across the room, catching and engaging Kella's gaze. It was almost as if the old man could read the policeman's thoughts.

'Did the devil-devil use a man to carry out the murder?' he asked.

The bow flipped again briefly in assent and was still. Throughout the hut the men rose angrily to their feet, demanding to know who was the killer among them. The ghost-caller shuddered and slumped forward, his job done.

Kella hurried out of the *beu*. The ghost-caller most certainly had not kept to any pre-ordained script. As a result, there could now be a lot of trouble in the village, perhaps even the start of a blood feud.

3

THE DEATH CURSE

Outside in the noon sun, the villagers gathered in animated and apprehensive knots, discussing what they had seen and heard inside the *beu*. Kella saw the headman complaining to the ghost-caller. He drifted over casually, in time to hear the headman refuse to pay the remainder of the custom man's fee.

'You've stirred up too much trouble,' howled the headman. 'You'll get no more from me.'

'I passed on the answers of the gods,' replied the other man stubbornly. 'A devil used a man from this village to kill Senda Iabuli.' He could not possibly have heard Kella approaching, but still turned to face the sergeant. 'It is not my fault if there are unbelievers present,' he said pointedly.

Kella realized that all eyes were on him. Get out fast, he told himself. You caused enough trouble on Malaita last time. Your record won't stand another court of inquiry. All the same he knew that he was not going to walk away while the village was still in such turmoil.

'*Aarai*,' he said quietly, using the Lau term of respect to the headman, 'you must pay this man what he is owed.'

'Who says that I must?' asked the headman.

'I do,' said Kella. 'I speak as the government's policeman.'

A large crowd was gathering to see how the headman would

deal with this threat to his authority. Several burly islanders began to shoulder their way through the throng towards the police sergeant. Kella knew that these were the headman's bodyguards, paid monthly in valuable porpoise teeth and cans of beer to do his bidding about the village.

'And', the police sergeant added, raising his voice, 'I speak as your *aofia*, directed by the spirits to keep the peace. If you shame the ghost-caller I shall call upon the shades for payback.'

Kella surveyed the crowd impassively. There were enough level-headed men and women present to accept what he said. Even the bodyguards looked uneasy and stopped pressing forward. The voice of tradition would often be heard when the white man's law was ignored. With the antenna of a politician, the headman sensed the change in the atmosphere and responded swiftly but with ill grace.

'I shall pay the fathom of shell money I promised the ghost-caller,' he growled. 'I am a true chief of my people and always keep my word. That is known among all the islands.'

The ghost-caller turned, satisfied, and walked towards the trees surrounding the village. Kella accompanied him, in case the bodyguards experienced a change of heart.

'You shamed me in your thoughts, *aofia*,' said the ghost-caller quietly as they walked. 'You believed I had been bought by the headman and would only give him news he wanted to hear.'

'I was wrong,' acknowledged Kella. 'I have been too long away overseas. Sometimes I lose touch with the old ways.'

The ghost-caller stopped and turned to face the sergeant. The old man's red-rimmed eyes searched Kella's face, as if looking for something. For a moment Kella sensed that the old man was going to confess something to him, but the moment passed.

'You use the ghosts but do not always believe in them,' said the ghost-caller. 'You tread a dangerous path, peacemaker. Dangerous for others, and for yourself.'

'Sometimes I don't know what to believe,' admitted Kella. 'As for my path, others chose it for me when I was a child and I must follow it for as long as I can.'

The ghost-caller sighed. 'Senda Iabuli and I were young together many years ago,' he said unexpectedly. 'We were friends. Like you, we did not always follow the appointed path. We did good things, but we also did bad things together. Now he is dead, and soon I shall follow him.' The ghost-caller walked through the outer fringe of trees without looking back at the policeman. 'Find your path, *aofia*,' he called. *'O lelea vasi amiua.* Go your way, as it has been appointed.'

The villagers were still milling restlessly as Kella walked back to the huts.

'Who is the closest living relative of Senda Iabuli?' he asked, determined to sort the matter as quickly as possible.

'I am,' said a youth, coming forward warily. 'I am Peter Oro. Senda Iabuli was my grandfather.'

Unlike the other men in their faded aprons or *lap-laps* he was wearing the black shorts and white shirt of the local mission senior primary school. Still to be in full-time education at the advanced age of sixteen meant that he was one of the potential high-flyers identified by the expatriate missionary priests to be processed quickly through the system. Soon he would be sent to King George VI Secondary School in the capital and then dispatched to Britain or Australia to gain a degree, and return to work in the government service in the long run-up to independence.

That meant that already the boy would be torn between the fading memories of his custom upbringing and the new and strange Western influences to which he was being subjected. Kella, who had been there, did not envy the youth what lay in store for him. He guessed that it was Peter Oro who had demanded the ghost-caller's investigation into the death of his grandfather. Kella wondered why.

'Show me your grandfather's house,' was all he said.

Peter Oro indicated one of the huts. It was fashioned like all the others in the village. The roof and walls consisted of layers of pandanus leaves sewn on to bamboo frames with vines. A series of bamboo uprights, each of exactly the same size, were bound to a betel-nut framework. Thatch eighteen inches thick on the roof was designed to keep out the heat of the day.

Peter accompanied the police sergeant to the door and started to follow him in. Kella raised a restraining hand. 'If you don't mind,' he said in English, 'I'd rather look round by myself.'

'What are you going to do about my grandfather's death?' demanded the youth hotly. 'You heard the ghost-caller say that he was murdered.'

'Ghosts cannot be produced as witnesses in the white man's court. But I shall investigate the matter, never fear!'

It was cool and dark in the single room of the hut. In the centre of the living space were a few blackened stones used as a fireplace on the earthen floor. Other fire-stones were scattered across the floor. This indoor fire would only be used for cooking in bad weather, but normally would be kept alight with damp wood all the year round to repel mosquitoes. A bamboo bunk had been built into one of the walls.

The dead man's personal belongings were kept in the thatching of the roof. Systematically Kella took down the spear, bow and arrows, wicker fish basket and paddle which were stored there. As far as he could see, there was nothing untoward about them.

He turned his attention to the rest of the room. There was a sleeping mat in a corner. Presumably it belonged to Peter Oro. Only the dead man's closest relative would be allowed to sleep in the hut during the six-month mourning period.

The hut was strangely untidy. As the home of a man whose spirit had not yet made the final journey to the far island, it

15

should have been maintained in an immaculate condition by Iabuli's next-of-kin. Kella walked round the interior of the hut several times. He frowned. This was not the neglect of a careless schoolboy. Peter Oro had been searching for something.

Kella went outside. The waiting youth regarded him with overt hostility. The villagers stopped milling around, and watched the police sergeant. Kella ignored them. Slowly he walked round the perimeter of the hut. On the far side he found what he had been looking for.

A pile of large round stones was balanced against one of the betel-nut supports. To a casual observer the cache was just a support used to keep a piece of timber in place. Kella was relying on Peter Oro's ignorance of local customs. It would have been some years since the youth had lived in the village. He might have no idea of the significance of the heap of round stones.

There was a horrified murmur from the villagers as Kella dislodged the pile with his foot and started separating the rocks from one another with his hands. They were comfort stones, used by the old and afflicted. Specially selected for their size and smoothness, they would be heated over a fire until they were too hot to touch, and then pushed with a log until they were under the bunk. The heat radiating through the slats would ease most aches and pains, of which Senda Iabuli assuredly would have had plenty since his fall. By also providing heat to drive out sick spirits, the stones were regarded as holy and must not be touched by outsiders.

Sullen growls of 'White blackfella!' emanated from the horrified crowd as Kella discarded the sacred stones. It was a phrase to which he had long grown accustomed and it did not deter him.

Nobody else in the village would have dared to approach the pile, while Peter Oro probably would not have remembered their significance. If Senda Iabuli, or anybody else, had wanted to conceal something during the villager's last days, this would be as good a place as any in which to do it.

Kella found what he had been looking for towards the bottom of the pile. A hollowed-out bamboo container was secreted behind the largest boulder. Kella removed the wooden top and shook out the contents. He held up the package for all in the village to see. Then he unwrapped the large celeus leaf. Inside was a piece of dried ginger sprinkled with lime.

Kella saw the headman gaping at his discovery. 'You know what this is?' the police sergeant asked.

The headman nodded, all traces of pride wiped away. 'The death curse,' he whispered.

Kella nodded. 'Now we can be sure that someone intended to kill Senda Iabuli,' he said.

Carefully he replaced the contents of the container. He glanced at Peter Oro, wondering how the youth would react to the vindication of his belief that his grandfather had been murdered.

The boy was not even looking at him. He was staring aghast at the scattered sacred rocks. Kella followed his gaze. Something else had been hidden at the base of the pile. The sergeant stooped and picked it up. It was the bone of an animal, carved, polished and trimmed roughly into the shape of a quill, some six inches long.

Peter Oro backed away fearfully, breathing hard. Then he turned and raced off into the trees. Kella swore and hurried after him, ignoring the stinging branches whipping into his face as he tried to overtake the boy. He should have anticipated such a flight. He caught up with him a hundred yards along a track leading to the village gardens. Defiantly Peter faced him.

'I thought you wanted my help,' panted Kella.

'I've changed my mind,' spat the boy, almost in tears. 'You bring too much trouble. Go away!'

Kella was suddenly aware that they were not alone. Thirty yards away at a bend in the track stood a tall elderly islander with a helmet of grey hair. It had been years since they had last met but Kella recognized him at once. For a moment the two men stood with their eyes locked. Slowly, almost reluctantly, the old man lifted a short carved bone on to which he had impaled a bladder of a bonito fish glowing with phosphorous. The islander pointed the stick at Kella. At the same time, with his other hand, he lifted a bag made from a pandanus leaf and rattled the contents viciously. Abruptly he turned and was lost to sight among the trees.

Peter Oro looked at Kella. All traces of the youth's truculence had vanished. Suddenly he was just another frightened village boy brought against his will into contact with the ghosts.

'That magic man has cursed you, Sergeant Kella,' he said, his voice shaded by misery and despair. 'Now surely you will die!'

The schoolboy turned and ran.

4

CUSTOM MAGIC

The Roman Catholic mission station at Ruvabi was situated on a bluff overlooking a river winding through the trees towards the placid blue sea a few miles away. The thatched bamboo classrooms stood along one side of a grassy square while the dormitories and the huts of the teachers were across the way. The ramshackle sprawling mission house and a neat red-roofed stone church were a hundred yards off, on the far side of the station, close to the ever-encroaching bush. Scattered haphazardly about the area were the huts of those Christian families who had abandoned their villages over the years.

Kella climbed the steep path from the river to the school buildings in the early afternoon. He had departed from the village three hours earlier, leaving the headman sullenly promising to keep the dead man's hut intact. Kella had added a few succinct words as to what he would do to the headman if anything untoward should happen to Peter Oro. On his journey Kella had kept his eyes open in vain for the schoolboy, who had not returned to the village.

Solomon Bulko, the headmaster, was sitting in a cane-backed chair at the head of the path, strumming idly on a guitar as he waited for the police sergeant. He was wearing the black shorts and white shirt worn by pupils and staff alike at the school.

'Which way now, bigfella?' inquired the headmaster casually, playing a complicated riff with spectacular ease.

'Speak English,' Kella admonished with mock severity. 'Pidgin is a bastard colonial mish-mash of a language. Set an example to your charges.'

Bulku grinned. He was a plump, jet-black, laid-back islander from Choiseul in the Western Solomons. His indolent manner concealed an incisive brain. He was the closest that Kella had to a friend in the islands.

'They let you come back then,' observed the headmaster. 'I thought they'd banned you from Malaita. I suppose they needed you to do some dirty work for them.'

He stood up and placed his guitar on the chair. He ambled across the bluff towards the school buildings with Kella, equably making no effort to carry the sergeant's pack.

'What are you doing here?' he asked.

'Routine patrol,' Kella told him truthfully. 'I'm looking for an American anthropologist called Mallory. Have you seen him?'

'He was stopping at the mission house until last week,' replied the headmaster. 'Then he went walkabout into the mountains. Haven't seen him for four or five days. Is something wrong?'

'Shouldn't think so,' Kella said. 'He was supposed to fly over to Honiara for a meeting with the High Commissioner this week. When he didn't turn up, the authorities thought they'd better check.'

'It's a long walk up into the high bush,' observed Bulko. 'I was up visiting schools there only last week. Don't worry. He'll stagger down in a day or two looking embarrassed and the worse for wear. Then he'll go away and write a book about it: *The Devil-Devils of Kwaio: an in-depth study.*'

'Why should he be different from the others?' agreed Kella. 'What's he like?'

Bulko considered. 'About forty, tall, thin, bald. Inhibited, buttoned-up. Decent enough but not a laugh a minute.'

They had reached the line of classrooms. A dozen of the older students were sitting on the grass, carving war clubs to be sold to tourists in the capital. The boys looked bored as they scraped away at the wood with their penknives.

'What are you making?' Kella asked one of the pupils.

The boy shrugged. 'A club,' he yawned.

'I can see that,' said Kella patiently. 'What sort of club – *dia*, *subi* or *alavolo*?'

The schoolboy looked blank. Some of the other students began to pay attention, welcoming any break in the tedium of the hot, empty afternoon.

'They're all the same,' answered the youth indifferently. 'They were for fighting and killing in the time before.'

Kella shook his head. 'That's where you're wrong,' he said. 'They used the *alavolo* for hand-to-hand fighting. The *subi* had another purpose.'

'What was that?' asked one of the other pupils, a faint spark of interest in his eyes.

Kella hefted the half-finished club in his hand. The balance felt all wrong. 'It was used to smash in the sides of the huts of enemies and then to finish off the wounded,' he said, handing back the club. 'This isn't a proper *subi*. You're making the head too sharp. Which island are you from?'

'Ada Gege.'

'The chief Kwaisulia came from Ada Gege. He was the greatest warrior in all of Malaita. He used the *subi* in his battles. You owe it to his memory to make sure that each one you make is carved properly. If you're going to do it, do it right.'

Bulko caught up with Kella as the sergeant walked over towards the mission house.

'That's right,' said the headmaster, panting slightly. 'Undermine my authority, why don't you?'

'You could use the carving lessons to teach the boys about their traditions.'

'For God's sake,' scoffed Bulko. 'They're only for the tourists. We ship the things out by the crateload every month. Who's to know?'

'The *mamiski*,' said Kella. Bulko was a good man but he did not care enough. 'The spirit people. They would know.'

The portly headmaster put his head on one side and regarded Kella. 'I never know when you're serious these days,' he said. 'Sooner or later you're going to have to make up your mind whether you're the progressive, technologically trained black hope for the future, or just another cosy, old-fashioned witch doctor. Where are you going now?'

'To talk to Father Pierre.'

Bulko smirked. 'Don't count on it. Things have changed since you were last here.'

'I always see the father.'

'Now he's got himself a watchdog, one with sharp teeth,' said Bulko. 'Go and see for yourself.'

Kella increased his pace. Bulko called his name. Kella stopped and looked back. For once the plump headteacher seemed serious.

'I'm sorry about the trouble you had at the killing ground,' he said. 'Whitey overreacted.'

'I made a mistake and was punished for it,' said Kella. 'A man was killed because of me.'

'How many degrees do you have?' asked Bulko, apparently inconsequentially.

'You know how many,' Kella said, suspecting one of the headteacher's wind-ups. 'The same as you. A BA from Sydney and an MPhil from London. So what?'

Bulko shook his head. 'So much education and so little sense,' he sighed. 'You didn't get dumped on by the old colonials because you ballsed-up an assignment. They tried to break you because you're an educated islander and they don't want you taking over one of their cushy jobs at the top. These islands will get independence just as soon as there are enough educated islanders to run things. We're threats. Especially you. They've got you pegged as a big man. That means you're a potential troublemaker.'

Kella shrugged and headed for the mission house. It looked different. The verandah fence had been repaired since his last visit, and the front of the building was freshly painted. A sister in the white robes of the Marist mission came out on to the verandah and regarded him suspiciously. She was small and trim, attractive in a severe manner, in her mid-twenties. Her skin had the soft pallor of someone unaccustomed to the tropical sun. When she spoke, it was with an American accent.

'Something I can do for you?'

'I've come to see Father Pierre,' said Kella.

'He's resting,' said the sister, shaking her head. 'He's an old man. He needs his sleep.'

'You're new here,' said Kella. 'Who are you?'

'Sister Conchita,' said the nun, bridling slightly, as if not used to being challenged.

'Conchita?'

For a moment the sister lost some of her assurance. She looked almost embarrassed.

'When I finished my training, I thought I was going to be sent to South America. I took a name I thought would be appropriate there. Then I was posted to the Solomons instead.' She stopped suddenly, flustered. 'Now just why am I telling you all this?' she wondered aloud.

'It could have been worse,' offered Kella. 'If they told you that you were going to the South Pole you might have called yourself Sister Igloo or Sister Husky.'

There was a sound of shuffling footsteps and Father Pierre appeared from the interior of the house. He was in his eighties, wizened and bowed with a few wisps of white hair drawn across his scalp. Spectacles with bottle lenses were perched on his nose. He was wearing faded black shorts reaching to his knees and an old blue shirt. A small wooden cross, inlaid with shell, hung around his neck. When he saw the police sergeant his face lit up.

'Ben!' he said joyously. 'I heard you were on the island. How are you? *E Diana asiana kufi riki oe lau.*'

'I'm well, father,' said Kella.

'Well, don't just stand there. Come in, come in.' The old man looked at the disapproving Sister Conchita. 'Ben's an old friend,' he explained. 'He was a student here once. I hoped he would be the first Melanesian priest in charge of the mission, but it didn't work out that way.'

The old priest took Kella through to the living room. Sister Conchita went into the kitchen, closing the door with a thud. The room had been renovated since Kella had last been in it. Most of the decrepit old furniture had been replaced and the wooden floorboards had been polished to a high sheen. Several open-topped crates of carvings from the school were in the process of being labelled before being dispatched to Honiara. One or two of the artefacts seemed to have been blackened with floor polish to give the carvings an aged effect.

Sister Conchita could be heard moving noisily about the kitchen. Father Pierre glanced in the direction of the sounds.

'Nothing personal,' he grinned. 'She's only been here a month and the girl's genuinely concerned for my well-being, bless her.'

'She'll soon learn that you're as tough as old boots,' Kella assured him. 'How many housekeepers have you seen off in the last forty years?'

'Nine or ten,' said the priest vaguely. 'And five bishops. Don't forget the bishops. They came and went with all the impact of the fluttering of butterfly wings. One of them wanted to move me out once.' Father Pierre grinned with yellow-toothed relish. Sister Conchita came in, radiating disapproval and carrying a tray with two glasses of lime juice. She lowered the tray on to a table.

'It was in 1942, eighteen years ago,' went on the priest. 'You know what it was like then. The Japanese were about to invade and everybody was panicking. The bishop wanted me to leave Malaita. Nonsense, of course. There was too much to do here. After all, the priest is responsible for the safety of everyone on the station.'

There was a clatter. Sister Conchita had upset one of the glasses. Red with embarrassment she muttered a word of apology and hurried out to return with a cloth with which to mop up the spilt lime juice.

'Time for the radio sked,' said Father Pierre, ignoring the disturbance. 'Do you have any messages to send to Honiara?'

Kella shook his head. Father Pierre went over to the antiquated radio transmitter and receiver taking up most of one side of the room. He sat down and switched it on in time for the daily scheduled hour when the bishop in Honiara contacted all the mission stations in turn.

Precisely on the hour, the booming voice of the bishop forced its way through the crackling overlapping frequencies. Kella noticed that Sister Conchita was standing near the door, listening to the messages. The different missions began to call with their requests. From one transmitter on Guadalcanal came a particularly plaintive appeal, 'My lord, we're out of whisky and fags!' A priest on Santa Isabel asked for permission to conduct the burial of a child from a non-Christian village who had died in the mission hospital. When she heard this request Sister Conchita shifted position abruptly.

Throughout Father Pierre sat huddled in evident pleasure over the radio, providing a running commentary on the incoming messages. 'Father Joseph has been called to Honiara – he's in trouble with the bishop! . . . Father Michael has been moved to another station – he can't handle the people where he is!' At one stage the old man bristled indignantly when the bishop broke into his native German to talk to a compatriot. 'Secrets!' spat Father Pierre with disgust.

Eventually came the call sign for Ruvabi. Father Pierre picked up the microphone and answered eagerly. 'All present and correct, my lord! Sergeant Kella has just arrived.'

'I expect he's looking for Dr Mallory, the anthropologist,' boomed the prelate. 'Has he returned yet?'

'Not yet, my lord. But if he is in the high bush Ben Kella is the right man to find him.'

'Tell him to take care,' warned the bishop. 'There are rumours that Pazabosi is on the move again. It is important that no one disturbs him. I'm sure that the police commissioner will agree with me. Please pass my message on to Sergeant Kella. By the way, I hear there's been an earthquake in your region. Any damage?'

'Minimal, my lord. A few trees uprooted, some rocks disturbed. Nothing we can't handle.'

A worried look had appeared on Sister Conchita's face. The nun caught Kella's inquiring gaze and looked away in annoyance.

'How is Sister Conchita settling in?' went on the bishop.

'Very well. She's cleaned places I didn't even know we had. She's looking after the native sisters, exports the carvings, keeps the books, supervises the medical centre, inspects schools and runs the farm. She is fully occupied.'

The bishop bade farewell to Ruvabi with a blessing. Father Pierre waited until the scheduled hour was over and then switched off the radio.

'You will take care with Pazabosi, won't you?' he asked Kella, returning to his armchair. 'He's a vindictive fellow. Weren't you friends once?'

'In the war,' Kella replied. 'We were in the same patrol boat.'

'Oh yes,' chuckled the priest. 'Deacon's pirates.'

'As a matter of fact,' said Kella, 'I ran into Pazabosi again this morning. He even placed a curse on me.'

He told the old man of his encounter with the magic man in the bush. Father Pierre rubbed his chin uneasily.

'I don't like the sound of this,' he said. 'Why has Pazabosi come down from the mountains? He hardly ever leaves his village these days.'

'I can think of two possible reasons,' said Kella. 'One is that he's putting another cargo cult uprising together.'

Sister Conchita was collecting their empty glasses. 'Do you know what a cargo cult is, sister?' Father Pierre asked her.

'They sometimes occur when a tribal society comes into contact with a more affluent one,' said the nun. 'The local people become jealous of the possessions – the cargo – of their visitors. Sometimes they try to use custom magic to empower an uprising, believing that the cargo will then become theirs.' She paused. 'There was something like that on Malaita after the war, wasn't there?'

'Marching Rule,' said Kella.

The sister nodded and went out.

'What other reason do you think that Pazabosi might have to leave his village?' asked Father Pierre.

'He particularly doesn't want me on Malaita. I'm the *aofia* and maybe Pazabosi doesn't want a peacemaker on the island at the moment. I'll keep my eyes open when I go up after Mallory tomorrow.'

Father Pierre looked alarmed. 'Do you really think you should go into the mountains?' he demurred. 'After what happened last time—'

'If that's where Mallory is, I don't have much choice,' said Kella.

'No, I suppose not,' said the old man sadly. 'But take care.'

Suddenly the priest looked tired. Within a few moments his chin was on his chest and he was breathing evenly as he slept.

Kella sat on in the living room, trying to put his thoughts in order. In the six months during which he had been banished from Malaita, too many things had been happening here for his liking. There was the strange custom death of Senda Iabuli, and the subsequent panic-stricken flight of Peter Oro to investigate. Were they linked to the sudden appearance of Pazabosi the magic man and his effort to deter Kella by placing a curse on him?

And there was something badly wrong at the mission too, he thought. He wondered why Sister Conchita was so uneasy. She was as jumpy as a three-week-old kitten, yet Kella could have sworn that normally the nun was a most self-composed young woman.

In fact, the whole area seemed in a state of disarray. His superior Chief Superintendent Grice might not like it, but Kella would have to stay and investigate.

5

THE BONES TABU

Kella had been lying for several hours in the dark behind the clump of ngali nut trees at the side of the graveyard. The oppressive night was humming with mosquitoes. Fireflies darted in vicious groups, like tracer bullets. He could hear the swelling chorus of cicadas and hunting owls. Squads of the fruit bats known as flying foxes headed aggressively through the air for their feeding grounds.

Kella prepared for a long stay. After he had left the sleeping priest that afternoon, he had made a tour of the huts on the station, pursuing the elders among his *wantoks*, those people on the mission who shared his language. Because the station was so close to Kella's home among the artificial islands, most of the local islanders were members of his clan and owed him both hospitality and the truth. Even so, there had been an unusual number of shifty silences and uncomfortable evasions from the old men and women he had encountered.

Kella suspected that most of the elders knew that something of moment was occurring but were not sure of the details. His feeling had been reinforced when he showed the islanders the carved bone he had found under the comfort stones in the neighbouring village. They admitted that it was a bones *tabu*, issued by a magic man to a potential victim, but claimed to have

29

no knowledge of Senda Iabuli or the dead villager's grandson Peter Oro.

Of all people, Mendana Gau had taken him closest to a solution. Gau was a scruffy, middle-aged entrepreneur from the Santa Cruz island group. For a number of years he had lived by his wits on the mission station, mainly by acting as the local agent for a Chinese trader in the capital. Gau ran a small store on the edge of the station, selling tinned rice and meat. Sometimes he would go on mysterious and probably illegal trading trips into the interior of the island.

Kella had run Gau down in the back room of his store, first brushing by the truculent but suddenly circumspect islander who was serving behind the counter. The sergeant found Gau engaged in easing the metal casing of a wartime shell into a large sack of copra amid a pile awaiting collection by the next boat. The trader's instinctive malevolent glare changed to a look of worried servility when he recognized the policeman.

'Sergeant Kella,' he said unconvincingly. 'What a pleasant surprise!'

'You really should move with the times,' Kella told him, indicating the reinforced sack of copra. 'Even the Brits open the sacks and check the contents before they weigh them these days.'

'Ballast for the boat,' muttered Gau. He was small and rat-like, wearing dirty khaki shorts and a tattered T-shirt revealing a substantial beer belly. A cigarette end dangled constantly from his lower lip. His flickering red-rimmed eyes met Kella's sceptical gaze. He shrugged. 'If the Customs officials are busy they don't always open the sacks at the wharf,' he explained.

'Gau, your whole career of petty robbery has been a triumph of optimism over bitter experience,' Kella told him, sitting on the edge of a rickety table. 'I'm here because I want some information from you.'

'I know nothing,' said the trader humbly. 'I am a mere outcast here, a poor itinerant exile from the Eastern islands.'

'And rightly so,' agreed Kella, 'because without a doubt you are also the biggest thief and liar on the station. However, on this occasion you might be of use to me. What do you know of the bones *tabu*?' From his pocket he produced the carved and polished bone he had found among the heating stones.

'Nothing,' whined Gau. 'These things are of the Lau culture.'

Kella stood up. The trader flinched and cringed away. Ignoring him, Kella walked over to the rusty weighing scales in a corner. He picked up four of the heavy metal counterweights lying on the floor.

'I wonder what would happen if I took these back to Honiara to be checked?' he mused aloud. 'If they proved to be wrong you would lose your licence.'

A spasm of fury contorted Gau's unshaven face. As if by accident he knocked a tin of corned beef off the table. It fell to the floor with a clatter.

'If that's supposed to be a signal to your hard man out there, don't bother,' said Kella mildly. 'He'll be long gone by now. He is of the Afena Kwai tribe on the foothills above Gwau Rate. Good enough for bullying women and children who complain about your prices, but I doubt if he'll stand up to a Sulufou man.'

'There would be no question of opposing the law in this establishment,' Gau said hastily. 'Especially when that law is also the *aofia*.'

'Don't you dare talk about the *aofia*, you miserable little man,' Kella told the trader. 'That name is for the Lau people only. You degrade it even by breathing its name.'

Gau looked genuinely frightened at the sudden change in the other man's attitude. He scuttled as far away from Kella as he could, throwing up his thin arms in supplication.

'Just ask me what you want to know,' he snivelled. 'Ask and get out!'

'Bones,' said Kella, half-ashamed of losing his temper. 'That's all I've been hearing today. What do you know about them?'

'There's a bones *tabu* on the station,' said Gau cautiously. 'So the old people say. It came about two days ago.'

'Who is it from?'

'I don't know.'

Kella looked hard at the trader. Gau capitulated. 'They say it is from Pazabosi, the old magic man,' he said with a rush.

'Is this bones *tabu* over yet?'

'I don't think so. Soon. Very soon.'

'Who is mixed up in it?'

'I don't know. You can hit me if you like, but I still can't tell you. Business bilong whitefella.'

Kella questioned the other man closely for another ten minutes, but it was evident that the resentful trader knew no more.

'Very well,' he said finally, walking towards the door. 'Thank you for your help, Mr Gau.' Kella nodded at the weights he had discarded. 'I'll be checking those before I leave. If they still give false weight tomorrow I'll tear your store down plank by plank.'

Afterwards he had dined on a roast chicken prepared by Bulko in his hut by the light of a battery-operated lamp over a substantial stove. They had eaten the meal in comfortable basket chairs while they listened to a Hank Williams LP on a portable record player. He had not bothered to question the headmaster. The Roviana man would never be told anything by the local islanders. Nor, with his attitude of benevolent self-interest, would Bulko want to know what was happening, unless it threatened his comfort or well-being.

Instead Kella had inquired about Peter Oro, the missing schoolboy. Bulko had been typically vague. Yes, the boy was away on personal leave to arrange the funeral of his grandfather.

No, he did not know much about the pupil, except that he was both bright and rebellious, but who wasn't at that age? Wearily the headmaster promised to make inquiries among the teachers who knew the boy.

Bulko was plainly less than enchanted with his charges. As he poured a beer for the sergeant he embarked upon a litany of complaints.

'Just because they've been selected for higher education they think they need never get their hands dirty again,' he grumbled. 'They'll do anything to avoid working in the gardens. They slope off into the trees and go walkabout, make up sob stories, go sick. Why, last week some of them even broke into the tool store and scattered the gardening equipment all over the place, just to avoid working on the land. We're still looking for some of the missing stuff.'

'What a shame,' sympathized Kella. 'Especially after the example of unrelenting manual work you set them.'

'That's different,' said Bulko firmly. 'They only think they're special. I *am* special.'

After the meal, under the cover of darkness, Kella had gone to work, making his way by a circuitous route to the graveyard on the northern boundary of the station. Several hundred white wooden crosses extended over the well-tended ground leading into the trees. Kella crouched behind a bush. For several hours no one approached the cemetery. Even the converted islanders shared the Lau religion's fear of death. Few would willingly come near the bone-yard after dark.

It was past midnight before Kella heard approaching footsteps and the creaking of wheels coming from the direction of the mission house. The sergeant shifted his position. He was feeling so stiff that he was sure that some of the corpses around him would be able to give him a start and beat him over a twenty yards sprint.

Three figures approached through the gloom. One was undoubtedly Sister Conchita in her white robes. She was accompanied by two frightened young island sisters wearing the blue habits of the Daughters of Melanesia. With some difficulty, the American nun was carrying three spades. The two island girls were pushing a wheelbarrow carrying something long and bulky encased in woven mats.

Kella looked on as the three women started inexpertly to dig a grave. For fifteen minutes they worked doggedly at their task. Maliciously Kella let them get a couple of feet down into the ground. He did not move until the sisters had lowered their spades and were lifting the bundle from the wheelbarrow. Then he stood up and walked quietly towards them. The Melanesians saw him first. They screamed, dropping the mats and their burden. The mats separated, dispersing their contents of darkened bones on the ground.

'Place im e fall down no good too mas,' said Kella, making one of his infrequent forays into pidgin. He translated for the benefit of the astounded Sister Conchita. 'This is a bad place for a man to fall down.'

The American recovered her self-possession quickly. 'What is the meaning of this, Sergeant Kella?' she demanded, in a voice that, for all her visible efforts, she was unable to prevent quavering. 'You do realize that this is consecrated ground?'

'An appropriate enough place for a skeleton,' agreed Kella. He was on his hands and knees, reassembling the framework in some sort of rough order. Sister Conchita was silent for a moment.

'How . . .' she began uncertainly. 'I mean . . .'

'Bones,' said Kella, not looking up, his fingers working busily. 'Ever since I landed on the island two days ago I've been hearing nothing but bones. There was a suspicious death at a village near here after a bones curse had been placed on the dead man. A magic man came down from the high bush just to frighten me

34

off with a bones *tabu*. When I reach the station I find that there are rumours that a bones curse has been put on something here as well. There's only one place where a bones curse could really operate and that's in a graveyard. So I decided to keep watch here for a couple of nights.' He paused and then added, 'Then there was the way you were behaving this afternoon.'

'Me?' asked Sister Conchita, startled.

'You were apprehensive about something. You knocked over a glass when Father Pierre said that the priest was responsible for the safety of everyone on his station. When the father at the Santa Isabel mission spoke over the sked asking permission to bury a non-Christian in his cemetery, you looked really upset. That made me wonder whether you knew something about what was going on here.'

'You've been very observant,' said the nun in a small voice.

'Believe me,' said Kella grimly, 'I haven't even started yet.'

His groping hands had found the skull. Quickly he turned it in his hands. At the back of the cranium there was the unmistakable indentation of a bullet hole.

6

LOFTY HERMAN

'Kella wants a coffin,' said Inspector Lorrimer.

'Surely not?' said Chief Superintendent Grice. 'He can't be more than thirty. Years ahead of him yet. More's the pity.'

'It's not for him,' said Lorrimer patiently. Grice sometimes overdid his bucolic act. 'Apparently he's found a corpse on Malaita.'

'So what else is new?' asked Grice dispiritedly.

The two men were in the chief superintendent's office on the second floor of the police headquarters building in Honiara. Lorrimer was standing at the window, looking down at the parade ground where a squad of recruits was being drilled noisily by an immaculate sergeant in a white *lap-lap*. On the other side of Mendana Avenue, which ran through the centre of the capital, were the white walls of the Guadalcanal Club, with its verandah running down to the beach behind and the slow, white-topped breakers of the deep-blue sea.

'Why a coffin?' burst out Grice petulantly. 'Doesn't Kella usually bury the people he kills in a hole in the ground and hope we don't hear about it?'

'We've never been able to prove that he's killed anyone,' Lorrimer pointed out reasonably. It was a wonder they ever caught any criminals at all, he thought. There were only three hundred officers and men in a police force responsible for the hundreds of tropical islands extending across the Coral Sea for almost a thousand miles in the chain lying north-east of Australia.

'Only because he's a little tin god on Malaita. What native is ever going to give evidence against a ju-ju man, for God's sake?'

'He's an *aofia*,' Lorrimer corrected his senior officer. He had researched the subject while preparing the papers for Kella's court of inquiry the previous year. 'It's a position peculiar to the Lau region of Malaita. Every few decades, a man of the line of chieftains appears who is of such probity and strength of character that he is appointed while he is still a child to maintain peace among all the people of the Lau region. It's a heavy responsibility. He's a sort of paramount chieftain.'

'He's supposed to be a bloody policeman,' pointed out Grice violently.

'Kella thinks he can be both.'

'How the hell can Ben Kella be a peacemaker? He's as wild as an alley-cat sometimes.'

'He doesn't have to be a pacifist to be an *aofia*. The reverse, sometimes. I agree it's not an easy concept to grasp.'

The two policemen were silent in a rare moment of concord. The atmosphere between them was usually one of armed neutrality. Grice was a permanent and pensionable officer, a member of what in its pomp had once been the Colonial Police Force, now better known locally as the African Retreads. Lorrimer was on a temporary secondment from the Metropolitan Police in London.

'Kella could have had it all, you know,' Grice complained, almost sadly. 'He's a Malaita man, so all the other islanders are scared shitless of him. He was the first native graduate to join the police force. He's been on half a dozen attachments to forces all over the world. If he would just keep his head down he could be the first Melanesian Commissioner of Police, when independence comes. But what does he want?'

'Kella's his own man,' said Lorrimer.

'He wants to be a bush policeman, that's what,' said Grice, ignoring his subordinate. 'Spends half his time poking around the jungle. And look at the trouble that got him into.'

'He got an official reprimand for it,' Lorrimer pointed out.

'Bit of a mate of yours, isn't he?' sniffed the chief superintendent.

'Kella's an interesting man,' said Lorrimer non-committally. 'Honest, too. He could have lied his way out of trouble after that missionary was killed last year.'

And he knows the islands, he thought. He wished that Kella was back in Honiara. The case presently occupying Lorrimer concerned two feuding neighbouring villages on Choiseul in the Western District. The occupants of one village were Methodists and the other comprised Seventh Day Adventists. The dispute had originated over a garden plot situated between the villages and claimed by both. Trouble had escalated to such an extent that the Methodists were waiting until Saturday, the Adventist day of church worship, and then pillaging the SDA gardens. For their part, the Adventists were retaliating by raiding the Methodist gardens on Sundays while their owners were at church. Kella would know how to deal with such a situation.

'If you'll take a word of advice,' said Grice portentously, 'you won't get too close to the natives, Lorrimer. I've never forgiven Kella for the way he let me down over the rugby.'

'Rugby?' asked Lorrimer. He was not interested in sport.

'Best wing forward the Solomons team ever had.' Grice had the rapt look of a man who invested as much enthusiasm in rugby football as other men did in sin.

'Did I ever tell you about the time the Solomons played Fiji?'

he asked. He paid no attention to the other man's indifferent nod. 'Never seen anything like it. Everyone thought that the Fijians would put sixty points past us. We had the usual rag-bag of a side. Half a dozen expats from the timber company, and then the usual mixture of odds and sods – Malaitans, Tikopians, a poofter British teacher from King George VI School, who was supposed to be captain.'

'What happened?' asked Lorrimer, dutifully excavating his superior from the shallow grave of his reverie.

'Kella was playing, that's what happened,' said Grice, looking almost happy for once. 'Open-side wing forward. It was bloody marvellous. From the kick-off nobody paid any attention to the expat skipper. The whole team was looking to Kella for a lead. He didn't want it, anybody could see that, but the leadership was foisted upon him. They just knew he was their natural chief. We tonked 'em, 25–9. Kella led the team as if it was a war party. No prisoners. Then he let us all down.'

'How did he do that?'

'With him in the team we could have won the South Pacific Cup that season. What does he do? I'll tell you. He goes off to Australia on a degree course, and while he's there he plays professional Rugby League, which meant he couldn't play Union again when he came back.'

'Needed the money, I suppose.'

'Don't you believe it. His family owns a copra plantation and I don't know what else on Malaita. No, he played League just to stick two fingers up at me.'

Grice sat simmering, the memories of a dozen similar betrayals of colonial benevolent paternalism in almost as many former colonial territories seething in his time-expired brain.

'About Kella's corpse,' Lorrimer reminded the chief superintendent.

'Forget it. It'll just be another inter-tribal feud.'

'That's the point, sir. The corpse found by Kella is that of a murdered white man.'

Chief Superintendent Grice looked at the other officer beseechingly, mutely imploring him to retract the last sentence.

'A white man?' he spluttered.

'Kella believes that the body has been dead for some years. The skeleton is six and a half feet tall, much bigger than any islander.'

'Six and a half feet?' said Grice. 'I've never known an expatriate that tall, and I've served here for twelve years.'

'I've looked it up in the files,' Lorrimer told him. 'The only white man of that size known to have lived on Malaita was an Australian beachcomber called Lofty Herman. The drawback is that Herman disappeared eighteen years ago, back in 1942.'

The telephone rang. Not taking his eyes from the inspector's face Grice lifted the receiver and listened. His back stiffened. Without a word carefully he replaced the receiver, as if taking part in a laboratory experiment which required absolute precision.

'That was the chief secretary,' he told his companion. 'You'd better get yourself over to Malaita straight away and fetch Kella back. Apparently the silly sod's in trouble again!'

7

WHITE MAN'S WAYS

'How did you know that Sister Conchita was going to bury a skeleton last night?' asked Father Pierre. The old priest was looking frail and small, as if physically reduced by the news the police sergeant had brought him.

They were sitting in the living room of the mission house. It was eight o'clock in the morning. Kella had been waiting patiently for the other two when they returned from celebrating Mass. Outside, the normal routine of the mission was being observed. Bare-breasted women in grass skirts were making their way up the wooded slopes on three sides of the compound to work in their gardens in the clearings. Men in loincloths were sitting outside their huts, mending fishing nets.

'It seemed likely that there was a dead body on the station,' Kella replied.

He told them about finding the bone under the pile of stones in the neighbouring village. He described how Pazabosi, the old magic man, had pointed a bonito fish impaled on a bone at him, to warn the policeman that he would anger the spirits if he pursued his inquiry. He explained how the trader Mendana Gau had confirmed his suspicions.

'How do you associate bones with an unexpected death?' asked an unusually subdued Sister Conchita.

'Local tradition,' said Father Pierre automatically. 'If a magic man brings a bone curse to an area, it means that there has been a strange death which will trigger off evil events, unless the *tabu* is observed and people keep away from the place where the death occurred.'

The old man was silent for a moment and then addressed Kella. 'Do you think there could be a connection between the death in the village and the bones *tabu* placed on the mission station?'

Kella shook his head. 'I doubt it. I also found a piece of ginger sprinkled with lime among the stones. That means that a separate curse had been placed on Senda Iabuli, the villager who died. You wouldn't have a lime curse and a bones *tabu* placed on the same corpse.'

'I agree,' said the priest, nodding. 'The two deaths weren't part of the same curse.'

'The only connection between the two is the schoolboy Peter Oro,' said Kella. 'I think he had been searching the hut for signs of a curse, but it hadn't occurred to him to look outside among the comfort stones.'

'All this talk of magic!' burst out a scandalized Sister Conchita. 'Surely you can't believe it! This is a Christian area.'

'Part-Christian,' Father Pierre corrected her. 'Much of the interior of Malaita is still pagan.' He cast an apologetic glance at the impassive sergeant. 'I'm sorry, Ben. I meant that many people still worship in the old ways there.'

Sister Conchita restrained herself with an obvious effort. 'All right,' she said to Kella. 'So you worked out that something connected with a body was going on here at the mission. You still haven't told me why you were waiting at the cemetery.'

'Last night Mendana Gau, the storekeeper, told me that the bones *tabu* would soon be over. That sort of curse usually ends when a body is reinterred. Gau also hinted that one of the expatriates on the station was involved – business bilong whitefella. With all respect, Father Pierre is a bit beyond grave digging, so I assumed it would be you. Especially as you seemed a bit upset yesterday afternoon when I arrived at the mission.'

'So much for my careful dissembling,' said Sister Conchita.

'Perhaps, sister, it is time for you to tell us how you came to be involved in this odd affair,' said Father Pierre.

The nun nodded, marshalled her thoughts and started to speak, gaining in confidence as she went.

'It started a couple of days ago,' she told her listeners. 'I was teaching at the mission school. A woman ran down from the gardens to tell me that a skeleton had been found at the foot of the cliff. By the time I got there a crowd of islanders were trying to carry it away.'

'Presumably to hide it somewhere before I heard about the incident,' nodded the priest.

'I told them that you would have to be informed,' said Sister Conchita. She dropped her head. Her hands trembled in her lap.

'Then what?' prompted Kella.

Slowly the nun raised her head. 'I've never seen the mission people like it,' she said. 'Normally they're so happy and pleasant, but now they'd found the skeleton they were in a dreadful state.'

'Presumably an aspect of their past had come back to revisit them,' said the priest. 'I'm sorry. Please go on.'

'I didn't know what to do,' confessed Sister Conchita. 'I know I should have come to you, but the people seemed convinced that the body had something to do with you, and that you would be badly affected if you heard about it. I didn't want to risk upsetting you, especially as you hadn't been well lately. So I, well, I kind of took it upon myself to bury him.'

She looked across the room at the thoughtful Kella. 'You guessed right. I couldn't bring myself to put the skeleton in unconsecrated ground, so I brought him to the cemetery last night.'

There was a long silence. Father Pierre closed his eyes. Sister Conchita stared at the floor. 'I had better see this skeleton,' the priest said, his voice tired.

'There's no need,' said Kella. 'I used your radio last night to contact Honiara, while you were asleep. They'll ship the bones back there for examination, but I believe it's Lofty Herman.'

A sound, which was half a groan and half a sigh, escaped from the priest. Sister Conchita rose to minister to him but the old man waved her away.

'The man was very tall,' Kella told him. 'No islander was ever that size and very few whites. It has to be Herman.'

'And he's been secretly buried on the mission station with a bullet in his head for all that time?' asked the priest.

'It looks like it.' Kella rose and glanced at his watch. 'I'd like you to show me where you first found the skeleton,' he informed the nun. 'Say in thirty minutes? I'll come back for you after I've spoken to one or two people.'

After Kella had left the room, Sister Conchita approached Father Pierre. 'I'm sorry,' she said in a small voice. 'I reckon I don't come out too high on obedience or humility.'

'You did what you thought was right,' said the priest. 'That's important.'

'Sergeant Kella seems to be on the ball,' ventured the sister. 'Maybe he'll get to the bottom of things.'

'That's what I'm afraid of,' said Father Pierre. He saw the surprise on her face. 'Don't misunderstand me. If there's anything untoward going on at the station I want it investigated, and Ben Kella's the only man who could do it. But I'm afraid of the effect it might have on him if he gets dragged too far back into the past.'

'He looks tough enough.'

'None tougher.' The priest was making one of his increasingly frequent forays back into the past. 'Ben was twelve when he first came to the mission school. We had a very aggressive bunch of Roviana lads ruling the roost here then. They picked on Kella as a Malaitan boy, from the start. At the end of his first week here six of them beat him up and left him unconscious in a ditch.'

'What did he do?'

The priest smiled. 'He picked them off, one by one,' he told her. 'Stalked the mission like an avenging angel, or as he would probably have put it, a devil-devil. He caught the first alone in the bush, the second out on a reef, and so on. Waited for each one on a different night and then half-killed him.'

'And you let this happen, father?' asked a shocked Sister Conchita.

'Kella was different,' said the priest. 'That was apparent from the beginning. I could see that he was working out his destiny. He came here to learn the white man's ways, but he had to develop the warrior bit, too. He's a Sulufou man. The Malaitans are the hardest men in the Solomons, and the ones from Sulufou are the pick of the bunch. They don't only build their own houses, they construct whole islands, stone by stone, out in the lagoon, when they're not fighting the bush people inland, or taking their canoes hundreds of miles out to sea. Once he had defeated the Roviana boys Ben could devote himself to his studies.'

'I take it he was good at those, too?'

'Oh yes. Brilliant. It was soon obvious that he was a man for the future. Unfortunately, we almost destroyed him in the process.'

'How did that happen?' asked Sister Conchita.

Father Pierre looked unhappy. 'By the time Kella came here he had already been picked out by the Lau people as their *aofia*, the hereditary bringer of justice to the island. The custom priests had trained him in their traditional ways. Then we tried to turn him into a good Catholic. It was too much of a burden for a young boy, expecting him to cope with two different faiths and philosophies. For a time he ended up pretty cynical about them both. That didn't stop him passing out at the top of his year at the secondary school and going on to university overseas. Then he came back and surprised everyone by joining the police force.'

'Why did he do that?'

'I think he wanted to be sent back over here to Malaita to sort things out. We're in a transitional state at the moment. One day the British will leave. What will happen when independence comes? On this one island alone we have thirteen different clans, each speaking its own language. It's a powder keg. Kella's trying to calm things down. As a policeman he can get out among the people and do his *aofia* peacekeeping. I thought he was getting things under control, until . . .'

'Until what, father?'

'Oh, he had some trouble six months ago,' said the old priest vaguely. 'It set him back a little. I hope he's all right now. That boy is a lot more sensitive than he lets on. The last thing he needs now is to get mixed up in another controversy, especially if it's a custom murder.'

8

THAT'S WHERE ALL THE DANGER IS!

Kella met Sister Conchita outside the mission house. He noticed without surprise that she was looking at him with renewed curiosity. Father Pierre would have been telling her about him.

He wondered how much the priest knew about what was going on. The old man was losing his grip on the station, there was no doubt about that, but he was still held in high regard by the islanders.

Doggedly Kella had questioned one or two of his *wantoks* about the discovery of the skeleton. All they knew was that the earthquake had driven the bones to the surface. The older men had remembered that this was supposed to be an act of custom magic, said to presage some great happening. They had persuaded the new white sister to rebury the body secretly, so that the bones *tabu* on the area would be lifted and life could go back to normal.

They had told her that Father Pierre would be upset should he be informed of the situation. This had only been a ruse on their part to get the body safely under ground again. The old priest, even in his present distracted state, would have insisted on making inquiries about Lofty Herman. This would have entailed the continued presence of the skeleton above the ground and the prolonging of the bones curse.

Sister Conchita led the way through the station to the school compound.

'I'm sure that Father Pierre will be all right,' Kella started to say.

'If you don't mind, Sergeant Kella, I'd just as soon you didn't patronize me,' said the nun, staring ahead. 'I know when I've screwed up big-time.'

They passed the trading store. Mendana Gau and several villainous-looking Santa Cruz men were stacking crates of Australian 4X beer against the side of the ramshackle building. The trader directed a malevolent glare at the police sergeant and snarled something in low tones to one of his helpers. The labourer sneered briefly and spat on the ground when he saw Kella looking at him.

Sister Conchita and Kella scrambled down the steep path leading to the broad, fast-flowing river cutting its way through the densely packed trees below the mission. Half a dozen canoes belonging to staff and pupils were stored on one bank in an *obala*, four poles supporting a thatched roof with no sides.

Most of the canoes were simple dugouts, but one was more substantial. It had been carefully constructed, with two long twelve-foot planks forming the bottom, and two more for the sides. The planks had been waterproofed with gum from the putty-nut tree and lashed together securely with pliable bamboo. Smaller pieces of wood had been used for the panels in the raised bow and stern. Fitted cross-planes reinforced the body of the craft. The exterior was decorated with inlaid mother-of-pearl shell, shaped into outlines of frigate birds.

'Just who was this Lofty Herman anyway?' Sister Conchita asked. She spoke unwillingly, as if the words were being chiselled out of her, syllable by syllable.

'He was an Australian beachcomber who lived here before the war,' Kella told her. 'I was only a boy then, and I don't remember much about him, apart from his height. He went missing before the Japanese landed in 1942. Everyone assumed he must have been killed by a Japanese patrol in the bush.'

'Perhaps he was,' said the nun, a breath of hope stirring in her dejected tone.

Kella shook his head, not wanting to give the nun false hopes. Lofty Herman had been murdered, he was certain of that. 'I doubt it,' he said. 'For one thing, why would the Japanese have bothered to bury him? And if any of the islanders had found his body, they would have brought it back to Father Pierre for a proper burial.'

'You think someone killed him and hid the body?'

'That's the way it looks.'

Sister Conchita fell silent again. She led him inland from the river, through the trees to the foot of the bluff. Part of the base of the cliff had split away and was lying in a pile of scattered rubble among the trunks of the towering trees. Some of the fallen rocks had cracked; their distorted shapes sprawled across the ground. A few were smooth and round, others were oddly scratched and pitted, like great scarred termites.

'Mr Herman must have been buried right up against the foot of the cliff,' she indicated. 'The earthquake broke some of the cliff away and churned up the ground immediately in front of it. One of the women saw Herman's arm poking through the rocks and fetched the men to dig his skeleton out. I had them carry it to an empty hut after dark, and then I wrapped it in some mats.'

Kella thought that it would have taken courage on the expatriate sister's part to have dealt in such a way with the bones and then disobey all the tenets of her faith, merely in order to prevent the mission priest from being upset by an unexplained incident from the past. She must be fond of the old man to risk the wrath of the church authorities in this way. Plainly Sister Conchita could be a very determined young woman.

Kella decided not to say so. The nun also had an acerbic tongue when she wanted to use it. He stared at the scene. It was quiet here among the trees. No islander would approach until the bones curse placed on it by Pazabosi had worn off.

Kella was about to turn away, when there was a loud crack. For a moment he thought it was a coconut plummeting to the ground. Next he heard a soft thud as something embedded itself in one of the trees. Then there was yet another report. This time a clod of earth and a whirl of leaves spun up into the air, less than a foot away.

Sister Conchita looked at Kella in bewilderment. Her expression changed to one of puzzled annoyance when the police sergeant seized her urgently by the wrist.

'Run!' shouted Kella, dragging the startled and protesting nun after him. 'Somebody's shooting at us!'

The two of them ran out of the trees and scrambled across the grass towards the bank of the river. No more shots were fired. Kella tried to listen for the sound of following footsteps. He could not be sure if anyone was behind them.

If he had been on his own he would have drifted through the trees at an angle and taken a chance on outflanking the other man. He dared not risk that with Sister Conchita at his side. Instead he concentrated on getting the young nun safely across to the water's edge.

When they reached the river Sister Conchita automatically turned to run towards the path leading up the bluff to the school buildings. Kella tightened his grip on her wrist.

'Not that way!' he shouted, expecting at any moment to hear the report of another shot as the marksman cleared the trees behind them and got a clear view of them both. He pushed the largest canoe out into the water with one hand, dragging Sister Conchita after it with the other.

'Get in!' he urged, steadying the side of the rocking craft.

Sister Conchita looked uncertain. 'Surely we'll be safer back at the mission,' she faltered.

'Haven't you got it into your head yet?' snarled Kella. 'That's where all the danger is. Move!'

Startled by the authority in the police sergeant's voice, the sister scrambled unwillingly into the canoe and crouched at the back. Kella pushed the craft farther out into the main current and leapt into the front. He picked up one of the two paddles lying on the floor and began to propel the canoe rapidly down the centre of the river in the direction of the sea. With deft, practised strokes he thrust the paddle into the water, first on one side and then the other.

The canoe began to buck unsteadily. Alarmed, Kella glanced over his shoulder. Sister Conchita had picked up the other paddle and was digging it unsteadily into the water. Her tongue was protruding with the effort of the unaccustomed exercise.

'Put that down!' Kella yelled. 'You'll unbalance us!'

'I was only', called the nun acidly, 'trying to help.'

'Do me a big favour. Don't!'

Kella turned back and ignored her, watching the river ahead. If the man with the rifle should still be behind them, he would not get an easy shot at them through the overgrown foliage on the bank. If the shooter had appropriated one of the smaller dugout canoes it would not keep pace with the custom-built craft they were now in. Kella estimated that they had at least a twenty-minute start over any pursuer.

He discarded the idea of confronting the marksman. He was unarmed and the other man had a rifle of some sort. Judging by the length of the intervals between shots and the fact that they had been so wide of the mark, Kella guessed that the weapon was probably an antiquated .303 of the type carried by the Armed Constabulary in the islands before the war and still in use among the villagers for hunting. At their best they had been notoriously difficult to use. Anything more modern would have released the shots much more quickly and accurately.

He skimmed the canoe over the water, taking care to keep it in the centre of the river. The trees growing along the bank were even thicker here, their branches forming an interlaced canopy overhead, blotting out the sun.

As they made progress along its length, the river was growing wider and more desultory, its colour a dirty brown from floods caused by heavy rain breaking down its banks up in the mountains of the interior. Kella looked for a suitable place to land. He saw a fairly clear area of bank and steered towards it.

'Where are we going?' demanded Sister Conchita.

Kella did not reply. He brought the canoe up against the bank and signalled to the nun to get out. Unwillingly she did so and stood tottering mutinously beneath a mangrove tree growing crookedly out of the slime of the river bank at the edge of the jungle. She wrinkled her nose at the all-pervading, sickly sweet, putrid smell, as heavy as incense. Lizards crawled sluggishly out of the mud, hunting for worms and insects. A turtle slithered unexpectedly out of the trees, its head bobbing and thrusting erratically out of its shell, before cascading softly into the river. Frogs grunted and exploded out of the mud like dirty brown and green corks propelled from buried bottles. The huge tortured roots of mangrove trees protruded across the water.

Kella dragged the canoe out of the water and into the trees, covering it quickly with leaves and brushwood so that the craft could not be visible from the river. He picked up several large fallen palm fronds and whisked them up and down the stretch of muddy bank where they had come ashore, obliterating all traces of their footprints. When he was satisfied that that there was no apparent trace of their landing he started forward into the trees.

'Pardon me if I've got this wrong, sergeant,' came Sister Conchita's sarcastic voice from behind him, 'but aren't you supposed to be the cop? Shouldn't you be chasing the bad guys, not running away from them?'

She had a point, acknowledged Kella, but he was in no mood to debate it with the nun at this particular moment. Their feet were sinking inexorably into the mud as they moved, making progress through the trees and over the all-pervading roots difficult. Kella made for the ridge of firm land to his right that he knew led out of the mangrove swamp to the higher, safer ground of the jungle of the interior. He remembered that the hidden path rose to a height of six feet above this morass around it. Once they were on this track they would be able to make faster time.

After half an hour Sister Conchita started to complain. Kella paid no attention to her. He waited until another thirty minutes had passed and they had reached the outskirts of the relatively dry forested land before he allowed her to stop.

The sister sank breathlessly to the ground. Kella walked over to a coconut palm and scaled the slender, swaying tree. He detached two green young coconuts and dropped them to the ground, thirty feet below. Descending from the tree he picked up a thick bough and sharpened both ends with a few strokes of his penknife. He stuck one pointed end of the branch into the ground and then impaled a coconut on the other end, boring a hole in it. He handed the husk to Sister Conchita, who drank the liquid eagerly.

Kella smashed the other coconut against the bole of a tree, breaking the nut in half. With the blade of his penknife he scooped out the soft white meat and gave it to the nun to eat. When she had finished she gave a satisfied sigh.

'However, don't think that I'm going to stop asking questions just because you've wined and dined me, Sergeant Kella,' she warned him.

'I wouldn't dream of it,' said Kella. 'What do you want to know?'

The sister gestured around her at the matted undergrowth choking the ground beneath the trees. 'What we're doing here, for a start,' she said.

'Where did you expect me to take you?' asked Kella. He recalled a hectic six-month attachment he had undertaken a few years ago. 'The East 67th Street station house in Manhattan, maybe?'

'If only,' said the sister with feeling.

'This is Malaita, not New York. The nearest police sub-station is at Auki. That's three days' walk across the central mountain range. The safest place for us at the moment is at the edge of a mangrove swamp.'

'And there was I thinking you were just trying to show me a good time. Couldn't we have gone back to the mission house instead of trying the white-water surfing stuff on the river?'

'No. The mission is where all the trouble started.'

'How can you possibly know that?'

'I just do,' said Kella. He paused and then added reluctantly, 'The spirits told me so.'

'Oh, fine!' burst out Sister Conchita. 'I'm dragged down a river and across a marsh because, I'm informed – me, a Christian sister, mind you – you're getting messages across the ether from trolls?'

'This is my island and they're my spirits,' said Kella. 'Just bear with me. We'll wait here until it gets dark and then I'll take you down to the lagoon. My village is there and we'll be safe.'

'Why can't we go there now?' asked Sister Conchita rebelliously. 'You got something against daytime travel?'

'The man who fired at us may still be looking for us. If he finds our track he'll have to approach us through the swamp. Only a local man could get to us from any other direction; the going's too hard.'

'Suppose this guy is local?'

Kella shook his head. 'Out of the question,' he said decisively. 'No one from the Lau area would try to kill the *aofia*.'

'Now we're back to that old thing again,' sighed the sister. 'You sure put a lot of trust in your status, Sergeant Kella.'

'Don't knock it till you've tried it. Why don't you get some sleep? I'll wake you when it gets dark.'

Sister Conchita muttered something unladylike but Kella knew that she must be exhausted after all the walking she had done in her thick habit under the morning sun. Reluctantly the nun stretched out under a tree and closed her eyes. Within minutes she was asleep, breathing heavily.

Kella sat down and prepared to wait. He was glad that the sister had been so tired. Had she been more alert she would probably have worked out that her companion was really waiting to find out who had been following them. The place where they had come ashore was one of the few landing spots along the length of the river bank. Sooner or later the man with the rifle would explore it and probably find their canoe.

The scorching, somnolent afternoon burnt away endlessly. Towards evening Kella heard the sounds of a crab-hunting party from a coastal village moving along the river bank. The islanders were lighting their candle-nut torches as darkness began to fall. The distant unseen villagers moved on in a cacophony of mutual insults and laughter until the noise died away. Kella continued to wait beneath the tree. An hour later, with the few remaining orange fingers of daylight gone with the setting sun, Kella heard someone moving laboriously across the swamp from the direction of the river.

The man was alone. He did not seem to know his way, because he was making too much noise as he struggled waist-deep through the mud between the trees. He made no effort to look for the relative comfort of the ridge path. Presumably he did not know of its existence.

With a glance Kella checked that Sister Conchita was still asleep in the gloom. Silently he dropped on to all fours and began to crawl along the ridge path back towards the swamp and the heedless din being made by the approaching man. There was no moon, so Kella could not see his pursuer, but he knew exactly where the man was. He was moving almost painfully slowly. Perhaps he was old or unaccustomed to physical activity. Maybe he was just exhausted, especially if he was trying to keep his rifle dry by holding it at arm's length above his head.

Kella maintained his measured stealthy crawl along the high ridge path, back into the heart of the swamp. He did not stop until he was certain that he was at least several hundred yards away from the sleeping Sister Conchita. Then he waited for the man with the rifle below him in the swamp to continue his unsteady forward progress.

The sergeant did not move until the splashing, grunting man was level with him, about twenty yards to his right. Judging the distance as best he could, Kella stood up abruptly. At the same time he shouted in alarm, as if only suddenly aware of the presence of his stalker. He heard the man flounder to a halt. Kella flung himself to the ground.

There was the report of a rifle. Kella did not move. The other man started to push uncertainly through the mud again. Now he was heading for the high ridge, in the direction of the shout in the dark. As he drew closer, a thin pencil of light from a torch illuminated the night before him. This man must be sure that his quarry was unarmed to be so careless in his approach, thought the police sergeant.

Kella waited until the light of the torch was hovering uncertainly along the ground near him. Then he stood up and ran crouching along the ridge path, back towards the river. He heard another shot echoing through the night. Kella ran for another hundred yards, vaulting the tangles of roots before him, and then stopped and sprawled behind a fallen tree on the wide ridge.

The moon drifted out from behind a cloud. Kella could just make out a figure pushing through the mud in his direction. The sergeant prepared to run again, in order to lead his pursuer into the densest part of the mangrove swamp, close to the river. Kella had spent much of his childhood digging for crawfish in the mud there. If necessary, he could lead the other man round in circles for hours, until he was so tired and lost that he would be begging for someone to come in and fetch him out.

At last the stalker found the ridge and hauled himself gratefully up on to the path. He was still too far away for Kella to be able to distinguish his outline properly. In order further to encourage the man, Kella stood up. The stalker let off another shot without aiming, firing so quickly that the bullet came nowhere near the sergeant. Kella dropped back behind the tree trunk.

Suddenly, to his alarm, he heard Sister Conchita calling his name. He could see the sister standing uncertainly among the trees on the ridge, her white habit standing out vividly against the dark background. She hesitated and then started running towards the sound of the last shot.

Kella shouted to her to go back. The sister continued to run. She thinks I'm in trouble, thought Kella. She doesn't know where she is, or what is going on, but she's coming to help me.

Sister Conchita was heading in the general direction of the elevated ridge path but in the darkness she misjudged the angle and floundered into the stinking swamp. She stopped, but then pushed forward again, almost waist-deep in the mud and brackish water. Crazy with courage, thought Kella. It was a pity about the complete lack of common sense.

The stalker was looking back in obvious bewilderment over his shoulder at the nun. To distract him Kella stood up again and started running along the ridge. He ran upright, in order to present the man with a target. No shots came. Kella stopped and looked round. The shooter had turned and was heading back purposefully towards the sister.

Kella swore softly. The stalker was now on the ridge and able to make good progress, while Sister Conchita's movements were hampered by the all-pervading mud and ankle-deep water of the swamp.

Kella changed direction and sprinted back along the ridge towards the retreating man with the rifle, shouting meaninglessly as he did so, in order to distract him. The stalker looked back and hesitated. Realizing that the police sergeant would be on him before he could reach the nun, he turned and deliberately raised his rifle to his shoulder.

Kella hurled himself off the ridge into the swamp below. The rifle exploded. Kella felt as if he had been savaged in his right shoulder by a cornered wild pig. He sprawled on the ground, pain jolting through his chest and upper arm. His mud-soaked shirt turned even darker as blood started to pump out of the wound.

The moon scudded back behind a cloud. He could see nothing. Kella forced himself to his feet and staggered through the night in the general direction of the marksman. At the same time he shouted to Sister Conchita to go back to the dry high ground, where the trees grew thickly.

Waves of nausea swept over the sergeant. Once, he fell to his knees and had to drag himself to his feet again and reel onwards. He remained down in the swamp, trying to shelter in the shadow of the ridge, presenting as small a target as possible and listening intently for the sound of the stalker's approaching footsteps. Kella was guessing that the man would come back to finish off the job, in case his last shot had not killed the policeman.

Tensely Kella waited beneath the ridge. After a few moments he heard the cautious shuffle of the man walking back along the ridge above him. Kella was too tired and weak to crawl up on to the ridge. Instead, he hauled himself along the side, squirming a painful few inches at a time, using his left hand to gain a purchase on the bank above. He stopped and used the same hand to take his penknife from his pocket. Opening it with his teeth, he waited until the stalker was directly above him. Kella gathered his remaining strength and propelled himself upwards, at the same time striking out viciously with his knife at the man's leg.

He had hoped to sever the tendons of the stalker's ankle, but he was too weak and tired. The blade entered the shadowy figure's leg, just behind the knee. The man screamed. Almost fainting with the pain of his exertions, Kella dragged the blade down the man's calf viciously, slicing it open for a length of six inches. The man yelped again and fell, in the same movement rolling over into the swamp on the far side of the ridge, almost instinctively putting the high land between himself and the sergeant.

Kella tried to crawl after him, but he could not move. He wondered how much blood he was losing from the wound in his shoulder. He lay panting for breath on his back on the slope of the ridge. When he heard footsteps pounding along the ridge he tried in vain to raise himself on to one elbow to defend himself, still clutching his knife.

He was dimly aware of flickering flares approaching rapidly above him. Then Sister Conchita was bending over him, accompanied by a group of solicitous crab hunters, bearing their flaming torches. Dimly he was aware of their awed voices, murmuring, '*aofia!*'

'Lie still!' commanded the sister tersely, taking command.

She pulled the shirt away from his bloodied shoulder. Gently she took the penknife from his hand and used it to cut the shirt away from the wound. She turned away. Kella heard tearing sounds. Sister Conchita turned back. She padded his wound with strips torn from her habit, tying it into place with more strips of the cloth. Kella drifted off into unconsciousness.

When he came round, he was being carried through the bush on a makeshift stretcher of stout branches bound roughly with vines. Sister Conchita was walking beside him, looking concerned.

'These guys say they know your island and they're taking us there,' she told him. She saw the flicker of apprehension on the police sergeant's face. 'Things aren't that bad,' she assured him. 'They taught me a little light nursing at the seminary.'

It was the opening Kella had been hoping for. He opened his mouth and tried to speak. The sister bent to hear him.

'Please stay with me,' begged Kella. 'They could harm me with custom medicine. Promise you won't leave me on my island until I'm better.'

He lay back exhausted. Sister Conchita looked surprised but touched by his unexpected display of dependence on her. She nodded reassuringly. 'I won't go, Sergeant Kella,' she said. 'That I promise.'

Kella let the men carry him towards the lagoon a mile or so away. He was conscious of his strength ebbing again. All the same, he felt oddly satisfied. At least by his stratagem he might have secured the sister's safety, until he was well enough to look after her again.

There was no doubt in his mind that she needed protection. Back in the swamp earlier that evening, as soon as the stalker had seen Sister Conchita he had turned to go after her, leaving Kella. It looked as if all along it had been Sister Conchita he had been intending to harm.

The distant, familiar and much-loved sound of lapping water soothed his ears. A few minutes later, through the swirling mists of his mind, he was dimly conscious of being loaded carefully on to a canoe at the lagoon's edge.

Suddenly a thought struck Kella. He tried to sit up to speak. Gentle but strong hands pushed him back on to his stretcher at the bottom of the canoe. As he floated into oblivion, the sergeant groaned.

He had assured the sister that no Lau man would ever harm him. That was true. But it did not mean that the same applied to Sister Conchita.

9

ARTIFICIAL ISLANDS

The gigantic *baekwa*, the man-eating crocodile, powered towards Kella through the waters of the lagoon, its massive tail thrashing violently, grotesquely swollen jaws opening and closing in heart-stopping slow motion. Kella turned to swim away, but his arms and legs seemed powerless. Screaming silently, he waited for the savage representative of the gods to devour him.

He woke up on the mat on the floor of his hut, trying to recall the details of his dream and the terrifying part that the menacing custom ghosts had again played in it.

Painfully he stood up and walked to a corner. He picked up a length of bark cloth. Carefully he unwrapped it and took out a string of Lau shell money. It was ten feet long, looped several times. The decoration consisted of alternate red and white shell discs strung along a length of bush vine. At each end of the string was a large grey mussel shell.

The necklace had been made by his mother before he was born. She had given it to him just before her death. She had hoped that one day he would use it as part of the bride price he would have to pay to the family of the woman he wanted to marry. Kella reckoned that it should be considered valuable enough even by the most demanding of the spirit people for his present purpose.

Kella carried the shell money to the door. His strapped shoulder still felt sore but after four days of drifting in and out of consciousness he was beginning to regain his strength. The bullet seemed to have passed through the fleshy part of his upper arm, doing no permanent damage.

He came out into the afternoon sunlight and walked down to one of the island's stone jetties. As always, he felt comfortably at home in his village of Sulufou, the largest artificial island in the Lau Lagoon. Forty or fifty thatched huts were crammed together on top of the great stones which formed the base of the island, eighty yards long and thirty yards wide. Other houses on stilts surrounded the island.

In the small square in the centre of the village stood a stone church, painted green and white, with a galvanized iron roof. The church had three small towers with spires. Outside the door of the church was a wooden drum used for summoning the islanders to prayer every morning and evening.

Brown-skinned children were swimming in the sheltered lagoon or skimming in tiny canoes across its placid surface. Most of the women were on the mainland, working in their gardens. Out in the open sea, on the far side of the coral reef, the younger men shouted excitedly as they controlled their bobbing outrigger canoes against the crashing waves. Blue herons swooped over them, waiting for fish to surface. The men were beating the water fiercely with their paddles to drive into the lagoon sea-bass, snapper, mackerel and mullet through the narrow fissures in the coral walls.

Inside the lagoon, older men were treading water, spears in their hands, ready to impale the fish as they were frightened into the enclosed area, and then stuff them in floating wicker baskets.

Farther out to sea, the occupants of other canoes were fishing with crude kites. Each kite was floating in the air, attached to its canoe by a length of vine. Another piece of vine, with a shell hook, dangled in the water from the kite, attached to a small stick that acted as a float on the surface of the water. Greedy large fish often mistook the kite for a bird hovering in wait for a shoal of smaller fish, and would hurry over to impale themselves on the hook.

The entire length of the Lau Lagoon, two miles wide and constantly refreshed by more than a dozen rivers pouring down from the mountains of the main island, was dotted with smaller artificial islands, each with its collection of houses. Over a period of a hundred years they had been built, stone by stone, by men and women from the mainland seeking to avoid the malarial mosquitoes and the constant warfare between saltwater dwellers and bushmen. The closely knit, sea-going Lau people spent much of their lives on their stone fortresses, going ashore only to hunt and tend their gardens.

Kella wrapped the length of shell money around his hand and muttered a *ngara*, the prayer made when an object was surrendered to the ancestral ghosts. He hesitated and then hurled the shell money as far as he could out into the lagoon.

He was aware of someone standing behind him. He turned to find Sister Conchita staring in surprise at him. The nun had come out of the women's hut in which she was living.

'What are you doing?' she asked.

'Making an offering to my ghosts,' Kella told her.

'For heaven's sake, why?'

'I must have offended them. Otherwise I would not have been wounded. Anyway, they've been entering my dreams, and I want them to leave.'

'Do you really believe that?' asked the sister.

'Sometimes,' said Kella. 'It depends.'

Sister Conchita sank on to a pile of stones. She had washed her habit and sewn a patch over the piece she had used as a bandage for him. Her face was red from exposure to the sun. She was looking more relaxed than he had ever seen her. He found it hard to remember that less than a week ago she had been thrusting through the mud of the mangrove swamp, putting her life at risk in order to help him.

'How are you feeling?' she asked, obviously deciding from the expression on his face that there would be no point in asking the sergeant about the resident gods and devils of the lagoon.

'Good.'

'I'm glad, because I'd like a word with you.'

'Can't hide from you for ever.'

'I'm pleased you appreciate that. So, what have you got to say for yourself, sergeant?'

'About what, Sister Conchita?'

'You know full well what,' said the nun calmly. 'All that garbage you gave me about you needing me here to nurse you back to health. Telling me that you were afraid of custom medicine.'

'Oh, that,' said Kella.

'Yes, that! What custom medicine? The morning after we arrived a guy came over from the mainland with a supply of penicillin and sulfa tablets for you.'

'My brother Henry. He runs the government medical clinic at Atta.'

'And the smart-looking guy who turned up in a speedboat with ointment, bandages and aspirin?'

'My brother Samuel. He's a mate on one of the government ships.'

'Just how many brothers have you got?' asked Sister Conchita.

'Five. The other three live here on Sulufou with my father and work our land over on the main island of Malaita.'

'Looks like you boys have the district pretty much sewn up between you.'

'We try. It's all a matter of line.' The young sister looked blank.

'Family,' Kella explained. 'My bloodline owns most of this island and some land on the coast. One way or another, I'm related to just about everyone in the lagoon and the saltwater villages along the shore.'

'Great,' said Sister Conchita resignedly. 'I've teamed up with the Melanesian mafia.'

She shaded her eyes and looked out over the lagoon. The fish-laden canoes were on their way back to the island with swimming escorts of noisy children. Women were beginning to paddle dugouts over from the mainland, their craft heaped with supplies of taro and sweet potatoes.

'Is there somewhere we can talk?' asked Sister Conchita.

'Sure,' said Kella. 'I know just the place. I wanted to show it to you anyway.'

He conducted her across the public dancing ground and past a *bisi*, one of the houses in which women remained for thirty days after they had delivered their babies. Kella untied a canoe from the jetty and paddled the nun out towards the reef.

They passed over coral gardens, beautifully designed fragile shapes and patterns shimmering at the bottom of the pellucid water. Kella used the short period of calm to consider some of the problems that had been brought to him as the *aofia*, since he had regained consciousness.

A palm tree had been toppled in a garden on the mainland after the recent earth tremor. During its lifetime the tree had belonged to one family, the nuts to another and the land upon which it had stood to a third. All three families had requested him to give judgement as to the disposition of the tree, its roots and fruit.

In another case, a young man from Sulufou was in dispute with the family of a girl he wanted to marry, about the amount of bride price he would have to pay for her. There were also complaints from one of the coastal villagers that the aged hereditary tree-shouter had lost his *mana*. For decades if a tree had proved too big to be felled by hand, islanders had approached the shouter and begged him to hurl incantations at it. Generally within a month the tree would begin to lose its leaves and branches and then die. Now it appeared that the old man had lost his powers. The villagers wanted him replaced. Kella would have to give rulings on these matters, and several others, before he left the lagoon to resume his police duties.

He stopped paddling and steadied the canoe against a ridge of stones. They had reached a small deserted artificial island, close to the outer reef. So far it was little more than an extended pile of rocks. Kella held the craft firmly while Sister Conchita stepped gingerly ashore. He tied the craft to one of the outcrops of coral and followed her on to the baking stones of the artificial island.

'Who lives here?' asked Sister Conchita, looking around.

'I will one day, when it's finished,' Kella told her. 'I'm building it myself. I get a little help, of course.'

'Naturally,' said Sister Conchita, 'What with you being so well connected and all.'

He led her to the solitary makeshift thatched hut on his island. The roof was supported on poles and there were no walls. They sat facing one another on rush mats in the shade.

'Right,' said Sister Conchita with a dogged resolve to get at the truth. 'That guy with the rifle who you frightened off in the mangrove swamp – it was me he was trying to kill, wasn't it?'

'What makes you think that?' asked Kella cautiously.

Sister Conchita gestured impatiently. 'Because I am neither blind nor stupid, Sergeant Kella! You deliberately tried to draw him away from me. As soon as he saw that I wasn't with you, he turned back and came gunning for me again. He would have got me, too, if you hadn't slowed him up by making him shoot at you.'

'It's hard to be sure—' began Kella, but by now the sister was in full spate.

'Afterwards,' she went on, 'you suspected that I might still be in danger. So you concocted that cock-and-bull story about being afraid of custom medicine, whereas really all you wanted was to keep me safely on Sulufou until you were better. Am I right, sergeant?'

'Possibly,' said Kella, wondering how much he could tell the nun without frightening her.

'Of course I'm right!' snapped Sister Conchita, reverting for a moment to a trace of her former impatient self. She stopped and controlled herself with an effort. 'I'm sorry. I'm grateful, I really am. It's just that I can't imagine who could want to harm me. Well, apart from a few senior priests, and maybe a church administrator or two, and perhaps some of the instructors at the seminary.'

'Hardly anybody at all,' agreed Kella. 'What did you do with your Novice of the Year plaque?'

The sister laughed in spite of herself. 'All right, all right, so I can be a pain in the butt. However, not to the extent of making anyone want to hire a hit-man to dispose of me. They'd be too cheap to spend the money, apart from the ones who would prefer to do it themselves.'

'Perhaps you've discovered something that you shouldn't have,' suggested Kella. It was a thought he had been mulling over during his periods of consciousness during the past few days.

'What? So far I've been moved from one dull job to another – administration, archives, comparative religions, you name it, I've done it. If you ever want to know anything about ancestor worship and pagan ceremonies, just come to me. I'm practically an expert on the recondite.'

'Have you upset anyone on the mission station?'

'Even *I* haven't been there long enough for that,' said Sister Conchita. 'I've had two weeks in Honiara, and now less than a month with Father Pierre at the Ruvabi mission. I'd really have to try hard to make someone want to kill me in that short period of time.'

Behind her flippant attitude Kella could sense that the sister was worried. That made it easier for him to broach the next subject. 'I'd like you to go back to Honiara for a while,' he told her. 'You'll be safe at the mission headquarters in the capital.'

'No way,' said Sister Conchita. 'No one's chasing me off with my tail between my legs. I'm going back to the mission, where I belong. I've got work to do there.'

'I wasn't thinking about you,' Kella told her. 'I'm worrying about Father Pierre. He's too old to look after you, and as long as you're on his station you'll be a liability. He deserves better than that.'

The nun looked horror-stricken. 'I hadn't thought about that,' she confessed. 'I was too busy giving my impression of a hot-shot, I guess.' She considered the matter, her head bowed. Finally she nodded. 'All right, Sergeant Kella, you win.' She looked appealingly at him. 'Will you be coming back with me to Honiara?'

Kella shook his head. 'It's my job to find out who was shooting at us,' he said. 'One of my jobs, anyway. I'll get a friend to take you back to Guadalcanal, maybe tomorrow.'

The sister looked across the lagoon at the mainland. Dark clouds were forming over the forested mountain range which formed the spine of the island. Despite the heat she shivered.

'I don't envy you on your own over there,' she said with feeling.

Kella followed her gaze. 'That's not the hard part,' he said.

'What is then?'

'The fact that you're involved,' Kella told her frankly. 'We don't often get expats involved in island problems. When they do, it gets complicated. I'm telling you this because I want you to be on your guard, even in Honiara.'

'Don't worry,' said the sister fervently. 'After that night in the swamp, I'll make sure of that. How about you? It can't be easy for you, representing the police force and trying to be the *aofia* as well. Father Pierre said that because you've rejected parts of both worlds you'll always be on your own.'

'I've still got a job to do,' said Kella, shying away from the probing intimacy of her remark. 'That reminds me. What can you tell me about the American anthropologist, Professor Mallory? I've been sent to Malaita to look for him.'

And that's all I'm supposed to be doing, he thought. If Chief Superintendent Grice found out that he was meddling in so many other inquiries as well, his superior officer would have apoplexy. That was just too bad. He had to search for Peter Oro. Solomon Bulko had sent a message from Ruvabi by canoe saying that the schoolboy still had not returned.

'I hardly know him,' answered Sister Conchita. 'When he was at the mission he spent most of his time with Father Pierre.' She hesitated. 'It seemed to me that he was always pumping the priest for information.'

'What sort of information?'

Sister Conchita shook her head. 'I don't know. When the professor discovered that I was new here, he lost interest pretty quickly.'

'There must have been something he wanted,' said Kella. 'Think!'

The sister looked surprised at the sudden urgency in the police sergeant's tone, but she closed her eyes in concentration.

'I believe,' she said, opening her eyes again, 'that he wanted to know about something called a *havu*.' She looked at Kella. 'What's that?'

Kella did not answer at once. It had never occurred to him that Mallory would be moving in that direction. Yet now it all seemed so simple. He would have to find the anthropologist quickly, before the American got into serious trouble. He realized that Sister Conchita was speaking again.

'I'm sorry I can't be of more help,' she said humbly, 'especially with you going to so much trouble to look after me.'

'I must,' said Kella. 'I have no choice. You are one of the *neena*, the unprotected. As long as you're in the Lau area, it is the duty of the *aofia* to see that you come to no harm.'

'Well, after all, I have my own God to do that,' said the nun calmly. 'But the way things are going, I don't want to be too picky. I guess I'll take all the help I can get.'

'Good! Now you're talking sense,' said Kella. 'I'm sorry you're going to have to be on your own here for the next couple of days, but I've got to arrange your transportation back to the capital.'

'No problem,' said the nun. 'I'll find something to do.'

They stood up. Kella beckoned to one of the passing fishing canoes. Immediately it pulled in to the side of the island. The islanders on board helped Sister Conchita down into the craft. Before it had pulled away she was already enthusing over their catch in halting pidgin.

10

MANA

Kella walked round his island, ostensibly checking on its development, as he tried to marshal his thoughts. He had started building his new home three years ago. First he had hammered four tall, sharpened guide-posts into the corners of the site. Then he had felled tree trunks on the mainland to make a raft. Loosening large boulders on the coral reef, enduring the huge pounding waves that sometimes drove him into the sea, he had loaded them on to the raft, a few at a time, and poled them over to the site he had marked out, and dropped them into the water between the four posts. When the rocks had reached the level of the waterline he had started to mould his island into shape, staggering across the surface with more boulders in his hands.

After the rocks had emerged from the lagoon to a height of six feet he had ferried huge quantities of sand from the beach and poured the sand between the gaps in the rocks as they shifted and settled into position. Now that the boulders and water had soaked up the sand he could start building a thatched house and plant alu trees for shade and palm trees for their fruit. And then, perhaps, he would find a wife.

But not just yet, he thought, staring out beyond the reef to the rolling open sea. He had other work to do first. Too many things were suddenly going wrong in his area. If he did not do something about them no one else would.

His first task would be to find out what had happened to Mallory. If the foolish American had gone in search of the *havu*, he would have climbed into the almost impenetrable high bush of the Kwaio area in the central mountain range, a dangerous journey for any man, let alone a middle-aged white academic.

Kella decided to send a message back to Honiara that he had gone in pursuit of the anthropologist. That should keep Chief Superintendent Grice off his back for another week or two. It would also give Kella time to investigate the spate of other crimes in the vicinity.

There was the matter of the skeleton of Lofty Herman, found with a bullet hole in its skull. Almost certainly that was a crime committed eighteen years before, when the Japanese had invaded the Solomons in 1942.

Of more immediate concern were the attempts on the life of Sister Conchita. What had the sister done or seen in the short time she had been on the mission station to impel someone to strike out at her, even when she was under the protection of the *aofia*?

Kella turned and stared over at the dark mass of the mainland. There was also the matter of the unexplained death of the old man Senda Iabuli in the saltwater village and the sudden flight of the dead man's grandson Peter Oro into the bush. That had been precipitated, he was certain, by Kella's discovery of the bones *tabu* and the subsequent placing of a curse on the police sergeant by Pazabosi, the magic man.

Pazabosi was also the paramount chieftain of the Kwaio bush, the area into which Mallory had been blundering. Kella unhitched his canoe. Matters were assuming an ominous shape, like one of Malaita's constantly changing but always threatening rain clouds. The discovery of Herman's skeleton had led to

Pazabosi placing his bones curse on the mission station. Pazabosi had left his bush home to make an almost unprecedented visit to the saltwater area. Almost at once, someone had tried to kill Sister Conchita.

Kella slipped into his canoe and began paddling it reflectively back towards Sulufou. The answer to many of his problems undoubtedly lay in Pazabosi's remote Kwaio district. That was where he would have to go next, even if the magic man had placed a bones curse on him. Kella had no fear of any incantation laid against him in the saltwater Lau region. Here his *mana* was strong. However, in the mountainous bush of Kwaio, all the magic would belong to Pazabosi. There he would find the devil-devils.

11

SIKAIANA WOMEN

Pazabosi sat cross-legged in the village clearing, under the shade of a banyan tree. He was thinking seriously about the past and the future. With so little time left it was important to get both into balance. He knew that the most important period of his long life still lay before him, and that what had happened in the past would have a great bearing on what was to come.

He was finding it hard to walk the long distances he had once covered with ease, and his sight and hearing were declining. But, thank the spirits, he still had his reputation as a tribal leader; he retained his *mana*. He knew that it was rumoured among his people that he had gained much of his power through eating the hearts of the enemies he had killed in battle. In addition to his wealth in land and possessions, it was also widely acknowledged that he even possessed the ultimate gift of being able to stop the sun in its passage to allow travellers to reach home in the light.

Images of the past unfolded in his mind as he waited for what was to come. Sometimes it seemed to him as if his whole life had been one long bloody pageant of plotting and fighting. He had been born into a pagan family in the most mountainous area of the bush, more than seventy years ago, and his earliest memory was of being hidden in the long grass by his parents as his father went off to fight the saltwater men.

While he was still a young man, Pazabosi had met some time-expired labourers returned from working on the Australian sugar plantations. He had admired their tall stories of life in the cane fields and had coveted the strong iron chests full of iron tools they had brought back with them. As a result, after much thought, he had undertaken the perilous three-day walk down to the coast. None of the saltwater men had attempted to stop him. They were pleased to see the departure from Malaita of such a dangerous foe.

At the end of his journey down from the mountains, he had made his mark with the captain of a three-masted labour-recruiting vessel at anchor in a bay. The blackbirder who had signed him on had been the first white man Pazabosi had seen.

It had all been a long time ago, he decided. Now the future was important to him. The old chieftain went over in his mind the arrangements he had made for the important few weeks to come. With one exception everything was now in place.

Pazabosi pondered over the one possible weakness in his plans. Sergeant Kella, the *aofia*, still stood in his way. Despite the bush chieftain's efforts to discredit the policeman, Kella was once again on Malaita. And Kella always represented a threat.

Pazabosi knew that he had the high inland bush region and much of the coastal strip, except for the artificial islands of the Lau Lagoon, under his control. He was aware also that the white administrators, remote and ineffectual in far-off Honiara, would never have the local knowledge or the manpower to forestall him.

But Kella was different. He was neither wholly a Lau man nor yet a white lackey. He occupied a strange, undefinable middle area and so was unpredictable. If Kella decided to come looking for Pazabosi, he would surely find him. So be it. Pazabosi was ready for him.

Two ancient bushwomen emerged from one of the larger huts in the village, shepherding before them three beautiful young

Sikaiana women in their late teens. The girls were naked, except for brief thongs of banana fibre between their legs. True to the traditions of their island they were lovely almost beyond belief – high-breasted and slim-legged.

They were Polynesians, their smooth skins a burnished dark gold. Their lustrous dark hair had been brushed to a high sheen and fell luxuriantly to their shoulders. When they smiled respectfully at the old chieftain, they revealed perfect, gleaming white teeth.

All the torments of sexual passion had long since departed Pazabosi but he returned the smiles of the young women. Sikaiana girls from their outlying atoll north-east of Malaita were reputed second in comeliness only to the extroverted women of New Georgia in the Western Solomons. For Pazabosi, the Sikaianans possessed the additional advantage of belonging to a clan committed to his movement. Their island leader had been perfectly happy to send three of his most prized practitioners in the art of love on the long voyage across the seas, to the Malaitan bush.

Pazabosi nodded his satisfaction and stood up. 'Come.' He instructed the giggling and acquiescent women. 'I will show you where you must go.' He paused and added drily, 'I'm sure you already know what to do!'

12

COCONUT BOSS

As the sun appeared over the horizon, Kella beached his canoe on the shore of the bay of John Deacon's copra plantation. He dragged the canoe up the sand and then walked along the footpath between the coconut palms towards the Australian's house.

Green-grey clover, planted to keep down quick-growing weeds, spread densely between the palms. Kella flexed his shoulder gingerly. It was still sore but mobile enough for his needs.

He noticed with approval that the plantation was still well maintained. Deacon was a harsh and unforgiving man but a good coconut boss. Hundreds of acres of straight grey trunks, thirty feet apart, admitted the same amount of sun everywhere.

At the tops of the trees, attaining a height of sixty feet, were the massive coconuts, half-hidden among great palm fronds. The large leaves that had fallen to the ground had already been swept into piles, ready for burning.

Hearing the approach of the police sergeant, Deacon came limping out of his wooden bungalow in a clearing.

'No appointment,' he chided. 'Jeez, you're growing slack, Kella.'

The sergeant grinned, aware of the whisky on the other man's breath. It was widely known that visitors to the plantation were discouraged. Even touring government officers had to use the radio network in advance if they wanted to drop by.

'How do you know I'm not here to take my land back?' he inquired softly.

'You wouldn't know what to do with it,' said Deacon. 'It takes magic bilong whitefella to run a place as inherently crook as this. Want some breakfast?'

'I've eaten,' Kella told him. 'I'm here to ask a favour.'

'So what else is new? Tell me as we walk. I haven't made my morning rounds yet.'

The two men fell into step. Deacon was short and stocky, in his mid-fifties, with a florid complexion and an irascible manner. He limped as he kept up with the islander. One leg was shorter than the other as the result of taking a raft of Japanese tracer bullets in his leg when he and Kella had raided an enemy ammunition depot on Guadalcanal eighteen years before.

The Australian had lived in the Solomons for almost thirty years, following a variety of nomadic occupations, including gold miner, trading-boat skipper, and bêche-de-mer fisherman. None of these ventures had paid off and it was generally assumed that Deacon also engaged in less legal practices on the side. Soon after the war had ended, unexpectedly he had produced enough money to take out a long lease on the copra plantation from Kella's father.

'How's it going?' asked the policeman.

'With first-grade copra falling to less than seventy dollars Australian a ton? Don't ask, mate!'

Deacon was always overly pessimistic. On this plantation he was able to produce three-quarters of a ton of copra to the acre, compared with the half ton grown by most. Kella also knew that, strictly against the terms of his contract, the Australian was also earning another couple of thousand dollars a year from the seashells he was taking clandestinely from the beach and lagoon.

The labourers, all Lau men, were beginning to emerge from their dormitories to start their day's work. They recognized Kella and waved cheerfully at him. Deacon shouted at them in pidgin, ordering them to get to work. Philosophically the men spread out among the trees in groups of four. Each labourer carried three sacks, which had to be filled with fallen coconuts and carried to the processing plant. Tractors began to cough to life and head for the passages between the trees.

Outside the drying sheds more islanders sat cutting coconuts into halves with machetes and gouging out the white meat in two movements. The raw meat was being carried by other labourers into the sheds, where it would be raked out and dried on wire racks above rows of wood-burning ovens.

Kella inhaled the familiar sickly-sweet odour of burning wood and roasting copra. One day several of his brothers would want to take over the plantation. So far Kella had persuaded them to wait. Deacon was aware of this. Kella could not be sure whether the Australian was grateful or not.

'So what do you want me to do?' asked Deacon.

'I want you to take someone to Honiara for me in your cutter boat,' said Kella. 'Today, if possible.'

'Sure,' said Deacon sardonically. 'Bring me a bucket of sand and I'll sing you the Desert Song.' He saw Kella's expression. 'You're serious, aren't you?' he asked. 'What's the game?'

'Somebody's trying to kill a sister from the mission,' said Kella. 'She's not safe on Malaita. I don't know anyone I can trust to do this, except you.'

He told Deacon about the attempts on Sister Conchita's life at the mission station and in the swamp. When he had finished the Australian nodded thoughtfully.

'You were lucky in that swamp, mate. Four shots fired at you, and all you end up with is a flesh wound. Either the other bloke's a bad shot, or he liked you too much to want to hurt you badly.

I wish I'd been that lucky in the war. That female God-botherer goes around asking for trouble, if you ask me.'

'I heard that she reported you to Customs for trying to smuggle shells out of the country,' said Kella. 'What are you worrying about? I bet you had them well stashed away before they searched you.'

'That's not the point. She reported me.'

'I was going to do the same thing myself one day, when I got round to it.'

'You're different. You're . . .'

'Black?' suggested Kella.

'I didn't say that, mate.'

'You meant it though. I can report you because I'm a copper and Melanesian. But the sister's white. She broke the code, didn't she? Whities stick together.'

'By God, we've had to in this place!' burst out Deacon. 'If we didn't we'd all have had our throats slit by now.'

'Thanks,' said Kella.

'I didn't mean you, Ben; you know that. You and me have always got on all right, but us expats have always been in a small minority in the Solomons. I've been in the islands for thirty years. We've only survived because we've looked out for each other. Anybody who didn't help his oppos didn't last long. And this kid comes out and starts reporting me. It ain't right.'

'If it's going to be a problem I'll get someone else to take her to the capital.'

'No, you're all right, mate. I'll take her. Screw her. I owe you big-time. She'll be right.'

'All right,' said Kella, unconvinced. 'But if you do take her, behave. Once you hold a grudge against someone—'

'I told you, she'll be right.'

They rounded a corner and the plantation manager let out a bellow of wrath. One of the labourers was throwing stones at the green young coconuts in an effort to dislodge them. The islanders were paid by the number of sacks they filled in a day. If there were not enough fallen ripe nuts some of them would surreptitiously try to increase their rate by shaking the immature fruit from the trees. Cursing vigorously, Deacon hobbled in the direction of the offending young islander.

Kella walked back towards the beach. He wondered how much longer Deacon would last on Malaita. The crude, blasphemous courage which had made him such an effective guerrilla leader against the Japanese was not endearing him to the new brands of islanders, who had at least a junior primary education and were well enough aware of the increasing drift to get rid of expatriates from the islands. The days of the old colonial taskmasters were almost over. That was probably the main reason why Deacon was hitting the bottle so hard.

An old and rusted American landing barge was half-submerged out near the reef. Kella's mind went back to the days in 1942, when he and Pazabosi and half a dozen others had served under Deacon on a whaleboat equipped with several machine guns, in which they had made a number of raids on Japanese coastal positions.

It had been a close thing as to which of the pair had been the most bloodthirsty, thought Kella. Deacon had fought with a cold, controlled anger, while Pazabosi had been the more frenzied and volatile in their bloody skirmishes in the war, which lasted a little more than six months before the Japanese had been driven out of the Solomons.

Deacon hobbled up behind him. He seemed to know what Kella was thinking about as the islander stared out at the wreck of the landing barge.

'How old were you when you joined us on the *Wantok*?' he asked.

'Fourteen,' said Kella.

'Christ! As young as that? I suppose you must have been. I remember when they brought you back from secondary school in Fiji to act as an interpreter between the Yanks and the natives. You stuck it for about a month and then got yourself back here and asked if you could do some real fighting with us on the whaler.'

'I soon got enough of that.'

'You were bloody good at it, mate. So was that old bastard Pazabosi. Sometimes I thought you were both going to heave me over the side and fight your own war against the Japs, because I wasn't tough enough for you.'

There had been little chance of that, thought Kella, remembering the iron discipline imposed by the Australian skipper on malcontents, supplemented by vicious floggings over an oil drum with a rattan cane.

'Have you heard anything of Pazabosi lately?' he asked.

'Haven't seen him for years. We were never mates. He went to ground and lay pretty low when the Marching Rule uprising collapsed after the war. I did hear lately that he was recruiting the natives for another go at the Brits, but there are always stories like that going the rounds. Why are you interested?'

'An American anthropologist has gone missing up in Kwaio country. I'm supposed to find him and bring him back.'

Deacon whistled. 'Well, if he's gone up into the mountains, Pazabosi will certainly know about it. If he gives the word the Yank will be chopped down like a small tree. You're not going to be crazy enough to go after him?'

'I thought I might go as far as the killing ground.'

'Then you're out of your bloody mind,' said Deacon vehemently. 'I would have thought your last caper up there would have warned you off that place.'

'I'll be careful.'

'You always had to do things your own bloody way,' said

Deacon, 'even when you were a kid. All right, I can't stop you. I'll pick up your nun and run her back to Honiara for you.'

After the plantation manager had left, Kella continued to stare out at the reef. He wondered why the normally heedless Deacon had been so eager to stop him going up into the mountains. The Australian had always been a shrewd operator, with an eye to the main chance. Perhaps he had his own agenda. With his days in the Solomons numbered he could be looking round for one last money-making venture.

Then there had been his reaction to Kella's account of the pursuit in the mangrove swamp. Deacon had claimed to have heard nothing of the matter. Yet he knew that four shots had been fired at them. Kella was sure that he had not mentioned this when he had given Deacon an edited version of the events of that night.

13

PRAYING MARY

The queue of women and children outside the Sulufou clinic already snaked around the island, although it was only ten o'clock in the morning. The news that the Praying Mary had reopened the island clinic had spread all over the lagoon. Across the water, canoes were heading for Sulufou from most of the other artificial islands.

The government rural health clinic consisted of a concrete floor and a tin roof, balanced on betel-wood posts. The walls were constructed of interwoven sago-palm leaves. The interior was divided into a large room used for medical inspections, and several small empty wards, each with a bed and a mattress.

On one of the exterior walls was pinned a poster issued by the Agriculture Department. In cartoon form it showed the amount of copra needed in order to purchase different items. The average amount produced after a day's work should earn the labourer enough to buy a bicycle, while seventy-five filled sacks were sufficient for the purchase of a motorcycle.

Sister Conchita stood at a table in the centre of the main room of the clinic, the sleeves of her habit rolled up, as she did her best to deal with the endless line of patients before her. After each one had left she entered the details of her diagnosis and treatment into a logbook.

She had come across the clinic on one of her earlier perambulations of the island. She had been informed that it was only opened for one day approximately every three weeks, sometimes not that often, when a government launch would deliver a medical orderly for a few hours, and then take him back to Auki, the district centre.

Sister Conchita had also noticed that the key to the main medicine cabinet had been deposited trustingly on a hook on the wall. Furthermore, the box was plentifully supplied with ointments, bandages, plasters, gauze, ether, tweezers, a magnifying glass and even several phials of aspirins and bottles of medicine.

Admittedly there were also handwritten warnings in pidgin, ordering the villagers not to touch any of the medical supplies. Sister Conchita consoled herself with the thought that she was not a villager and that she had ministered to plenty of patients at Ruvabi mission; it would be a shame not to offer her services to the islanders while she happened to be in the area. In any case, it had always been her philosophy that it was better to apologize profusely after the event than to neglect an opportunity when it arose. Besides which, she thought, the islanders had told her that it had been at least a month since a medical orderly had visited Sulufou.

There were no men in the queue outside the clinic, and no one at all from the bush villages. It was against the custom of the pagan mountain dwellers to adopt the white man's medicine, while the saltwater men would accept no help from a white woman. Even so, there was plenty to be done with the women and children who had come to be attended at the newly opened medical centre. Sister Conchita's morning passed in a whirl of bandaging and prescribing. She attended to pregnancies, doled out chloroquine to malarial patients and sulfa tablets for abdominal pains, massaged and put compresses on strains, and applied pressure to bleeding wounds.

At one o'clock in the afternoon, she took a short break and carried a bottle of water to the door. Shyly a village woman brought her a plate of taro. The queue waiting patiently outside seemed to extend as far as ever. As she watched, a small flotilla of canoes headed out from the mainland and pulled in at the artificial island's wharf. Half a dozen male malaria eradication sprayers, on a periodic anti-mosquito tour of the artificial islands, leapt out of the canoes and advanced cheerfully on the houses. They wore khaki shorts and shirts and were carrying backpacks, jets and nozzles.

The old village men gossiping lethargically in the shade of a canoe shelter glared at the noisy new arrivals. The itinerant sprayers, trained and dispatched in groups by the Department of Health, had a not undeserved reputation for routinely trying to seduce local girls on their travels. Oblivious to the disapproval of the elders, the sprayers carried on with their work, leering and calling out licentiously to the younger women in the line for the clinic.

Sister Conchita looked on idly, preparing to go back inside the clinic. She became aware that one of the malaria sprayers was looking at her with some intensity. He was the biggest member of the team, broad-shouldered and tall. The nun recognized his stare. It was one that she had encountered a number of times since she had come to the Solomons. Most of the islanders were perfectly prepared to welcome expatriates, or at the very least ignore them as alien beings beyond their comprehension. A few, however, especially the better educated, actively resented the presence of the white strangers in their land. The big worker was plainly one of these. He was glowering at her, making no effort to disguise his antagonism.

Sister Conchita wondered whether she should try to talk to the big islander, but decided against it. There was something forbidding about his lowering presence that made it seem likely that he would resent any overtures made to him by one of the outsiders he so clearly disliked. In any case, she had work to do. She went back inside the clinic.

The first part of the afternoon was as busy as the morning had been. Sister Conchita continued to attend as best she could to fractures and dislocations. She dabbed arnica on bruises and placed cold compresses on skin rashes, weighed babies and stitched wounds. She was in the process of making a paste of water and soda bicarbonate powder to apply to a sea-urchin sting suffered by an eight-year-old boy, when the clinic door was flung open and a flustered middle-aged woman thrust her head into the room.

'Come hurry-up, sister,' she begged.

Sister Conchita ran through the crowded huts to a space in front of the island church. There the malaria sprayers were huddled in consternation around one of their number, who was screaming in agony next to a large fire. On the ground, upside down next to the fire, lay a large wooden bowl. Desperately Sister Conchita tried to muster enough of her scanty pidgin to find out what was happening.

'Whichway now thisfella—' she began haltingly.

'I speak English,' said the large sprayer with whom earlier she had made eye contact, turning away from the others towards her. Impatiently he indicated the stricken man writhing on the ground. 'We were boiling water for tea. Isaac knocked the bowl over and the boiling water has scalded him.'

Isaac screamed again. The sprayers looked at him helplessly. 'Bring him to the clinic!' ordered Sister Conchita. The men did not move. Of course, thought the sister. They would never allow a woman to look after a man. To do so would go against tradition. Yet the stricken man was in urgent need of attention. She looked across at the big sprayer. His command of English was excellent; he must have been educated overseas. Had that taken him sufficiently far from the constraints of custom? Would he have the moral courage to allow her to help?

'Do you know how to help your friend?' she asked. The big man shook his head. Sister Conchita pounced. 'Well, I do!' she said. 'Bring him to the clinic quickly. It's the only chance he's got.'

The big man hesitated. Then, after what seemed to the sister a very long time, he nodded and turned to the other sprayers, talking urgently to them. The men shuffled their feet, plainly unwilling to move. The big man spoke again vehemently, waving his hands in the direction of the clinic. Finally two of the sprayers ran to the clinic and came back with one of the stretchers piled in a corner. Under Sister Conchita's supervision they lifted the groaning man on to the stretcher and carried him into the clinic.

'Put him on the table,' ordered Sister Conchita. She waited until the men had done so and then made shooing motions with her hands. 'All right, leave him with me now.'

The sprayers looked at their leader. He nodded and said something in dialect. Dragging their feet the men left the room. The big sprayer remained. When Sister Conchita glanced at him he shrugged. 'I must stay,' he said. 'They do not like leaving one of their own with a mary – a woman. I cannot leave him.'

'Very well,' said Sister Conchita. 'If you must, you must. Perhaps you can make yourself useful. What's your name?'

'Jimmy.'

'Stand over by the door while I examine him, Jimmy.'

Bracing herself, Sister Conchita bent over Isaac. Carefully she cut away part of the sprayer's sodden shirt, taking care not to remove any of the cloth adhering to his skin. It was plain that most of the water had been spilled over the man's chest area and stomach. Already angry blisters were forming on his blotched skin.

'We've got to cool his wounds,' announced the sister. 'That means training a constant flow of cold water over the afflicted parts.'

'There aren't any taps on the island,' Jimmy pointed out. 'How can we keep a steady supply of water coming?'

'This way,' said Sister Conchita, and told him exactly what she wanted done.

Five minutes later a long line of islanders was extending from the large concrete freshwater stand in the centre of the island to the medical centre. A variety of slopping containers of all sizes, from buckets to gourds, were being passed, hand to hand, from the stand to the door of the clinic, where Jimmy seized each one in turn and hurried over to Sister Conchita where he emptied it carefully into a small funnel held by the sister.

The nun stood over the prostrate Isaac, carefully pouring a constant stream of cool water over him through the funnel. Jimmy ran to and from the door, taking the new, filled pots and returning the empty ones, to be passed back along the line to the concrete water stand.

For a quarter of an hour Sister Conchita stood over Isaac, emptying the water over his quivering body, concentrating only on maintaining an even flow. The concrete floor of the clinic was awash, but gradually her ministrations seemed to be having an effect. Isaac had stopped whimpering and was gazing dazedly at the roof. After a time he made no sound at all, although he was still conscious.

'I think we've done it,' said Sister Conchita, with relief, conscious of the aching of her arms. 'At least Isaac's not in so much pain now. I'll cover his wounds with a dry dressing and give him some aspirins. Then we've got to find a way of getting him to a hospital.'

She wrapped bandages around the sprayer's body and placed a blanket over his unaffected legs.

'You've done good work,' said Jimmy grudgingly, standing next to her.

'Not too bad for a mary,' agreed Sister Conchita.

Jimmy walked to the doorway and ordered the villagers to send no more water across. Suddenly it seemed as if he did not want to leave. He loitered in the doorway, avoiding the nun's gaze. When he spoke it was in a rush of words.

'You are a good woman, Sister Conchita. Everyone says that the Praying Mary is here to help us.'

'If I'm allowed to.'

The islander shrugged. 'It is not easy. We must find our own way, not depend on others. All the same, this afternoon you saved Isaac because you were the only one who knew what to do.'

'I was only able to help because you convinced the others that a mary was capable of taking charge,' said Sister Conchita. 'That's the way it should be – working together.'

'Soon, I think, it will be too late for that,' said Jimmy, shaking his head. 'Whitey must leave and give us a chance on our own.' He raised a hand to forestall her reply. 'This is not the time to speak of such things. Today you helped my team and I am grateful. It is custom that I must now do something to help you.'

'I don't expect—'

'It is custom,' repeated Jimmy in a tone that brooked no argument. 'Would you shame me in front of my men?' Sister Conchita forced herself to shake her head. 'Good,' said the malaria sprayer approvingly. 'You are learning, Praying Mary. Listen to me. This week we have been working along the coast. We visited Ruvabi mission and Deacon's copra plantation. There has been much gossip about you in both places.'

'I bet there has,' agreed Sister Conchita with feeling.

'And,' went on Jimmy inexorably, 'there has been talk that you are in danger.'

'If you consider getting shot at in the swamp dangerous, I'll go along with that.'

Jimmy did not respond to the sister's attempt at flippancy. 'That was only a part of it. You have got involved in the smuggling. You will find it difficult to shake yourself free. Custom is involved, as well as theft. Be very careful. Do what your *aofia* tells you. He is the only one who can help you.'

She should never have got involved with John Deacon's attempts to take the glory shells out of the islands, thought Sister Conchita. Before she could question Jimmy, one of the other malaria sprayers poked his head around the door.

'Boat come!' he said excitedly

Leaving the sprayer with Isaac, Sister Conchita and Jimmy ran down to the wharf. A government launch had anchored just outside the lagoon. A small rowing boat was pulling through the rocks of the reef, heading for Sulufou. Two uniformed seamen of the Marine Department were rowing, while a third sat in the prow, with several canisters at his feet. Most of the women, children and old men still left on the artificial island were streaming down to the wharf to greet the newcomers.

'It's Kovara, the medical orderly,' said Jimmy as the rowing boat drew closer. 'He's come to take his monthly sick-call at the clinic.'

Sister Conchita's heart sank at the news. She looked back at the open door of the clinic and thought of the medical supplies she had appropriated and used so freely that day, without permission, and of the diagnoses she had made without consultation. It had all seemed so right and proper at the time, helpful even. Now, with the bespectacled and rather prim-looking medical orderly being dragged in the dinghy up the beach by the two seamen from the government launch, the nun wondered if he would take the same free-spirited attitude as she had done to her random use of government medical supplies. Somehow she doubted it. It looked as if she was in trouble again.

Kovara, the medical orderly, was now splashing through the shallows towards her. As he approached he was staring open-mouthed over her shoulder at the line of would-be patients waiting outside the clinic. Inspiration struck Sister Conchita, as it so often did in times of trouble. She raced to meet Kovara, taking his hand and shaking it gratefully.

'Oh, thank the Lord you've come, Mr Kovara,' she gabbled, hoping that she was not overdoing the helpless little woman bit. 'I don't know what we would have done without you. One of the sprayers has been badly scalded. I've done what I can, but he needs to be taken back to the Auki hospital at once, under your expert care. Please, it's urgent!'

'I don't understand,' faltered the orderly. He gazed in dismay at the open door of the clinic and the table strewn with bandages and ointments. 'Who—'

'Please,' begged Sister Conchita, 'it may be a matter of death. Please turn the launch around and tend the poor man on your way back to Auki. I'll make sure that your clinic is looked after.'

Kovara still looked reluctant. Jimmy broke the impasse. He issued rapid orders to his fellow sprayers. Two of them ran to the clinic and emerged carrying their scalded co-worker on the canvas stretcher. Without looking at Kovara they bore the stretcher to the rowing boat in the shallows and loaded it gently on board.

'Get him to Auki now,' growled Jimmy.

Still the medical orderly hesitated. Jimmy and the other malaria sprayers advanced on him menacingly. Kovara took a pace backwards. In a moment he had scuttled to the dinghy and, his healing instincts taking over, was bending solicitously over the man on the stretcher, as the two seamen rowed them back towards the launch.

'Thanks again,' Sister Conchita said to Jimmy.

'Just take care,' said the malaria sprayer. He shivered despite the heat. 'This is a funny part of the Solomons. You never know what's going to happen here.'

He issued orders to the other sprayers and they struggled into their backpacks and equipment before continuing with their work. Thoughtfully Sister Conchita walked back to her waiting patients. It seemed common knowledge that she was in danger. The only problem was that she still had no idea what it was or where it was likely to come from.

14

CAVE OF DEATH

Kella reached the waterfall in the high bush by late afternoon, eight hours after he had left the plantation to start his ascent into the mountains. For the most part he made good progress up the steep and tangled paths beneath the trees. He was aware of being watched constantly from the undergrowth by many pairs of eyes. The hidden bushmen would recognize his police uniform and with luck would probably allow him unimpeded passage, as long as he did not transgress any of their customs.

The days of constant outright warfare between the bush people of the interior and the saltwater men of the coastal villages had passed, but there were still brawls between men of the two cultures when they met at the markets, where fish were exchanged for taro.

Sometimes, even today, a party of coastal warriors would raid the gardens of the interior. In return, bush fighters would attack and hole canoes left on the beach. Occasionally these fights would lead to a death or two, but they were seldom reported to the police authorities in the capital. Kella had always done his best to prevent such pitched battles. Until his recall to Honiara he had been having some success with his peacemaking endeavours.

He toiled through a solid wall of green vegetation. The thick grey trunks of the banyan and betel nut trees were almost obscured by trailing green vines and creepers falling in unlikely creases like stained and holed curtains. Bushes and tall grasses struggled for supremacy between the trees. Green snakes were inching their absorbed way up through the interlocked boughs in search of nesting birds.

Surely Peter Oro would never have ventured so far from the salt water? The youth was probably staying with *wantoks* down on the coast and would return to the school when he felt like it.

When he reached the waterfall he walked across the grassy plateau to a vine bridge leading to the sacred cave hidden behind the thundering torrent. He took a torch from his pack and dropped the pack on to the ground before starting to cross the swaying bridge, pushing his way through the booming avalanche of water to the dry calm of the cave beyond.

He switched on his torch. He saw the rows of skulls along the ledges of the *faatai maea*. He knew that he was in the presence of a vast orchestrated slaughter. Once a great bush chief had been buried here. According to custom, fifty of his bodyguards had been slain so that they might accompany him into the next world, and their heads brought to the *faatai maea*, as the Kwaio people believed that a man's spirit resided in his skull. The remains of the bodyguards had stayed in the cave ever since, a memory of the bloody past.

Kella remembered, with no lessening of the pain, the last time he had entered the cave of death, six months ago, to recover the body of the murdered missionary. He drove the thought from his head and tried to concentrate on his surroundings. The beam of his torch scoured the walls and roof of the pagan shrine. It settled on a ledge at the back. The carved outcrop was bare. Kella directed the beam around the interior again before he was satisfied. There was no *havu* in the sacred cave.

Back in the sunshine of the plateau the police sergeant conducted a rapid search of the area. The only addition since his last visit was a large, newly constructed hut on the edge of the bush. Kella glanced inside. It was unfurnished. A dozen coconut husks were scattered on the floor. In a corner a bowl of liquid stood fermenting. A mosquito net lay, tidily folded, on the floor. Presumably the owners had not yet moved in.

He walked back out on to the plateau and lay down on the grass to dry off. If the *havu* was missing, along with Professor Mallory, it could mean that both the icon and the anthropologist were together somewhere.

Despite the laws forbidding their export, some very distinguished academic visitors to remote areas of the Solomons had not been above spiriting away precious relics and impregnating local girls at the same time. It was possible that Mallory had stolen the carving and was now hightailing it back to Honiara and a Solair flight out of the Solomons.

Yet how could Mallory have got past the guards of the sacred cave? Kwaio tradition decreed that anyone attempting to steal one of its relics would be slain and his body placed by the waterfall as a sign of payback. The fact that there was no corpse in evidence probably meant that Mallory was still alive somewhere.

Kella was roused from his reverie by the sound of a soft hiss, the Solomons way of warning someone courteously that a newcomer had arrived.

'Good afternoon,' said a woman's voice.

Kella opened his eyes and looked up. A young woman was smiling shyly at him. She was light brown in colour, very beautiful, with long black hair. She wore a simple print dress. A Polynesian, judged Kella; she was probably from Sikaiana.

'Hello,' he answered, almost overwhelmed by the woman's radiance, highlighted against the background of the waterfall and the trees far below. He held out his hand. 'My name's—'

'Kella, Sergeant Kella,' smiled the young woman, shaking his hand. 'You lectured to us about law and order when I was a student at the British Solomons Teachers' Training College in Honiara. We were all most impressed. You were the first big man who ever bothered to come and talk to us. My name is Elizabeth Adomea. I am the village schoolteacher. You don't know how good it feels to be speaking English to someone again.'

'I didn't know there was a school in these parts,' said Kella, puzzled. There were very few schools in the high bush area.

'The Melanesian Mission sent me to open one,' said Elizabeth. 'I've only been here a couple of months.'

The Melanesian Mission was the Anglican Church in the Solomons. They must have thought highly of the young teacher to send her so far from home into such a wild area. It must be lonely for her, which probably accounted for her eagerness to greet him.

'What are you doing here, sergeant?' Elizabeth asked, frankly curious. 'You've frightened the village people. All day they have been calling to each other about you, using their *kuku* talk.'

'I heard them,' said Kella. *Kuku* was the name given by the inhabitants of the Kwaio territory to the long-drawn-out cries they used to make messages travel for long distances.

'Why didn't you hide like the others?' asked Kella.

'Do I have anything to be afraid of?' she asked softly. 'You must be hungry and thirsty. Come back to my house.'

The deserted bush village was in a clearing about half a mile north of the waterfall. There were thirty or forty huts in two straight lines, facing one another. Cooking fires smouldered outside some of the thatched houses.

Kella looked on as Elizabeth deftly made a meal of taro pudding, mixed with ngali nuts, over her fire.

'No meat,' she joked. 'I wouldn't like the police sergeant to think that I was giving him long pig just because he was in the bush.'

Long pig was the name given to human flesh. Many saltwater people thought that bush dwellers were cannibals.

'I would only eat someone I had killed myself,' Kella informed the schoolteacher with mock gravity. 'That way his *mana* would enter me and make me strong.'

'Eating these people wouldn't do you much good,' said Elizabeth contemptuously. 'They are ignorant and dirty.'

'Not all of them,' said Kella, choosing his words carefully and watching how they affected Elizabeth. 'Pazabosi has great *mana*.'

'He is an evil man who sups with the devil-devils,' said the young teacher.

'Have you seen him lately?'

She nodded reluctantly. 'He was here with some of his men a few days ago. They slept for a night in the *faatai maea*. Then they went back up the mountains. I was in the school when they left, but everybody here seemed very excited about Pazabosi's visit.'

'He doesn't often come this far down the mountain,' agreed Kella. 'It's a long trek for someone of his age.'

'It is time for his long rest,' agreed the girl. It was plain that she did not want to discuss the feared magic man. Kella decided to try just once more.

'Was there a white man with him?' he asked casually. 'A tall American called Mallory?'

'I didn't see a white man,' said the girl. 'The food is ready. Come inside and eat.'

They entered the tidy hut. Elizabeth cut the taro pudding in half and gave Kella his portion on a thick banana leaf. The sergeant was preoccupied as he ate, hardly noticing how good the taro was. He could hardly blame the teacher for being unwilling to answer his questions. She would still be living in the village long after he had left. He still decided to ask one more important question.

'Do you know anything about the *havu*?' he asked her. 'It's been taken from the killing ground. Perhaps Pazabosi took it with him when he left.'

The girl looked blank. 'What's a *havu*?' she asked, chewing with a good appetite.

'Oh, just a carving,' Kella replied vaguely. He put down his empty banana leaf and refused a second helping of taro. Attentively Elizabeth handed him a bamboo container of water, from which he drank deeply.

'What sort of a carving?' she asked.

'Nothing important.'

'Oh, come on, Sergeant Kella,' persisted the teacher, smiling. 'Is it something naughty? The bushmen make many sex carvings. Is this one of them?'

'Well, yes, as a matter of fact it is,' replied Kella, embarrassed. Polynesian women were notoriously uninhibited, even the educated ones.

'Oh, good! Tell me about it,' she begged, giggling. 'Have you ever seen it?'

'Yes,' said Kella. 'I saw it the last time I was here, six months ago.'

A vision swam into his mind of the crumpled, bloody body of the missionary.

'Well?' prompted the girl, leaning forward eagerly, placing a hand lightly on Kella's knee.

'It's very old,' said Kella, returning his attention to her, conscious of the girl's cool, gentle touch. 'It was supposed to have been put in the *fatai maea* when the shrine was first built, hundreds of years ago. It is the sacred symbol of the Kwaio people. It represents the conception of their whole clan.'

'Conception?' asked the girl.

'Beginning.'

'Oh, you mean *fakim*,' cried the girl, clapping her hands in delight. 'Twofella jig-jig.' She tried to look serious. 'What position are they using, Sergeant Kella?'

'The usual,' replied the sergeant, trying not to show his discomfort. Lau women most certainly did not tease their menfolk in the way that Elizabeth was now taunting him. He stood up with as much dignity as he could muster and took a towel from his pack. 'Thank you for the food. I'm going to wash.'

The teacher was still laughing when he left her hut. Kella saw no one until he was almost back at the waterfall. Then a bushman emerged from the trees ahead of him. The man was stunted and naked. He carried a spear. His face was a whorl of tattoo marks. On his forehead was the diamond-shaped *fuae alite*, representing the nut of the alite tree. On his cheeks were the *bubulus*, large circles with rays radiating outwards. Below the rays were the *tale kokosu*, the tracks of the hermit crab.

The man saw Kella and in the same movement turned and plunged back into the undergrowth and was lost from sight. Kella stripped by the side of the waterfall and bathed in the thick spray exploding over the plateau. Towelling himself down he dressed and walked back to the village.

The place was still deserted. Night was beginning to creep unwillingly over the mountainside. The huts huddled together in the gloom like whipped dogs. Kella stopped outside Elizabeth's hut. He hesitated. Then he heard his name being called softly from within the structure. He went inside. It was cool and quiet. He could just make out the young school-teacher's lovely naked body lying on a woven mat. Her long slim legs were drawn up and splayed languorously.

'Oh, Kella,' she whispered through the darkness, extending her smooth arms. 'Come to me. I will be much better than any silly wooden *havu*.'

15

PETER ORO

The early morning light streamed in through the cracks in the walls of the schoolteacher's house, awakening Kella suddenly. He lay on his back on the mat, trying to assemble his thoughts. Memories of the long and tender night engulfed him. He remembered the soft, brown enfolding limbs, the whispered endearments and urgent cries as he and Elizabeth coupled and climaxed time after tremulous time in the dark hours.

Kella stood up. With an almost overwhelming sense of disappointment and loss he realized that Elizabeth was no longer in the hut. She must have left to bathe in the women's section of the river below the falls. He dressed and picked up his towel.

Outside, the hitherto deserted village was slowly coming to life. The contrast with the emptiness of the previous day was acute. Naked children were playing between the huts. Old men sat cross-legged in groups, exchanging early morning lies. Women were cooking over open fires. Because there was a stranger in their village they were no longer naked but wearing flimsy grass skirts.

The inhabitants ignored Kella sulkily as he nodded to them. They were not necessarily hostile, he thought as he walked, warmed and gentled and made vulnerable by the events of the previous night; they were probably shy and unused to strangers.

He moved contentedly through the trees, immersed in thoughts of the soft ferocity of the Sikaianan girl. He stepped out of the fringes of undergrowth and trees on to the plateau.

Then he stopped. His world collapsed about him with a rush, like the fronds of a falling palm tree. On the edge of the plateau was a body lying in a grotesque arabesque of death.

Desperately Kella broke into a sprint. He drew closer to the crumpled form, expecting to find the body of Mallory deposited there. But it was not the anthropologist. The corpse was that of a boy in his teens, clad in black shorts and a white shirt. There was a deep, corrugated, bloody gash across the boy's exposed throat, reaching from one ear to the other.

Almost weeping with chagrin and remorse, the police sergeant bent over the inert body. Then he threw back his head and screamed in despair.

He was looking at the body of the schoolboy, Peter Oro.

By the time that Kella had run back to the collection of huts, his heart pounding and sweat obscuring his vision, the men of the village were lined up waiting for him in truculent, seething ranks. There were about forty of them, all carrying spears or clubs.

Kella knew that he should be circumspect but he was too angry to care. He had stopped to vomit among the trees and his stomach was still churning. The bushmen regarded him stonily. They knew no English but there might be one or two among them with a smattering of pidgin.

'Which way teacher bilong you now?' he asked loudly. 'Name bilong Elizabeth.'

There was no answer from the obdurate crowd before him. Kella was aware of frightened women and children peering at him from the safety of the huts.

'School!' shouted Kella. 'Where now thisfella school: place bilong piccanin?'

No one answered. The bushmen exchanged puzzled glances. Then a villager, older than the others, probably the headman, advanced, limping slowly, from the crowd.

'No school,' he said, shaking his head firmly. 'No school bilong thisplace-ia.'

Kella stared in disbelief at the old man and then broke away. He hurried from hut to hut, wrenching aside the leaf hangings and staring inside each dwelling. Children broke into shrill cries as he thrust his head through the doorways, while women jabbered at him fiercely.

Finally Kella abandoned the search and walked bemusedly back towards the mob of incensed men. Each hut was obviously an established home. There was no building in the whole village resembling a school.

'Me lookem long thisfella mary, place bilong him Sikaiana, name bilong him Elizabeth,' he said desperately.

'No catchem thisfella mary,' protested the old man in faltering pidgin. He turned and said something in dialect to the others. They shook their heads in tandem and growled fiercely, denying all knowledge of the Polynesian girl.

The sergeant knew that they were lying. Pazabosi must have arranged for Elizabeth to be spirited away from the village earlier that morning, while he slept. He wondered what her function could have been. Why had the girl gone to such lengths to seduce him? Presumably Pazabosi had wanted him detained in the village while Peter Oro had been hurried through the trees to the *faatai maea* and then so cruelly murdered at the side of the waterfall. It all bore the marks of careful planning.

'Who now killem thisfella Peter?' he demanded, knowing as he spoke that he was wasting his time.

No one answered. The armed bushmen began to drift away, ignoring the sergeant. Kella walked quickly over to the hut in which he had spent the night with Elizabeth. The interior was occupied by a woman and three young children. One of the bushmen followed Kella in and raised his spear threateningly.

Kella scrutinized the hut in search of any trace of Elizabeth. Then he saw on the earthen floor a mound covered with a length of tattered cloth. Kella darted over and tore the cloth off the pile, paying no attention to the threats of the bushman. The cloth had concealed two intricately woven skirts fashioned out of dyed banana fibre, in the traditional Sikaiana check pattern. Elizabeth had been living in this hut and the family had not had time to dispose of the clothing she had left behind after her rapid departure.

The bushman edged forward, making small, dangerous circles and thrusts with his spear. Kella backed off quickly, leaving the hut. The bushman followed him out, calling to the others. The rest of the men rushed over towards them. Kella backed up against the side of the hut. The bushmen crowded about him, jostling him angrily.

There was a cold rattle of rifle bolts and a shouted word of command. The startled bushmen turned. Six uniformed police-men were scattered around the edge of the compound, their rifles pointed at the crowd. Their facial markings showed that they were Choiseul men from the Western Solomons, old foes of the Malaitans and the only islanders who would have dared enter the high bush in this summary fashion.

Standing behind them, sweating profusely and holding his service revolver, was Inspector Lorrimer. He caught Kella's gaze and nodded calmly.

'Morning,' he called laconically. 'You're a hard man to find, Sergeant Kella.'

16

BEYOND THE REEF

At dawn two men from the artificial island paddled Sister Conchita out towards the reef. Skilfully they negotiated the natural coral walls protecting the lagoon from the snarling ocean and slipped their canoe through a narrow fissure out into the open sea.

The change from the calm of the lagoon was remarkable. Large waves seized the canoe and sent it spinning helplessly from breaker to breaker as the two Melanesians paddled frantically to keep their frail vessel on an even keel. The nun clung desperately to the sides of the canoe as it careered over the rough waters like a frightened horse.

Sister Conchita saw that they were headed towards a larger vessel pitching on a sea-anchor just outside the lagoon. As the canoe buffeted its way through the crashing waves to the side of the ship she could just make out through the stinging sea spray that it was a battered old pre-war cutter of the sort commonly used for coastal trading around the islands. The ancient rusty vessel bucked almost uncontrollably above her, dwarfing the writhing canoe and its occupants. Its fifteen-horsepower engine was crammed into a tiny space enclosed by a hatch in the centre of the single deck. The wheel and the rigging for the mast were situated just behind the hatch. There were two meagre cargo holds placed fore and aft.

A rough rope ladder suddenly cascaded down from the ship's rail like an uncoiled snake. One of the Melanesians in the canoe stood up precariously and grabbed the bottom end of the ladder as he swayed, briefly securing the canoe to the side of the cutter. Urgently he gestured to Sister Conchita to stand and climb the ladder as it rattled noisily against the larger vessel.

Trying to control her fear, the nun propelled herself to her feet. It was difficult to stand on the spinning craft. The islander clinging to the ladder called out to her again. Unless she moved quickly he would soon be torn from the canoe by the force of the rope ladder slapping violently against the side of the cutter.

Apprehensively Sister Conchita forced herself to edge to the side of the canoe. The cutter was heaving before her like the wall of a crumbling building almost disintegrating in an earthquake. From this close the trading vessel now looked both enormous and impregnable. The ladder billowed wildly out of control above her head. Impulsively the nun threw herself forward and clung to its twisting rungs, her feet scrabbling for purchase. It took several scrambled efforts before they twisted frantically into position on the slippery lower hempen steps. As she clung breathlessly to the unruly rope Sister Conchita was dimly aware of the canoe bouncing erratically away from the cutter, heading back for the security of the lagoon.

'Climb, woman!' demanded an irate voice from above her head.

The nun threw back her head to glimpse the unshaven face of John Deacon glaring vindictively down at her from the rail of the ship. Step by step Sister Conchita forced herself up the rope ladder, her habit soaked and achingly heavy, the muscles of her arms and legs screaming for relief, the waves chopping viciously below her, reaching up as if to drag her back. Doggedly she inched upwards, until her face was level with the deck. Rough arms grabbed at her and lifted her clumsily up over the rail and deposited her in a breathless heap on the scarred planks of the deck.

'Where do you think you are, on your holidays?' demanded the same gruff voice sardonically. 'I've got a schedule to keep.'

Determined not to reveal her feeling of utter relief at her deliverance, the trembling Sister Conchita hauled herself to her feet, gripping the rail for support. There were two Melanesians on board, seeming to make up the entire crew. One of them was already hauling up the rope ladder, while the other was disappearing into the engine room, from which soon emerged a guttural cough and a subdued howl of released steam as the engine came to reluctant life.

'Good morning, Mr Deacon,' she said to the short, broad-shouldered white man clad in shorts and a singlet before her. 'I hope you're carrying a legitimate cargo this time.'

'I've got two rules for you as long as you're on board.' growled Deacon, flushing. 'Keep quiet, and keep out of the bloody way!'

The trader stalked over to the wheel and took up his position there, rapping out instructions to the seemingly indifferent Melanesians. Within minutes the vessel was limping its way arthritically through the waves. Sister Conchita glared at the broad back of the Australian. One of the Melanesians emerged from the engine room. He winked at the nun and pointed over the side of the vessel.

'Good too much,' he said approvingly. 'Missus bilong God climb like a gecko.'

'Well, I'm glad you appreciate it,' said Sister Conchita warmly. 'If you want to know, I thought it was pretty darn good myself.'

A shout from Deacon sent the crew member loping over to take the trader's place at the wheel. The Australian stamped over towards the nun. Sister Conchita eyed his approach coolly.

'Thought up some more rules for me, buster?' she asked unblinkingly.

Deacon stopped in surprise. For a second a reluctant grin contorted his unshaven face. Then he was glowering at her again.

'Kella tells me someone took pot-shots at you,' he said brusquely. 'Any idea who did it?'

'I doubt it was anyone from the Solomons Tourist Board,' said the nun icily. 'Nor yet a prelude to a march-past with fixed bayonets welcoming me to the islands. How the heck would I know who it was?'

'You don't faze easy, do you?' grunted Deacon.

'Do I have something to be fazed about, Mr Deacon?'

'I don't know. But Ben Kella's been a friend of mine for a long time. That guy can look after himself. Yet inside a couple of days of meeting you they're carrying him away on a stretcher.'

'I'd like to say I usually have that effect on men, but I don't.'

'Strewth, you don't talk one bit like a sister,' complained the bewildered trader.

'There are people who'll tell you that I don't sister like a sister, but I hope I'll learn. I don't like being bullied, Mr Deacon. Not by anyone. I'm sure there are plenty of members of my order in the Solomons who will be willing to turn the other cheek. Why don't you look for one of them?'

Deacon took a deep breath. 'I don't want you getting Kella into any more trouble,' he persisted. 'That guy's got a big job to do in the islands over the next few years. He shouldn't be wasting time acting as a nursemaid to you.'

'That's the last thing I want as well,' said Sister Conchita. 'At least we agree about something.'

Deacon edged closer towards her. Despite herself Sister Conchita retreated slowly until her back was to the rail of the ship.

'Real rough seas,' said Deacon softly, looking over her shoulder. 'Anyone should go over the side, we'd never get them back.'

Sister Conchita suddenly felt afraid. Deacon was only inches away from her now, his face pressed against hers until she could smell the Australian's sour breath and was aware of the grey stubble dusting his projecting jaw.

'Back up, please, Mr Deacon,' she said, doing her best to sound calm. 'This isn't remotely funny.'

'You're right there, sister,' said the trader, not moving. The ship lurched as a wave broke over its bows. Sister Conchita felt herself being pressed backwards over the low rail by Deacon's solid, inexorable presence. The man's eyes were now flint-like and menacing. She did her best to remain upright but did not possess the strength to repel the pressure now being exerted against her by the Australian's body. With a chilling certainty she knew that in seconds she could be propelled backwards over the rail into the furious sea.

'Massa!' said a warning voice from behind Deacon.

The Australian swung round. The Melanesian who had hauled the rope ladder back on board was standing staring expressionlessly at Deacon. The other crew member was securing the wheel and hurrying over to join the small group. Sister Conchita walked away from the ship's rail and stood in the centre of the deck by one of the cargo holds. She was trembling.

'What the hell is this?' demanded Deacon furiously. 'I'm the master of this ship. You two do as you're told and keep out of the way!'

Both Melanesians were shaking their heads stubbornly. They had positioned themselves so that they were standing between Deacon and the nun. The crew member who had been at the wheel pointed at Sister Conchita.

'*Neena!*' he said loudly.

'What are you talking about?' demanded the Australian wildly, suddenly at a loss in the face of opposition from such an unexpected quarter.

'I think, Mr Deacon,' said Sister Conchita, doing her best to control her voice, 'that he is trying to tell you that I am a *neena*, one of the vulnerable, and that as such I am under the personal protection of the *aofia*, Sergeant Kella. I imagine that these two men are from the Lau region, so their ultimate loyalty is to the *aofia*, and not to you. In short, I believe that they are endeavouring to make the point that, despite appearances to the contrary, I am perfectly safe on this rust-bucket.'

For a moment she thought that the stocky trader was going to try to bluster his way out of the situation. His eyes raked the two Melanesians viciously. Studiously they avoided his gaze. Their heads were bowed respectfully, but still they did not move. Deacon relaxed abruptly.

'Hell, I didn't mean anything,' he expostulated, smiling falsely. 'Just having a little fun to see how you'd react. I'm like that, ask anybody. My bark's worse than my bite. You did all right, sister. Just like you did back at the shark-calling.'

'I'm glad to hear it,' said Sister Conchita, trying to control the overwhelming weakness threatening to destabilize her legs. 'I wonder how Sergeant Kella would react if I were to tell him about your little . . . joke?' Alarm flared like a beacon in the Australian's eyes. The nun continued, indicating the watching crewmen. 'However, I think we can forget all about it, as long as you take no action against your two colleagues for joining me in not seeing the humour of your little prank.'

'Sure thing,' Deacon assured her hastily. 'They're good boys. Real *kanakas*.'

'They are also gentlemen,' said Sister Conchita with heartfelt sincerity. She watched as Deacon resumed his place at the wheel, trying to appear unconcerned, and the Melanesians departed, nodding reassuringly in her direction. She wondered why the Australian had menaced her in such a forthright manner. Was he really trying to protect his friend Sergeant Kella from contact

17

MURDER TWICE OVER

Kella had been waiting fatalistically for almost an hour in the ante-room in the Secretariat, the administration building in Honiara. Chief Superintendent Grice and Inspector Lorrimer were already inside with the secretary for interior affairs.

The Guadalcanal girl sitting behind the receptionist's desk smiled across at him sympathetically, sensing an islander in trouble. Kella winked, but he was not feeling particularly jaunty.

He had arrived back at the capital from Malaita on a fast government vessel three hours ago. The previous day Lorrimer and his armed police officers had escorted him down to the coast from the Kwaio bush village. A waiting government speedboat had taken them round to the harbour at the Malaitan district station of Auki.

Kella sat immobile, trying to control his impatience. There was much to be done. He could not afford to waste time here. The door of the inner office opened. Lorrimer poked his head out.

'Sergeant Kella, will you come in, please,' he asked.

The office was large and air-conditioned. On one wall was an official signed photograph of the queen and on another were two crossed Nigerian assegais. The secretary, spare, white-haired and bristling terrier-tenacious, sat behind the desk. Grice sat upright on a chair before him. Lorrimer resumed his seat next to the chief superintendent.

'Sit down, Sergeant Kella,' invited the secretary.

The three men glared at Kella. The sergeant fixed his innocent gaze on the secretary. There was an extended silence. Kella resisted the temptation to look at his watch.

'Well now,' said the secretary with a noticeable lack of enthusiasm. 'Perhaps you'd better tell me just what you've been doing on Malaita over the last week.'

At different times over the past twenty-four hours Kella had already told his story to Lorrimer, Grice and the commissioner of police, with increasing degrees of incredulity on the part of his listeners. He repeated his version to his latest audience. Chief Superintendent Grice rumbled in the background, like a freshly activated volcano, as a counterpoint to his account.

'Extraordinary!' winced the secretary when Kella had finished. 'Quite extraordinary! Let me see if I've picked up the salient points. Chief Superintendent Grice sent you to Malaita to inquire as to the present whereabouts of Professor Mallory. Mr Grice gave you specific orders that you were to limit your activities to this alone. Am I right?'

'Yes, sir,' said Kella, sitting to attention.

'Yet you flagrantly disobeyed these instructions.' The secretary ticked off the infringements on pink, stubby fingers. 'On your own initiative you start an investigation into the custom killing of a villager. Then you discover a skeleton at a mission station and allege that it is that of a beachcomber who has been murdered. After that you become involved in a shooting incident with a Roman Catholic sister, and tell her that someone is trying to kill her. Finally you launch yourself on an expedition into the most dangerous area of Malaita. This time you encounter the corpse of a dead schoolboy. This drives you into a rage, which antagonizes the local people to such an extent that they were about to kill you when Inspector Lorrimer and his officers arrived providentially.'

Kella had to admit that put like that it did all sound unfortunate. Aloud he said, 'Sir, I believed that all these events were connected. In one way or another they were all involved in the disappearance of the professor.'

'How the hell do you make that out?' exploded Chief Superintendent Grice. He caught the secretary's baleful stare and subsided unwillingly.

'In my culture we don't believe in coincidences,' Kella told him. 'We consider that all things have meaning and are interlinked. I think that when the earthquake uncovered the skeleton of Lofty Herman at the mission, it gave rise to everything that followed. Pazabosi had been waiting for a sign to start a cargo uprising. Wittingly or unwittingly Senda Iabuli and his nephew Peter Oro became involved in the bones *tabu* that Pazabosi had placed on the area to stop people examining Herman's skeleton too closely. As a result, they were both killed.'

'Then how did Sister Conchita become involved?' asked Lorrimer. 'She's convinced that the man with the rifle was trying to kill her, not you.'

'I don't know,' confessed Kella.

Disbelief hovered like a cloud of mosquitoes over the other three. The secretary cleared his throat fastidiously. He may have been one of the despised expatriate dregs of Empire, but he was determined to get at least one more promotion on some neglected rock before the few remaining British overseas dependencies dwindled away. To achieve that he intended to do everything by the book, carrying out the wishes of Whitehall without needlessly upsetting an increasingly restless local population.

'It seems to me, Sergeant Kella,' he observed frostily, 'that once again you have allowed yourself to become too closely involved with events on Malaita. Earlier this year you had to face a court of inquiry after the death of a missionary in the same area. At the time there was a strong feeling in the court that had you done your duty strictly as a police officer, instead of allowing, er, cultural considerations to prevail, that death might have been averted.'

'I did what I believed to be right, under the circumstances,' said Kella.

'Didn't do much for the poor bugger who got killed, though,' said Chief Superintendent Grice brusquely, shifting his pendulous bulk in his chair.

'On this occasion,' went on the secretary equably, ignoring both interruptions, 'Father Pierre at the mission and Mr Deacon, the plantation manager, both knew that you were going up to the waterfall in search of Professor Mallory. That enabled Inspector Lorrimer, very courageously, to take his squad through the bush after you.'

'Why did you send Inspector Lorrimer to Malaita in the first place?' asked Kella. It was a matter that had been puzzling him.

'We had reports from a number of mission stations that Pazabosi had been seen outside the Kwaio district, a very rare occurrence. We assumed that he was intent on stirring up unrest again. The situation on Malaita is always a volatile one. Under the circumstances, the last thing this Administration needs is a loose cannon like yourself careering all over the island.'

'Pazabosi may have kidnapped Professor Mallory,' said Kella stubbornly. 'I can do some good over there—'

'You may rest assured, sir,' said Chief Superintendent Grice stiffly, 'that Sergeant Kella will not be returning to Malaita in the foreseeable future.'

'I'm glad to hear it,' nodded the senior official. He returned his attention to Kella. 'I'm sure that there is plenty for you to do here in Honiara. After all, despite your rather chequered career, you are still our senior indigenous police officer, Kella. The Protectorate has invested a lot of time and money in your development. There's still time to put these matters behind you and make a career for yourself in the force. It's simply a matter of overcoming your more impulsive tendencies.' He rifled through some papers before him dismissively. 'Thank you, gentlemen.'

Outside in the busy corridor Chief Superintendent Grice walked away without a word or a glance back. He was probably annoyed at having to start work so early that day, thought Kella. To his local staff Grice was known as Ten Fifteen, as that was the time he usually arrived at the office in the morning.

'Want a lift back to HQ?' Lorrimer asked him.

'No thanks, I've got things to do,' answered Kella. 'You can drive me along the coast and drop me off at Domo, if you like.'

Lorrimer nodded. He hesitated and then lowered his voice. 'Look, old son,' he murmured. 'Don't push things too far, eh? They don't want to sack you because it would cause a stink getting rid of someone as well-known as you are, but if you force them into it they will, and then find another local heir-apparent. You can always do your celebrated tilting at windmills bit when you're the boss man here in the islands.'

'I can't wait that long,' Kella told him, striding away down the corridor.

Outside the Secretariat building they walked in the 80 degree heat to the inspector's jeep. It was a hot, airless afternoon in the small town. Mendana Avenue, the capital's single main street, lined with flowering flame trees, was occupied on both sides by stores and office buildings. Many of the shops and the Point Cruz cinema were housed in old Quonset huts left standing by American troops when they abandoned the site in 1945. The office buildings, the two banks and the courthouse were of stone.

To one side of the main road, on the ridges above the town, were the residences of the government officials and their families. On the other side of the avenue, behind the row of buildings, were the placid bay and the harbour. About ten thousand people lived in and around Honiara. A tenth of them were expatriates – British, Australians, Americans, New Zealanders, Chinese and Fijians.

Lorrimer drove them out of town in silence. Normally he was friendly enough but this afternoon he seemed preoccupied. Kella knew that he was indebted to the other man for coming to his aid on Malaita. It would have taken courage for an expatriate with no knowledge of the island to lead his police squad up the forested mountains into Kwaio territory. The Englishman seemed a conscientious police officer and, as a temporary visitor, he had the advantage of not being an Old Colonial. For some time Kella had wondered if this was a rare white man who might be trusted.

They soon left the houses behind them. On their right, along the winding, pitted coastal road, were the smooth waters of Ironbottom Sound, so-called because of the number of Allied vessels which had been sunk off the coast during the war. On their left, palm trees gave way to the wooded foothills, which in turn climbed gradually to the central mountain range of the island of Guadalcanal.

'No chance of your telling me what you're going to do, I suppose?' asked Lorrimer resignedly.

'Believe me,' Kella assured him, 'best you don't know.'

The inspector tried again. 'Then at least tell me this. Why do you think that the killings of Senda Iabuli and Peter Oro are linked? Apart from the fact that the two islanders were related.'

'They were both custom killings,' said Kella. 'They're very rare. It's most unlikely that there would be two separate murders in such a short time. I'm sure the deaths were combined. And there's something else.'

'What's that?'

'I think', said Kella carefully, deciding after much thought to share his thoughts with someone for once, 'that Senda Iabuli might have been murdered twice.'

Carefully Lorrimer pulled into the side of the dusty road and stopped the jeep. He switched off the ignition and turned to face Kella.

'All right,' he said, 'I'll buy it. What was that supposed to mean? How could anyone be killed twice?'

'You see,' explained Kella, 'when I made my first investigation into the death of Senda Iabuli, I suspected that he had been killed by the other people in his village.'

'Why on earth would they want to do that?'

'Because of Iabuli's miraculous escape from death. Think about it. To take the fall that he did, and survive, seems impossible. How could he possibly have escaped death?'

'Are you saying that Senda Iabuli didn't fall from that bridge? There were witnesses—'

'Oh, he fell all right. Hundreds of feet. I went to the ravine and looked for myself. Iabuli had a simply miraculous escape from death. And by doing that he ensured that he would die.'

'What the hell are you talking about?' demanded Lorrimer.

'The people of the village could only have come to one logical conclusion when they found Senda Iabuli still alive. They would have believed that the old man had entered into a pact with a devil, who had saved his life.'

'Oh, come on,' said Lorrimer.

'Trust me,' said Kella. 'I'm a witch doctor. I know these things. According to custom, it was the only thing they *could* think.'

'Do you really believe that?'

'Never mind what I believe. I'm telling you the way it was in that village. The people there couldn't have someone wandering about who was in cahoots with a devil. It would be far too dangerous. They would have gone to the headman and demanded that Senda Iabuli be killed before he could harm anyone.'

'So the headman killed him?'

'Or had him killed. If the headman wanted to remain in charge he would have had Senda Iabuli poisoned. Peter Oro, the old man's grandson, remembered enough about the custom ways to guess that. That's why he insisted on the ghost-caller being summoned to find out the truth. Which he did, in a way.'

'Believe me,' said Lorrimer dazedly, 'murder inquiries were never like this at West End Central. How do you mean "in a way"?'

'Somehow or other,' said Kella, following the thread unravelling in his mind, 'Iabuli had also upset Pazabosi, the old bush magic man. I know that because I found a sign of the bones *tabu* outside Iabuli's house. That meant that Pazabosi had put it where Iabuli would have found it when he was getting the comfort stones to put under his bed.'

'You mean this was separate from anything the headman might have done?'

'Oh, yes,' said Kella. 'No doubt about it.'

'A bit like being slipped the black spot,' ruminated Lorrimer. 'So the poor old sod was being targeted by both the headman and by Pazabosi?'

'Not the luckiest of guys, was he? I don't know which of them got to him first, the headman or Pazabosi. Perhaps they both did it. That's what I meant when I said he may have been murdered twice.'

'Exactly how was Senda Iabuli killed?' asked Lorrimer. 'That might help us find out who the murderer was.'

'I don't know,' admitted Kella. 'Iabuli had already received a custom burial by the time I arrived at the village. Even the *aofia* couldn't insist on the body being dug up, supposing I could have discovered his grave. He was probably poisoned or suffocated. Perhaps both if my theory is correct. Somebody could have smothered Iabuli after he had been drugged.'

'What a mess,' said Lorrimer feelingly.

'Don't worry, it gets worse. There's also the matter of Lofty Herman's shooting, all those years ago at the mission station. As far as I can work it out, the whole thing – the two deaths and the subsequent attack on Sister Conchita – was sparked off when the beachcomber's body was uncovered.'

'I shouldn't bother too much about that one at the moment,' said Lorrimer, suddenly formal.

'Why not?'

'I can't tell you that. Just take my advice and leave the Lofty Herman killing alone.' The inspector turned on the ignition and let in the clutch. 'Suffice it to say that matters are in hand. You've got two other murders on your plate, and you aren't allowed to leave Honiara. That should be challenge enough, even for you.'

18

THE CUSTOM WAY

Thirty minutes later they reached the huts of Doma, a small village scattered around a creek on the Guadalcanal coast. Kella got out of the jeep and waited until Lorrimer had spun the vehicle around and, with a fatalistic wave of his hand, had headed back in the direction of Honiara. Then the sergeant walked down the sandy beach fringed by palms.

Half a dozen tough-looking Guadalcanal men were sitting on the sand in the shade of a tree, staring apathetically out to sea at a rusting landing barge anchored half a mile off the shore. They appeared totally unimpressed by the arrival of a police officer.

'Where-im now thisfella Sam Beni?' Kella asked.

The men took their time in replying. Finally one of them removed a clay pipe from his mouth and jabbed the stem in the direction of the barge.

'Me wannem for talk-talk long thisfella,' said Kella. 'Spose you wannem, you take me out long barge?'

The Guadalcanal men did not exactly laugh but it was plain from their attitude that the last thing any of them was going to do was to convey Kella to the barge and its dangerous cargo. Kella did not blame them. They had risked their lives a dozen times filling the tethered craft in the first place.

He indicated a small canoe drawn up under a palm tree. He

asked whose it was. One of the labourers indicated possession by raising an eyebrow. Kella asked if he could borrow it. The owner's scornful expression told him that if the police sergeant was foolish enough to want to approach the barge, he did not object.

'Side bilong you,' he yawned.

Kella thanked him and pushed the dugout down to the water's edge. He found that he was soon paddling even more slowly than the chopping water necessitated. When he was a few yards from the barge, he stopped, steadying the canoe with occasional thrusts of his paddle against the tide.

As usual the barge now looming above him was loaded with hundreds of discoloured, mildewed armament shells of all sizes, both American and Japanese. Among the heaving lethal piles Kella could discern small two-pound mortar shells, hand grenades, stick bombs, howitzer, armour-piercing and high-explosive anti-tank shells, all jumbled together in a tortured, constantly shifting, deadly parody of metal sculpture.

On top of the heap stood a sinewy islander in his mid-forties. He was clad only in a pair of tattered shorts. One by one he was throwing the shells carelessly into the sea. When he saw the sergeant he nodded, without pausing in his work.

'*Tua futa*,' Kella said respectfully, using the Lau term for a member of the artificial islands' extended family. By the use of the phrase, implicitly he was asking his *wantok* for help.

'Hello, Kella,' said the other man indifferently, continuing the use of the Lau dialect. 'What do you want?'

'I'd like to talk to you, Beni.'

'You do, do you? Come up here then.'

'I can hear you fine from here,' Kella said quickly.

Sam Beni shook his head. 'Oh, no,' he said. 'If any policeman wants to talk to me he can come aboard.'

Still steadying his canoe, Kella considered the situation. It was typical of Beni's caustic sense of humour that he would want to face down any representative of the law. The barge was a floating death trap, liable to explode at any moment. Beni's employer, a New Zealander, had a contract to find and dispose of the thousands of live shells and grenades left behind in the bush after the war on Guadalcanal. In order to do so, he had recruited the hardest and most reckless men on the island. They combed the bush, collecting the long-neglected and volatile ammunition, and loading the shells and grenades on to the barge. The New Zealander then towed it out to sea behind his powerful motor boat, and anchored it, before returning to the safety of the shore. Only Beni would remain on the barge, with the suicidal task of dumping the shells into the sea.

'Well, are you coming up?' taunted his *wantok*.

Kella took a deep breath. Gingerly he tied his canoe to a rusted projection on the side of the barge and clambered gingerly aboard. He stood balancing uneasily on the shells groaning and shifting ceaselessly beneath his feet. The barge creaked and swayed against its anchors.

Kella could see the small volcanic island of Savo on the far side of Ironbottom Sound. He knew that if he made the wrong movement, or if his luck ran out, two of the live shells could crash into one another, sending the barge and its occupants up in a sudden eruption of flame and smoke.

Beni waited, enjoying every moment, as Kella tiptoed across the ammunition to him. Then he sat on the side of the barge, lighting his pipe with a careless scrape of a match on one of the casings. His cold eyes surveyed the other man without a flicker of liking or emotion of any kind.

'Well?' he grunted.

'I want to ask you about Marching Rule,' Kella said.

'I don't give history lessons.'

'After that I need to find Pazabosi and arrest him.'

Beni bowed his head in reflection. When he raised it there was an unidentifiable glint in his usually dead eyes.

'That's different,' he acknowledged. 'I don't owe Pazabosi anything. What do you want to know?'

'What part did he play in the uprising?'

'Not as much as he'd like you to think. He was one of us at the beginning, but when the Brits started sending in armed policemen in 1948, he went off back to his mountain-top.'

'That doesn't sound like Pazabosi,' frowned Kella. 'I fought with him in the war. He was as brave as they come then.'

'Oh, the old man was never a coward,' acknowledged Beni disdainfully. 'He just wasn't interested in losing, and he knew by then that Marching Rule was doomed. While the rest of us went to prison, he stayed up in the bush, waiting for a better moment to arrive. He's making his move at last, is he? I'm surprised. I would have thought that by now he would be preparing for his long journey to the spirit world.'

'I'm not sure what's happening, but he's in the thick of something,' said the police sergeant. 'That's why I have to find him. Only you can help me. You were one of the big men in Marching Rule. The people on Malaita still respect you for that. If anything against the government is happening on the island, you will still be told about it.'

'How do you know I'm not still involved with Pazabosi?'

Kella shook his head. 'That's not your style. You think he ran away to fight another day. That's not good enough for you. You had one chance ten years ago, and you put everything you had into it. When you lost it took too much out of you.'

'Thanks,' said Beni bitterly.

'Well, look at you, perched on top of a rubbish heap, like a wounded eagle. This is no place for a warrior *ramo*. You won't try again. You may frighten me and your friends shitless with your recklessness with these shells out here, but really these days, Beni, you're one of the *neena*, the unprotected.'

Beni roared with incandescent rage and jumped to his feet.

Without taking his eyes off the sergeant he lifted a shell at random from the pile. He raised it above his head with a surge of muscle and suddenly hurled it back down on to the rest of the ammunition.

Kella leapt backwards, raising his hands instinctively to protect his face. He went sprawling on the shells. Involuntarily he closed his eyes and waited for the explosion. Nothing happened. When he opened his eyes again everything was as it had been. The precarious cargo was still grunting and shifting, the sea lapped against the side of the barge. Across the bay the volcano on Savo remained calm. Kella was only aware of the pumping of his heart.

'I do that most days,' said Beni, his anger replaced by melancholy. 'None of them have gone off yet.'

'Keep trying,' panted Kella, scrambling to his feet and trying to control the trembling of his arms and legs. 'You never know your luck. Are you going to tell me about Pazabosi?'

'Why should I? You're the white man's policeman. What did you ever do for the Marching Rule movement? I don't suppose you were even in the Solomons when we tried to throw the Brits out.'

'That's right,' said Kella. As soon as the war was over he had been sent back to a secondary school in Fiji and then on to the Australian university. By the time he had returned in 1952, the movement had collapsed and the ringleaders like Beni had been sentenced to prison terms.

The revolt had been based on the premise of cargo. It was rumoured among the people that the black GIs, who had so impressed everyone with their wealth and generosity during the war, had never really left the Solomons. They were said to be hiding in the bush with their vehicles and equipment. If the islanders rose against British colonial rule, the rebels declared, the GIs would emerge and aid them in their struggle against oppression. When that had been accomplished, shiploads of cargo would arrive from overseas for all the islanders.

'I spent three years in the white man's jail,' Beni went on. 'When I came out no expat would give me a job, except this crap one. The Lau fool who did it before me lasted three months until he made his final explosion. My land has been confiscated, and I won't go home as a cringing *neena*, begging for food. And you expect me to help the colonials!'

'I'm not doing it for the white man,' said Kella. 'I want to stop Pazabosi from tearing Malaita in half. Marching Rule didn't work, neither will Pazabozi's uprising. All we've got to do is to wait a few more years and we'll gain independence. If Malaita belongs to Pazabosi by then, the Lau people won't have a chance.'

'Do you believe everything the white sugar-lips tell you?' jeered Beni.

'I think for myself,' said Kella doggedly. 'Remember, I am the *aofia*.'

It was a card he disliked playing, but he had discovered over the years that sometimes there was no alternative.

Beni shrugged. After a time he nodded reluctantly. When he spoke again his tone had softened a little. 'I was present at your *maoma* feast, when you were anointed as *aofia*,' he said quietly. 'You must have been about ten then. The custom priests had already picked you out and started training you. There were thousands there. All the Lau people, from Suu down as far as Ataa Cove, came to witness it. They dedicated you out on the reef and gave you the areca nut to carry with you always, as a sign of peace. I hoped for a time that this might be the start of something important for Malaita, but then the war came, and when it ended, you had gone. So I decided to do something for myself.'

Abruptly Beni started tossing the shells into the sea again. Sparks and shards of rust flew as the ammunition collided noisily on its perilous descent over the side of the barge.

'You should have waited,' Kella told him. 'You should still be waiting. When the time comes, I shall do something. I promise. Now,' he persisted, 'when I get back to Malaita, where will I find Pazabosi?'

Beni stopped, the sweat rolling down his lean face and body. Kella reached into his pocket and produced something. He could not remember the last time he had been forced to use it. He handed it to Beni, who stared reflectively at the object in the palm of his hand. Beni studied the nut expressionlessly before handing it back.

'Nikona village, in the Kwaio high bush,' he said briefly. 'Whatever Pazabosi's doing, and I'm not saying he's plotting an uprising, he's doing it there. Now go away and let me get on with my work. And never pretend that we have anything in common.'

'There's certainly one big difference between us,' said Kella, climbing with stomach-churning relief back down into the comparative safety of his canoe.

'What's that?' asked Beni from the barge.

'I care whether I live or die,' shouted Kella, picking up his paddle.

Kella hitched a ride back into Honiara in a lorry taking a load of yams to market from Visale at the far end of the road. He was dropped off outside the Mendana Hotel. He looked at his watch. It was only four o'clock. He realized that he did not want to go back to his office and the company of the expatriate police officers.

Instead he walked up a quiet sloping side-street to the Roman Catholic headquarters building. It was an old, sprawling wooden edifice, which doubled as an administrative centre for the mission and a hostel for priests and nuns visiting the capital from the outlying districts.

In the hall, cooled by a ceiling fan, he asked the shy local Daughter of Mary Immaculate novice behind the desk where he could find Sister Conchita. The novice stood up and led him in silence through the building to a large back yard. In one corner stood an old, decrepit van. From beneath the vehicle projected a pair of slim ankles. The novice tapped the ankles with her foot. There was a whirling noise and a mechanic's flat trolley was propelled at speed from beneath the Bedford. Sister Conchita was lying on it, blinking up at him in surprise and some discomposure, a spanner in her hand. Her habit was flecked with oil and there were smudges of grease on her nose and cheeks. She scrambled to her feet.

'They soon put you to work then,' said Kella, indicating the sagging vehicle.

'Just running repairs,' said the sister. 'There's the blessing of the fishing boats tomorrow night. We'll need this to drive the sisters down to the wharf.'

Belatedly Kella extended a hand in greeting. Sister Conchita hesitated and took it reluctantly, releasing her grip almost at once. Kella wondered what was wrong. On his island of Sulufou he had thought that they had become almost friends. Now they were strangers again. Perhaps it was the black and white thing, once they were back in so-called civilization.

'I thought I'd see how you were,' he explained. 'John Deacon got you back here all right then? I must see him before he goes back to his plantation. How did you get on with John?'

'All right,' said the sister expressionlessly.

'Something wrong?' asked Kella. 'Deacon can be on the sharp side with strangers.'

'Everything's fine,' said Sister Conchita, not meeting his gaze. 'You'll have to hurry if you want to see him. He told me that he was filling up with supplies and catching the night tide back to Lau tomorrow.'

'Yes, Honiara will be a bit too respectable for John these days,' joked Kella. 'Well, as long as you're all right . . .'

He turned and walked back through the building. Sister Conchita followed him. He had reached the front door when the sister called his name. He turned back. She was standing very straight, her fists clenched at her sides.

'Why have you come here, Sergeant Kella?' she demanded, fighting back tears. 'Was it to gloat?'

'I don't know what you're talking about,' protested Kella.

'If you had any animosity towards the mission because of your own schooldays there, you've certainly got your revenge now. In pidgin, they call it payback, don't they?'

'I don't understand—'

'Of course you understand!' blazed the sister. 'You're a policeman. You know what's going on. They're bringing Father Pierre back to Honiara. They think he had something to do with the murder of Lofty Herman!'

19

CHINATOWN

Kella sat at his office desk ploughing through the paperwork that had been occupying him for most of the day. He opened the file on the sixth case submitted for his opinion. There was a dispute on Santa Isabel among the Bugotu people. A young man wanted to marry a girl within the same clan. This had been forbidden with horror by the girl's father, a strong follower of custom, which forbade marriages within the same tribe, as it led to poor stock. The youth had persisted in his attentions and had subsequently been beaten up by the girl's brothers. The case had come to the attention of a touring District Officer, who had reported the matter and optimistically requested a police investigation.

Kella sighed and on the paper before him scrawled the hieroglyphic indicating no official action to be taken. The battered youth would never give evidence against his putative in-laws. If he had any sense he would get his beloved pregnant as soon as possible and then offer a lavish retrospective bride price to her family. Before the war such an action would have resulted in both the youth and the besmirched girl being stoned to death, but even the most traditional of clan leaders were getting ever more philosophical about such transgressions, except on Malaita, where custom still ruled.

Kella closed the file and allowed his mind to return to Malaita and Father Pierre. He could hardly believe that the old priest was being brought into the capital for questioning about the murder of Lofty Herman. He had tried to find out more from the Catholic headquarters, but his telephone calls had met with obdurate stonewalling evasions. Both Chief Superintendent Grice and Inspector Lorrimer had been out for most of the day. No one else in the headquarters building seemed to know anything about the affair, or if they did they were not going to reveal anything to Kella.

He thought about the day that he had gone into the priest's study at the mission school. This had been in 1941, immediately before he was due to leave for his secondary education in Fiji. He had been twelve or thirteen, but already quite sure in his mind that the white man's religion was not for him. He had done his best to assimilate its tenets, but already he was sure that he would have to follow the custom way for the rest of his life. Father Pierre had heard him out in silence. To his surprise the priest had not been angry.

'You must do what you think is right, Ben,' he had told the boy. 'You have been brought up in the custom way for a special purpose, and one day your people will need you. If you truly believe that tradition makes you stronger than the way we have tried to teach you here, then you must follow that path. But don't disregard everything you have learnt here. Some of it will serve you well one day.'

Years later Kella had heard that the priest's attitude had got him into trouble with the church authorities. He had been told that it was his duty to dissuade his star pupil and ensure that he remained within the Church. Father Pierre, as usual, had been unrepentant.

'Ben Kella has been shown his path,' he insisted. 'Now he will follow it. It won't be easy for him. He is finding his way in two worlds. In the end that will make him strong and independent, but inevitably it will mean that he will suffer the occasional dark night of the soul. When he does, he will continue to need our help.'

Kella heard a vehicle pull up in the car park below. He walked over to the open window. Chief Superintendent Grice was getting out of his Volvo. Kella hurried to the door. He was waiting in the corridor outside the chief superintendent's office by the time Grice had stumbled up the stairs. The Englishman's eyes were glassy and he was moving with great care. When Kella walked forward to meet him he could smell the whisky on the senior police officer's breath. Grice must have been lunching at the Yacht Club again.

'Could I have a word with you about Father Pierre, sir?' Kella asked humbly.

Grice looked amiably perplexed. 'Pierre?' he asked with clipped enunciation, giving the consonant a final polish before allowing it to emerge pristine and clear. He frowned. 'Oh, the old priest! No need to bother, Kella. I'm dealing with that particular matter myself. Tricky situation, you see. Calls for tact and diplomacy.' Grice tapped the side of his nose conspiratorially. 'Political.'

Kella followed the chief superintendent uninvited into his office. 'Perhaps I could help,' he persisted hopefully. 'I know Father Pierre rather well.'

The official looked enraged by Kella's unexpected invasion of his territory. His air of bonhomie vanished as he swung violently into one of his mood changes. Suddenly his eyes were slitted with fury.

'Help?' he choked. 'I've had enough of your bloody help, thank you, Sergeant Kella. What you need to do is bugger off until we've sorted out your mess for you. Take some leave, or something. Just keep away from that priest! That's an order!'

Kella left the office without speaking. Grice slammed the door shut after him. As the sergeant walked dispiritedly along the corridor, Lorrimer came up the stairs. The inspector's uniform was dust-stained. He had left for Henderson Field, the small airport outside Honiara, that morning, to assist the Customs and Excise Department in a drugs operation connected with an incoming Heron aircraft on an Air Fiji flight from Nadi. He glanced briefly at the chief superintendent's door. It was still reverberating. Lorrimer raised an eyebrow at Kella.

'I got the bum's rush,' explained the sergeant. 'Don't ask! Never mind, I'm sure you can help me instead.'

'Now why does my heart always sink when you say that?' asked Lorrimer without rancour.

In his office the inspector sank gratefully into the chair behind his desk. Kella sat on the chair opposite.

'Have you had a chance to think about my Choiseul problem?' asked the inspector.

'The garden raids? Leave it alone.'

'But if I do it might lead to trouble.'

'There will only be trouble if you interfere,' said Kella. 'The Methodists and SDAs have been looting those gardens for years. The Methodists choose Saturdays because the SDAs are at church, and the SDAs attack on Sundays for the same reason. Each side knows they will never meet, so there will be no fighting. It's not much more than a game. It's not as if there's a lot to do on Choiseul.'

'Okay,' nodded Lorrimer. 'You know best.'

'Any luck with the smuggling?' asked Kella.

Lorrimer shook his head. 'Not a scrap,' he replied. 'The plane was clean. It seemed a good tip-off from the Fijian police, too.'

'I expect the smugglers offloaded the drugs at the stopover at Santo in the New Hebrides,' Kella told him. 'Then they would have put them on a ship and landed them anywhere along the Guadalcanal coast that they fancied.'

'Thank you for sharing that inspiring thought with me,' sighed Lorrimer. 'It fills me with a burning determination to continue the good fight, secure in the knowledge that the good guys are bound to win. So what can I do for you?'

'You can tell me about Father Pierre,' Kella told him. 'And don't pretend you know nothing about him. You hinted to me yesterday that Grice was investigating the case on his own. I just didn't believe that he would be stupid enough to try to implicate the priest.'

'I'm completely in the dark, old son,' said Lorrimer.

'Don't give me that, whitey. You're a paid-up member of the expats' cosy club. What do you really know?'

'All I've heard', said Lorrimer, raising his hands in a gesture of surrender, 'is that Chief Superintendent Grice received information from somewhere that Father Pierre could have been implicated in the killing of Herman in 1942.'

'Where did he get the information from?' asked Kella.

'I don't know,' said Lorrimer. 'Perhaps the Catholics shopped him.'

'Not a chance,' scoffed Kella. 'The mission hierarchy may regard Father Pierre as a maverick, but they look after their own. The old boy is a living legend on Malaita.'

'We'll have to question him when he arrives,' said Lorrimer.

'Don't hold your breath,' Kella told him, rising and going to the door. 'The old man will come in his own good time. He'll deliberately miss the first couple of boats bound for Honiara, then he'll get one going the long way round Malaita. You'll be lucky to see him in a month.'

'Side bilong big man-ia,' said Lorrimer in an unconvincing attempt at pidgin as Kella left.

If Lorrimer was right, thought Kella, descending the stairs, and all they had on Father Pierre was a raft of unsubstantiated allegations, from an anonymous witness, it did not seem to justify bringing such an old man all the way from Malaita. There must be more to it than that. Unless Grice was getting it all wrong, as usual.

The day shift was just going off duty. There was considerable traffic in both directions on the stairs. Some of the passing indigenous officers stared at Kella. Ever since the news had spread that he had discovered Peter Oro's body in the same place that the missionary had been killed on Malaita, Kella knew that there had been gossip that he might even have been responsible for both deaths, perhaps as a matter of duty as the *aofia*.

Few of the officers did more than nod awkwardly as he passed them. Some of them would be regarding him as inefficient. Others would attribute to him the much more dangerous trait of being unlucky.

Only Sergeant Ha'a stopped to talk to Kella, mainly because he needed the rest as he dragged his stubby, corpulent body up the stairs. He was from New Georgia in the Western Solomons. He was a rotund, cheerful extrovert, his glossy, jet-black features surmounted by a head of tight curls.

Ha'a was a skilful musician, adept on the guitar, and an efficient organizer. On his overseas police officers' course in Yorkshire, he had dragooned two Gold Coast inspectors and a sergeant from Northern Rhodesia into a money-making group he had called Curly Ha'a and his South Sea Island Hawaiians. They had raised a storm at working men's clubs all over the North of England, and had even appeared on television on *Opportunity Knocks*.

'Which way now, bigfella?' he asked, pumping for breath, with his hands on his knees.

'Are you still on the student beat?' Kella asked, remembering something he had meant to find out.

Ha'a grimaced. 'Too true! Bunch of over-educated, know-all bolshie gits. Want to swap jobs?'

'Not on your life,' Kella assured him. There had been rumours of unrest among some of the older, politically conscious students at King George VI Secondary School out on the road to Henderson Field. For the last year Sergeant Ha'a had been deputed to keep an eye on all student activities among the islands. In the process he had built up an impressive if constantly shifting list of informants.

'If I wanted to find out about a student from Father Pierre's school at Ruvabi, who would I need to see?' asked Kella.

'Is this the boy who got murdered up in the killing ground?' asked Ha'a, who was much shrewder than he looked. 'What's-his-name, Peter Oro? That was a bad business, bigfella. You must really be on whitey's shit-list, providing them with two corpses in six months.' He considered the question. 'There wouldn't be much use asking his headmaster. Solomon Bulko's a good bloke, but bone idle. Anyway, you know that; he's a mate of yours.'

Ha'a screwed up his face in thought, then snapped his fingers. 'As a matter of fact, there might be someone. Michael Rapasia only stopped teaching at Ruvabi last week.'

'Rapasia?' asked Kella in surprise. 'Is he still alive? He was teaching there when I was a student at Ruvabi. Guadalcanal man.'

'That's right. Compulsorily retired by the mission authorities without a pension when he reached sixty. I saw him get off the plane at Henderson Field only a few days ago. I'm not saying that he's all that reliable, but he might be worth talking to. He's mightily pissed off with the mission for not letting him stay on. He might well be in the mood to dish some dirt.'

'Where do I find him?'

'He's on the loose. Spoiled. Got a drink problem. That's one of the reasons Father Pierre got rid of him. Rapasia's staying with different *wantoks* all over the place. Better be prepared to spend this evening looking round all the bars in Chinatown.'

'It's a rough job,' said Kella, walking away, 'but somebody's got to do it!'

It had gone five o'clock when Kella left the police head-quarters building. Islanders were thronging along the pavements as he walked towards Matanikau Bridge at the western end of the town. The roads were crowded with the cars of the expatriates on their way home from the government buildings to their bungalows and duplexes on the ridges above the bay.

It took him a quarter of an hour to reach the bridge over the river running down to the sea. Once he had crossed it he had left the town behind him and was on the road leading out to the airport. On his right were the grey breeze-block dormitories of the Labour Lines, occupied by islanders employed by the different government departments. To his left were the shore and the sea.

Twenty minutes later he reached the fishing village, a collection of huts under a clump of palm trees near the beach. These were the remains of a much larger pre-war community, still defying the ominous spread of the capital.

Kella was entitled to a room in the police barracks, but the prospect of living in the centre of the town was abhorrent to him. For some years he had rented a hut on the outskirts of the fishing village, on the understanding that he did not conduct his professional activities in the area and had nothing to do with any of the local women.

He entered his hut and strip-washed from the bucket of water he had drawn from the communal standpipe that morning. He changed into a shirt and a pair of slacks from a locked chest next to his sleeping mat. He opened a tin of corned beef and ate the contents with a wooden spoon, finishing with a Coke.

As he ate he thought about Peter Oro and his grandfather Senda Iabuli. What could the pair of them have been doing that led to them both being killed? What connection, apart from the ties of blood, could there have been between an old saltwater villager and a promising young schoolboy?

Was the bushman Pazabosi the link that led to their murder? If so, why had the discovery of the bones of Lofty Herman sparked off their deaths and led to the attempt on the life of Sister Conchita? And where did Professor Mallory, the anthropologist, come into the equation? Could the American have been kidnapped, or even slain by the old Kwaio bush chieftain?

Night was falling as Kella left his hut and walked back into Honiara. He turned right past the bridge and entered the noisy, lively street that housed Chinatown. There were several dozen stores and bars crammed into Quonset huts and corrugated iron edifices, backed by ramshackle wooden dwelling houses, hand-constructed in many different styles, all running along the banks of the river at a right angle to Mendana Avenue. Even this early in the evening the stores were doing good business among the hundreds of Melanesians jostling up and down the street. Men and women were crowding into Joy Biscuits, Sweeties, Wong Pew, Ho Kee and the other colourful shops, each selling its jumbled, high-piled mixture of tinned food from Taiwan, rice, bottled beer, bread, tin plates, decorated china mugs, clothing and fishing tackle.

Kella pushed his way to the end of the street and entered the Everlasting Delight Bar. Despite its aspirational title it resembled most closely a tropical version of a Wild West spit-and-sawdust saloon of the 1880s. The room's entire length was occupied by a beer-slopped bar. The shelves behind were loaded with small brown bottles of 4X beer. There were a few plastic tables and chairs scattered about the room, but most of the occupants were lining the bar, three-deep.

The place was crowded with those Melanesian workers who still had a few dollars of their pay left this late in the week. They were drinking in island coteries, men from Malaita, Santa Isabel, Guadalcanal, Choiseul, Ugi, the Shortlands, and others. The air was filled with the sound of a dozen different dialects being spoken at a high volume. Between each group was a small but definable gap. Later that night a truculent drunk might spill over into the wrong throng, and then the brawling would start.

Kella stood on the edge of the Malaitan party and ordered a beer from one of the sweating barmen. He was served by Joe Dontate, a flat-nosed Roviana former boxer in his thirties.

A decade earlier he had reached the finals of the South Pacific Games middleweight championships in Suva. A savvy Australian manager had persuaded him to turn professional with enticing stories of the glittering prizes available to supporting contest fighters at the Sydney Stadium. Altogether Dontate had survived thirty bouts, in which he had been over-matched in only a couple, before returning to the Solomons with some scar tissue around his eyes, a perforated eardrum and enough money to open a trading store at Munda, which was now being run for him by his relations.

The ex-fighter had been unable to adapt back to village life and was apparently contentedly enough serving as a bouncer-barman for his Chinese employers. He was a watchful, philosophical character, with all the spontaneous aggression long since punched out of him, but still with enough steel in him to be able to control a tough bar like this one.

'You going to stay late and spoil the fighting?' he grinned, as he pushed the bottle across the counter and scooped up Kella's coins.

'I'll be gone inside the hour,' Kella promised.

'I'll hold you to that, sergeant.' Unhurriedly Dontate moved farther along the bar. He was still smiling but there was a definite edge to his attitude. He had made his point and he knew that the other man had taken it.

Kella sipped the lukewarm beer. He exchanged nods with some of the Lau men in the nearest group. They left him alone, knowing that he would edge closer into the crowd if he wanted company.

Kella remained where he was for half an hour, his eyes constantly flickering around the room. This was the most popular bar in the capital for the islanders. Expatriates mostly drank at the Mendana Hotel or in the whites-only clubs in the town.

Michael Rapasia did not arrive. Kella sighed and pushed his empty bottle back across the bar. When he emerged, the main Chinatown street was more crowded than ever. He looked in different stores and eating-houses without success. By the time he had finished his search he had reached the beach. It was quieter here. For the first time he was able to hear the footsteps of the men he had sensed for some time had been following him. He whirled round, clenching his fists.

'Easy, sergeant,' said Joe Dontate, coming forward, so that Kella could see his face. Accompanying the barman were two scowling Guadalcanal men.

'Business so bad you're throwing customers into the bar, instead of out?' asked Kella casually.

'Mr Cho wants to see you,' said Dontate. 'In fact he sent us to fetch you.'

'Which Mr Cho?'

'The boy.'

'What does he want?'

'How the hell would I know?' asked the barman. 'Do you think he tells me anything?'

Kella hesitated. He had no idea what the Chinaman wanted of him. When he did not respond immediately the two Guadalcanal men shuffled their feet restlessly. Kella ignored them. Even a former pro fighter like Dontate would not want to start trouble so near the main street. News would soon reach the Lau drinkers in the bar that the *aofia* was being roughed up. That would lead to a mass fracas that would greatly displease the influential Chinese store-owners.

On the other hand, thought Kella, he had nothing to lose. Perhaps Cho could aid him in unravelling part of the problem. It would be nice if somebody could.

'I'll come with you if you'll help me out with something,' he informed Dontate. 'I'm looking for Michael Rapasia. They tell me he's a serious drinker these days, so I expect you know where he is. Tell me how to find him and I'll come quietly.'

Dontate summed up the police sergeant unsmilingly. He walked closer to Kella. The Guadalcanal men moved to cut off any possible avenue of escape for the sergeant. Kella wondered if he had misjudged their mood. Dontate started to talk in an undertone.

'I sometimes wonder how long you'd last against me,' he said speculatively, as if discussing an algebraic problem.

'Must help pass the long evenings when you're watering the drinks,' agreed Kella. 'Maybe we'll find out some day. Just now we're both busy. Well?'

Dontate thought the matter through and then nodded. 'Crown and anchor game behind Jimmy Fat's,' he said, stepping back a pace. 'Rapasia will be there as long as he's got any money left.'

'Thank you,' said Kella. 'That wasn't so hard, was it? Now let's go and see young Mr Cho.'

20

LABOUR LINES

Sister Conchita came out of the chapel after evening service and joined the throng on its way to the refectory to eat. If she skipped the meal she would have several hours before she would have to take the older sisters to the beach for the blessing of the fishing boats. No one would miss her for that amount of time. The headquarters building was not run on the same lines of discipline as the mission stations. Too many itinerant priests and nuns were constantly coming and going on their way to postings out of the Solomons or to different areas of the island. Some stayed only a few nights before catching a ship or aircraft to their destinations.

Before leaving the house she hurried out to the back yard to examine the batttered Bedford faded red van that had been placed in her charge since her arrival in the Solomons. She had done her best to bring it up to scratch, but it was being held together largely by faith and rust. She hoped that it would survive long enough for her to be able to take her consignment of elderly sisters on their long-anticipated evening expedition.

For a moment she wondered if she dared appropriate the vehicle to take her on the immediate journey she had planned that evening. Firmly Sister Conchita put the thought out of her mind. She had been greeted with concern and sympathy upon her enforced return to Honiara but all the same she felt that she was being regarded with suspicion by the mission hierarchy. Too many inexplicable things had been occurring at Ruvabi mission lately for the peace of mind of the mission administrators, who were trying to pursue a policy of masterly inactivity. No one would tell her anything about Father Pierre and she had been emphatically denied access to the radio sked to talk to the old priest.

In that case, she decided as she slipped out of the side door into the gathering gloom of the evening, she would just have to use the bush telegraph instead.

Sister Conchita hurried down to Mendana Avenue where the stores and shops were mostly closed this late. She crossed the Matanikau Bridge over the river. Here there were no lights. She reached the Labour Lines, the long breeze-block buildings in which itinerant workers were housed. There were a dozen of these constructions, each one reserved for the workers of a different island. They were situated well apart from one another.

Sister Conchita headed for the block in which the Malaita men stayed when they were working in the capital. Shadowy figures glided about the dormitory buildings and she was aware of many eyes on her, but no one challenged the authority of her habit.

She approached a group of Malaitans huddled around a fire in the compound. In her halting pidgin she asked if she could see the latest arrivals from Ruvabi mission station. Without a word one of the men stood up and walked into the building. He returned a few moments later with a slight, grey-haired figure wearing a long green *lap-lap* and smoking a clay pipe. With relief the sister recognized him as Matthew Dauara. He was a deck hand on one of the Chinese trading boats that circumnavigated Malaita regularly. He was in his sixties, old for a seaman, but his knowledge of the reefs and tides around the coast made him a valuable relief wheelman on voyages. He also spoke English, a fact for which Sister Conchita was grateful.

'Sister Conchita,' said Dauara with surprise.

'I'm sorry to bother you, Matthew,' said the nun, shaking the man's hand, 'but have you seen Father Pierre lately? I'm worried about him.'

'We put in to Ruvabi two days ago,' said Dauara. 'I saw the father then.' He took her by the arm and guided her to a pile of logs stacked outside the concrete building, gesturing to her to sit down.

'How was he?' asked the sister anxiously.

Dauara hesitated. 'Sad,' he said finally. 'Father Pierre is unhappy. He does not want to come to Honiara.'

'I don't blame him,' said Sister Conchita. 'Is that why he is unhappy?'

'I think there is something else.'

'What?'

'It is about the time before.'

'The time before? Oh, you mean something that has happened in the past?'

Dauara hesitated, choosing his words carefully. 'The old men on the station say that he is sad too much because of the death of the big beachcomber.'

'Lofty Herman? I didn't think that Father Pierre knew him that well.'

'Oh yes. I visited Ruvabi many times before the war. Herman and the father were good friends. They did many things together. Some of the old people say that Father Pierre is blaming himself for the beachcomber's death.'

21

NIGHT TIDE

When Kella and Dontate arrived, John Cho was sitting behind a desk in a neat, uncluttered office at the back of the Happy Gardens general store. A pair of slim, discontented-looking Chinese youths were sitting on the floor, with their backs to a wall. They seemed terminally bored. Martial arts experts, Kella guessed. Joe Dontate could probably blow them apart without breaking into a sweat. The trouble was, Dontate was on their side.

The youths ignored Kella and scowled at the barman, as if their capabilities were being questioned by his presence. Dontate surveyed them and then leant against a wall, as far away from the youths as he could get. It looked as if Cho's bodyguards were not entirely one big happy family.

'Ah, Sergeant Kella,' said John Cho. 'So good of you to come. Please sit down.'

'I'm only here because Dontate gave me some information I needed,' Kella told him.

'Sure, whatever,' said Cho, flapping an impatient hand in the direction of a chair.

Kella nodded and took the seat opposite Cho. The Chinaman was in his twenties, wearing an expensive lightweight suit. On one wrist was a gold Rolex. He was slim and good-looking, with thick black hair brushed straight back over his head. His father, David Cho, was regarded as the most influential man in the Chinese community. A remote, shadowy figure, he was seldom seen outside Chinatown now that he was growing old. The rumours were that John was eager to take over from his father as soon as he decently could, but that he was a little short of the requisite weight for the job.

'I've been looking forward to meeting you, sergeant,' said Cho, flashing a mechanical smile. 'We should have got together a long time ago.'

It was all a little too pat and fluent. To Kella it seemed as if the young Chinese man was modelling his behaviour on one of the old black and white gangster films so often shown at the Point Cruz cinema. His father, on his rare public appearances, never struck attitudes. He had no need to.

'Why's that?' asked Kella.

Cho spread his hands in an expansive gesture. 'We're the two coming men,' he smiled, exaggerating an American accent. 'As it happens, I am assuming a little more responsibility in my father's various business affairs here in Honiara. You are commonly regarded as the leader of the Lau community. The Lau men are the hardest in the Solomons, that is common knowledge.'

Joe Dontate stopped leaning against the wall. One of the Chinese, who presumably understood English, translated to his companion, who grinned, revealing broken teeth. For a second, Dontate transferred his glowering attention to the first youth, before returning it to John Cho. The Chinaman continued to pay no attention to the islander.

'A lot of people would disagree with that,' said Kella.

Cho was not interested in what a lot of people, Dontate included, would disagree with. He leant forward eagerly across his desk.

'There are big changes coming up in the Solomons, Sergeant Kella,' he said smoothly. 'Big opportunities too. A smart man like you should be able to take advantage of the situation. Especially if you've got the right friends.'

'Like you?'

Cho shrugged modestly. 'Maybe. I've got influence and connections.'

And an influential father, thought Kella. Aloud he said, 'I've already got a job in the police force.'

'For how much longer, Sergeant Kella? It's a commonly accepted fact that the top brass among the Brits aren't going to give you a chance until you've grown a long grey beard. You're just their token Melanesian.'

'White blackman,' sneered Dontate.

'I wouldn't put up with it, if I were you,' urged the Chinaman. 'On the other hand, I respect your talents and ability. We could do a great deal together. You could retain your police job, and you'd still become Commissioner of Police when independence comes. Only by then you'd be a wealthy man.'

'What would I have to do?' asked Kella, too amused to be annoyed. After the subtle and elaborate manoeuvrings of old David Cho, the approach of his son seemed almost manic in its intensity.

'Just become a personal friend,' pounced John Cho. 'Pass on information about stake-outs, lose the occasional file, keep me in touch with what's going on at police headquarters, don't interfere too much. In general, become a friend at court. Is that too much to ask? As a matter of fact, there's one particular matter you can help me with straight away.'

'What's that?' asked Kella, suddenly alert.

'I'll tell you when we've agreed terms. I'll start you at a thousand dollars Australian a month. That's big money for a police sergeant.'

The young man was pushing altogether too hard. In the Solomons, everyone practised patience, especially the criminal fraternity. Cho was badly in need of advice. Only a very ignorant and naive man would attempt to bribe the *aofia* and treat a Roviana man like Dontate with contempt at the same short meeting. Kella knew that he ought to play the Chinaman along and find out what was bothering him enough to send for a police officer in this way, but he did not have the stomach for it. He stood up.

'Very big money,' he agreed. 'Now I'm going. You're wasting your time. Good evening, Mr Cho.'

John Cho went red. The two youths scrambled to their feet. Dontate had already stepped forward to stand in front of Kella before the pair of hired hands had had time to sort themselves out.

'Shall I slap him, Mr Cho?' asked the bartender.

'Don't be silly, Dontate,' snapped Cho. 'You're just a messenger boy.' He looked venomously at Kella. 'You're making a big mistake, sergeant. I was going to invite you in on a very good deal; one that you're already inadvertently involved in. You could have made a significant and lucrative contribution to the matter.'

Dontate was still standing close to Kella. The Roviana man had been made to lose face twice at the meeting. The former fighter would be resenting that. Kella decided to exacerbate the situation as best he could. It might serve his purpose to deepen the wedge between the two men.

'Tell your messenger boy to get out of my way,' he said, stressing the description.

'Stop interfering, Dontate,' snarled Cho, waving the glowering Melanesian away. 'You have made a bad decision, Kella; one you might later regret.'

'How do you like working for the Chinaman as an errand

boy?' asked Kella as he and Dontate came out of the store into the noisy, garish night.

'I suppose about as much as you enjoy working for the Brits,' said the Roviana man. His mind seemed far away.

'Is John Cho always in such a hurry?'

'Not that much,' admitted Dontate. 'Someone must have shoved a thorn up his arse to make him hammer away at you so obviously.'

'That's what I thought,' said Kella. 'Almost like I was getting close to something.' He eyed the bartender. 'I don't suppose you're going to tell me what this deal is that Cho was inviting me in on?'

'What do you think?' asked Dontate contemptuously. 'I'll tell you this for nothing though. You pissed the Chinaman off in there, and he ain't used to that. He's not a patch on his daddy, but he's got some say-so and a pot of cash. You be careful, Kella. I wouldn't like to see his hatchet men having a go at you before I get my chance.'

'You're all heart,' Kella told him.

He found the crown and anchor game lit by lanterns on poles in full spate on a patch of wasteland running down to the river behind Jimmy Fat's store. Twenty or thirty Melanesians were jostling around the large flat board divided into squares bearing different inscriptions. The banker, a Chinaman, with two watchful Guadalcanal minders, was throwing the three dice. The gamblers were thrusting notes on to different squares and greeting the results of the throws with cheers or groans.

Kella stood quietly in the background until he had made out Michael Rapasia. His old schoolteacher was on his knees in front of the board, squabbling with the other punters as he threw down his banknotes from the thin wad in his hand.

At first Kella could hardly recognize the man. The quiet, dignified figure who had taught him many years earlier had been replaced by an unkempt, snarling gambler, fighting for his place at the board. Rapasia was a slight, grey-haired man in frayed shorts and an old Hawaiian beach shirt.

He was not having any luck with his bets. Kella saw the last of the former teacher's money scooped up from the board by one of the Guadalcanal men. Rapasia stood up and slouched away from the game. Kella stepped forward.

'Good evening, Mr Rapasia,' he said. His old teacher stared blankly at him. 'It's Kella, sir. You used to teach me at Ruvabi.'

'Kella,' said the old man vaguely. He scrutinized the other man with dull eyes. 'Oh, yes,' he said. 'You became a policeman and sent a missionary and Peter Oro to the killing ground.'

'It wasn't quite like that, Mr Rapasia,' said Kella. He tried not to let the casual, offhand insult affect him. 'It's Peter Oro I wanted to talk to you about. Do you remember him?'

'Of course I remember him,' snapped Rapasia. 'I remember you all, even the killers.'

'I'm trying to find out who might want to murder him,' said Kella. 'Have you any idea who might have disliked him that much?'

'He was just an ordinary boy,' shrugged Rapasia. 'Brighter than some, and ambitious.' He tried to brush past the police sergeant. 'Anyway, I don't want to talk about the school. Did you know they have sent me away?'

'I heard that you had retired,' said Kella tactfully.

'Sent away!' repeated Rapasia vehemently. 'Dismissed! I was too old and ignorant for the bright young headmaster there.' He stared angrily at Kella. 'Do you remember the Lau incantation for an old man left alone and helpless, begging the younger men to fetch wood for his fire?'

'*Tutu taa'I nay. Ngwane ku aarai na,*' said Kella. It had been years since he had last heard the phrase. He was surprised that he could remember it. He translated. 'I am all by myself. I am an old man.'

'Precisely,' said Rapasia. 'Well, that's me now, thrown on the scrap-heap and left to fend for myself.'

He started walking away. Kella fell into step beside him, ignoring the old teacher's blatant hostility.

'What puzzles me', he said, 'is the partnership between Peter Oro and his grandfather Senda Iabuli, if there was one. On the one hand, you have an ordinary old uneducated saltwater villager, while on the other, there's a clever young schoolboy who's left village life behind him and will soon be off to secondary education and then an overseas university. What could the pair have in common?'

Rapasia stopped, his anger erupting again. 'Even the old and the ignorant can still teach the young,' he said.

'I know,' said Kella hastily, 'but in this case—'

'As a matter of fact,' said Rapasia triumphantly, as if producing a winning card, 'there was something between those two.'

'What do you mean?'

'I know for a fact that Iabuli came to the school at Ruvabi several times before he died. I don't suppose the other teachers noticed. One villager looks just like another to those *graduate* teachers.' The old man invested a lifetime of resentment into the adjective.

'But as you can see,' he went on with heavy sarcasm, 'I'm just a peasant myself. I noticed. Iabuli visited the mission school several times in the evenings during the last week of his life. On each occasion, he talked to his grandson down by the river. It seemed odd at the time; that's why I remember it. Iabuli certainly wasn't a Christian. I don't think he'd ever been to the mission before.'

'Did he talk to anyone else there?' asked Kella.

'Not that I saw.'

The police sergeant persisted with his questioning but Michael Rapasia either knew no more or was not prepared to divulge what he did know. Finally Kella nodded and took a five-dollar note from his wallet.

'Right,' he said. 'Thank you. Have another go on the board, on me.'

The old teacher looked at the note thrust into his hand. For a moment the sergeant thought he was going to refuse it. Then Rapasia's shoulders hunched. Without a word he turned and walked back towards the crown and anchor game. He rejoined the crowd and was lost to Kella's sight among the noisy, heaving mass of the gamblers.

Kella looked at his watch. It was eight o'clock. The tide would turn in a couple of hours. There was just time to get to the wharf and have a word with John Deacon before the Australian sailed back to Malaita. Before he left, Kella wanted to know why Sister Conchita had seemed to freeze the previous day when the Australian's name had been mentioned.

He walked along the deserted beach towards the wharf, wishing that he had approached Michael Rapasia in a more appropriate manner. During his questioning he had treated the former schoolmaster as an equal, which was right. However, once he had offered the old man money he had insulted him. Worse, Rapasia had demeaned himself by taking the five dollars. He would try to make things right with the Guadalcanal man the next time they met.

The only lights in the area came from the Yacht Club, where a dance seemed to be in progress. The music from the record player drifted over the sand and Kella could hear the shuffling feet of the dancers. He skirted the club building and resumed his journey along the beach towards the dark outlines of the vessels moored in the harbour.

He was only a few hundred yards from the silent wharf when rough hands grabbed at him and pulled him backwards. He snatched himself free and turned, but his feet slipped on the wet sand and he fell on his back, winded. He half rose but a callused bare foot crashed into his chest and sent him spinning back again.

Strong hands seized his arms and pinioned them behind his back, twisting them viciously, until tears of pain filled his eyes. The same bare foot drove again and again into his body. There were three men, one holding the police sergeant, and the other two punching and kicking him with sickening force.

Kella did his best to fight back but the islander clinging to him was enormously strong and he held on tenaciously to the sergeant as the other two rained punches and kicks on their victim, grunting and sweating with the effort. Kella was aware that despite all his efforts consciousness was already beginning to drain from him under the onslaught. Summoning all his strength he struggled to his knees but, given fresh life by his unexpected reaction, the blows and kicks redoubled in their velocity and after a moment he toppled helplessly over on to his side, waiting for the inevitable finishing blows.

The onslaught ceased abruptly. Taking advantage of the unexpected lull Kella forced himself on to his feet through a haze of pain. One of the islanders was lying unconscious on the sand. The other two were backing away from Joe Dontate. As Kella looked on helplessly the two remaining Melanesians turned and ran, disappearing into the shroud of darkness provided by the beach. Kella started to thank his rescuer but turned away, doubled up and was sick.

'Back in Sydney they used to call that the Technicolor yawn,' observed the bartender helpfully, sucking his bruised knuckles.

Kella raised his head. His body ached and his legs tottered like a colt's beneath him. Slowly he forced his limbs under control.

'Thanks,' he heard himself croak.

'It was nothing; I was just passing,' said the bartender.

'Like hell you were,' said Kella, struggling hard. Every word he uttered made his bruised chest and stomach ache. 'John Cho sent those guys after me and you followed them.' Dontate shrugged. 'Why?' asked Kella. 'I mean Cho sent his goons to beat me up because I wouldn't work for him, but why should you bother to get me out of trouble? You work for Cho as well.'

'Not any more,' said the ex-boxer. He indicated the islander still lying prostrate on the sand. 'That was my official resignation. I was going next week anyway. I've saved enough money to open a second store, in Gizo. Then I'll pass the word to my *wantoks* there that they're to use my places, not Cho's. David Cho's too old to do anything about it, and I'd like to see his boy come up against me on my own territory.'

'Lucky for me you were about to make an upwards career move,' acknowledged Kella.

'Nothing personal,' denied Dontate. 'I didn't do it for you. It was the quickest way I could think of to get up John Cho's nose, that's all.'

'Fair enough,' said Kella. 'But thanks again all the same.' He turned to resume his journey towards the wharf. Dontate put a roughly restraining hand on his arm.

'Where do you think you're going?' sighed the bartender, as if talking to a child.

'Deacon's sailing out on the night tide,' Kella told him, pulling away. 'He'll take me back to Malaita. Cho won't follow me over there.'

'Maybe not,' explained the bartender, 'but he's got twenty men strung out between here and the wharf to cut you off. You were wrong when you said he only wanted you beaten up. You'll never make it.'

'Shit!' said Kella vehemently. He really had upset the Chinaman that evening. 'Johnny Cho wants me killed?'

'He's protecting something big,' Dontate told him, beginning to move away. 'Don't take it to heart. You'll think of something.

What's the point of being a witch doctor if you can't conjure up the odd miracle?'

'Thanks a bunch,' said Kella bitterly. Dontate was several yards away now. 'One more thing,' he said plaintively.

'What?' asked the Roviana man.

'You must have followed those three Guadalcanal men all the way from town. Couldn't you have interfered just a couple of minutes earlier and saved my ribs?'

A rare grin creased the Roviana man's battered face.

'That's something you'll never know, Kella,' he chuckled. 'Drop in and see me the next time you're in the Western District. We'll have a chat about it.' Dontate nodded and turned and walked away along the beach, back towards the lights of Chinatown.

Kella stood thinking hard. The recumbent islander shook his head dazedly, struggled to his feet and started to run in the direction taken earlier by his two companions. Absent-mindedly Kella aimed a vicious kick at the departing islander's backside. It connected and the man howled in agony as he hobbled quickly away to safety.

The sergeant wondered which group his attackers had come from. In the heat of the action he had been unable to make out any tribal markings on his assailants. They were probably representatives of a new breed of Melanesians, men who had come to the capital as children and had never gone home. They retained no island or clan allegiances and offered themselves for sale to the highest bidders.

And according to Dontante there were a lot more of them lurking in the darkness to prevent his reaching the security of John Deacon's trading vessel moored at the wharf.

Kella became aware of the sound of concerted feet thudding on the sand farther along the beach. A group of some thirty white-robed priests and sisters, both Melanesian and European, were marching eagerly along the shoreline, following a large cross being held aloft by one of their number. At the same time the sergeant could see the first of a fleet of fishing boats moving furtively out of the harbour on the night tide and sailing slowly parallel to the shore to pass the assembled clerics. Soon there were about twenty of the vessels in view on the water, bobbing up and down daintily. Most of them were small and dilapidated, powered ineffectually by ancient, much-repaired engines. They had fragile, whiplash masts of scarred timber, decorated tonight in honour of the occasion with coloured lanterns adorned by garlands of flowers. Each fishing vessel was crewed by only two or three islanders.

Kella remembered that Sister Conchita had reminded him that the annual blessing of the fishing fleet was due to take place tonight. A few bored islanders were walking along from the town to witness the ceremony, but the event was not attracting much attention. Commercial fishing for bonito and tuna had hardly got off the ground around the main island of Guadalcanal yet. Most of the fishing in the area was conducted with simple rods and lines from canoes by individual islanders putting out from the coastal villages. The Solomon Islands was one of the few areas in the world where most of the fish in its waters still died of old age.

The bishop, a burly, middle-aged German with cropped hair, was standing up to his knees in the water as he performed his blessing. His cassock and cape stirred in the off-shore breeze as he prayed in a loud guttural tone for safe voyages, strong nets and abundant catches to be the lot of the small trawlers assembled precariously out in the bay.

Unobtrusively Kella joined the knot of earnestly praying priests and sisters. He saw Sister Conchita standing on the edge of the small crowd. She looked up warily as the police sergeant approached.

'Looking for salvation, sergeant?' she greeted him coolly in an undertone.

'No, just help,' muttered Kella, straight to the point. 'Is your van parked nearby?'

'I dropped the sisters off on the road and left it there,' replied the sister guardedly, indicating the stationary vehicle a hundred yards away. 'Why do you ask?'

'Tell me,' said Kella, apparently at a tangent. 'Do you still use it as the mission ambulance, picking up sick seamen from boats in the harbour and taking them out to the hospital?'

'Sometimes when it's necessary,' agreed the sister. 'What's this all about?'

'So if anybody saw the van speeding to the wharf, they'd get out of the way and let it pass?'

'They would if I was driving it.'

'Hmm,' said Kella. 'Could I borrow it?'

'Certainly not!' replied Sister Conchita indignantly, returning her attention to her prayer book. 'Immediately the service is over I have to drive the sisters back to the mission. The older dears will be more than ready for their cocoa by then.'

'It's rather important,' persisted Kella.

The sister ignored him, intoning a prayer with determined piety.

'You could almost say it was a matter of life and death,' Kella tried again. Still there was no response from the slight, devoted form in front of him.

'I'm in trouble and I need help,' said Kella loudly.

Several of the praying nuns were now looking curiously at him. Sister Conchita slammed her missal shut with exasperation and dragged the sergeant away from the group, her face flushed and vexed.

'What sort of trouble?' she demanded. 'And why aren't I surprised?'

'I need to get to the wharf but there are people who want to stop me.'

'Then send for a policeman.'

'I am a policeman,' Kella said, feeling like the straight man of a music-hall double act.

'You could have fooled me,' rapped Sister Conchita with asperity. 'What's so special about getting to the wharf tonight?'

'John Deacon's cutter is casting off at any minute. He can take me home safely.'

'Deacon?' asked the young nun sharply. 'You want me to help you get to that man?'

'Yes. What's so odd about that?'

'Nothing,' said Sister Conchita, biting her lip. 'Life is never dull around you, is it, Sergeant Kella?'

'You've been known to stir things up yourself just occasionally. Look, this really is important. If you could let me have the keys of the van—'

'No chance!' said the sister definitely.

'Right,' nodded Kella, giving up helplessly and turning away. 'Thank you for listening to me anyway.'

'That vehicle is in my charge,' called Sister Conchita after him. She produced a key from the folds of her habit. 'Where it goes, I go. I'll drive you to the wharf. Very much against my better judgement, if I may be permitted to say so.'

Now it was Kella's turn to be concerned. 'I can't let you do that,' he protested. 'It's dangerous.'

'Sergeant Kella, over the last week I have found and unsuccessfully tried to bury a skeleton, been shot at by an unseen assailant, chased through a swamp, forced to climb the side of an unsafe vessel in high seas and condemned to share a journey with an uncouth and extremely unprepossessing Australian. Now you seem to expect me to defy my bishop, abandon my fellow sisters and put a mission vehicle to what is almost certainly a most

159

secular, if not to say illegal use. Kindly do not lecture me about danger! Shall we go?'

As they walked along the beach towards the Ford van they could hear the soft chuckle of waves sneaking up the sand, overlaid by the booming voice of the bishop as he concluded his blessing:

'May the peace and blessing of Almighty God, the Father, the Son and the Holy Spirit, descend upon these ships and upon all who shall be in them, and remain for ever.'

As his closing words were still reverberating across the beach the other nuns turned with alacrity and hurried away from the fishing vessels towards the town. One of them caught sight of the departing Kella and his companion and called out to them.

'We're ready to go back now, my dear,' said the nun brightly, descending upon Sister Conchita.

In a moment all the sisters had caught up with them and were surrounding the couple, smiling with anticipation. Kella could not see one who was under sixty years of age. These were nuns who had spent many years of their lives in arduous work at isolated mission stations and only now were beginning to relax in various administrative tasks in the capital.

'Actually, I've promised to drop Sergeant Kella at the wharf,' faltered Sister Conchita. In the presence of so many experienced nuns the usually dominating sister seemed positively chastened, noticed Kella, amused in spite of his predicament.

'No problem,' said the nun who had first addressed them. 'Why, it's practically on our way back to the mission house. It will be no trouble to take the sergeant to the harbour. In you get, sisters.'

Trilling and cooing like the latest recruits to a welcoming aviary, the sisters climbed skittishly into the back of the Ford van. Sister Conchita looked helplessly at Kella.

'We can't take them,' hissed the sergeant. 'It could be dangerous.'

'Do you fancy telling them to get out again? No, I thought not. Get in the front with me, and try to keep quiet.'

In a moment the van was pulling away into Mendana Avenue. Kella noticed that the bishop and his priests were getting into a fleet of ancient and ill-matched cars. Sister Conchita drove past them without a sideways glance, studiously avoiding eye contact with any of the puzzled-looking white-robed men.

She steered the vehicle past the poinciana trees and hibiscus bushes bordering the main road. The sisters in the back were chattering together gaily. At the driver's side, slumped in his seat to avoid recognition, Kella kept a watchful eye for any figures lurking in the shadows on either side of Mendana Avenue. He did not expect an attack to be launched along the main thoroughfare. Any of Cho's men stationed there would be in the capacity of scouts, to alert the larger groups waiting for him down by the wharf.

At first he thought they were going to get away with it. After all, thought Kella hopefully, the Ford often came down here to pick up sick and injured seamen from incoming vessels. Dextrously Sister Conchita swung the vehicle off the avenue and started bumping down the unmade road towards the wharf at the bottom, a hundred yards away.

It was then that one of the men lurking by the waterside must have spotted the sergeant. His urgent warning yell alerted the others. Suddenly there seemed to be figures appearing from everywhere, racing towards the van.

Sister Conchita kept her nerve. With tightened lips but no change of expression she jammed her foot down on the accelerator. The Ford lurched forward, protesting mutinously at the unexpected turn of speed so unceremoniously demanded of it. The sudden difference in the tempo was enough to dislodge the two islanders who were already clinging to the side of the van. They dropped to the ground with cries of pain.

Within seconds Sister Conchita was applying her brakes vigorously, bringing the vehicle to a shuddering halt on the edge of the wharf itself. Kella's heart leapt at the sight before him. Instead of the area being dark and deserted, as he had expected, it was bustling with activity. Searchlights, powered by humming generators, lit the whole area harshly. Deacon's cutter was tethered between one of the Banks Line cargo vessels from Britain, and the smaller *Papuan Chief*, which regularly brought goods from Australia to the Solomons. Both vessels were being unloaded preparatory to a quick turnaround the following morning. Melanesian labourers were hurrying up and down the gangplanks of both vessels, carrying sacks and boxes of cargo on to waiting trucks. With relief Kella noted that there was a highly satisfactory element of exiled Lau men toiling at their tasks. They had already recognized him and were whispering to one another.

Farther along the crowded wharf was yet another vessel in the process of berthing, dwarfing the two cargo ships. This was a huge, modern American cruise liner, one of the types that were taking wealthy American tourists with increasing regularity around the South Pacific islands. Hundreds of them were even now on the decks of the vessel, rubbernecking at the cargoes being unloaded. As Kella stepped out of the Ford, the first of many gangplanks was lowered with impressive efficiency from the liner by its crew of tough-looking American seamen.

Cho's minions had also noticed the activity and the proliferation of labourers and seamen of all races who presumably would come to the aid of anyone threatened on the illuminated wharf. They hesitated amid the shadows at the far end, reluctant to advance in the face of so many potential foes.

'Are you going to spend all night here, Kella?' It was Sister Conchita, caustic and impatient.

'You're safe enough on the wharf,' Kella told her. 'I'll arrange for someone to escort you all back to the mission house.'

'When I need your help, sergeant,' said the nun, 'I shall ask for it. Kindly leave this to me.'

As the stupefied sergeant looked on, Sister Conchita descended from the van and walked round to the rear. 'Come along, sisters,' she said briskly, banging on the side. 'I've got a little treat for you. We're going to look round this lovely cruise ship. Would you like that?'

Chirping their assents gamely, the elderly sisters scrambled down from the van and excitedly followed Sister Conchita along the wharf to the gangplank of the liner. Before the tolerant eyes of the surprised and unresisting officers and crew members she led the nuns up to the lower deck of the luxurious vessel.

'I'm sure that one of these handsome gentlemen will give us a guided tour,' Sister Conchita informed her charges, bearing down on a transfixed, large and uniformed master-at-arms, who stood hastily to one side to allow the sisters to board the ship.

'And do you know what I'm going to do while we're on board?' went on Sister Conchita, raising her voice to clarion strength, ensuring that any of Cho's hired hands still in the area could hear her. 'I'm going to ask the kind radio operator to send a message to Honiara police station to dispatch an armed escort to take us back to the mission house when we've had our tour. Won't that be fun?'

The sisters cheered enthusiastically and disappeared from sight among the entrails of the vessel. Shaking his head in disbelief and wonderment Kella walked across to Deacon's cutter.

'What the hell was that all about?' asked Deacon, who was on deck staring blankly across the wharf in the direction of the cruise ship and its sudden influx of white-robed sisters.

'Don't ask,' said Kella. 'I'm not sure that I know myself.'

Suddenly he felt tired. Gratefully he subsided on to the warped and ancient planks of the cutter.

'What happened to you?' asked Deacon. 'You look as if you've been in a fight.'

'I think I've just been warned to mind my own business.'

'Not a bad policy,' Deacon agreed. 'Bit hard to enforce if you're a cop though. You look really crook. I'll send one of the boys to fetch you a taxi to take you to the hospital.'

'No,' said Kella, using the rail as a support to haul himself back on to his feet. 'I'm coming back with you to Malaita.'

'Suit yourself, mate,' said Deacon, raising an eyebrow. 'It's not like you to run away from trouble, though.'

'I'm not running away from it, believe me,' Kella assured the plantation manager. He winced as bolts of pain shuddered through his body. 'I'm going back into it.'

A Guadalcanal girl emerged shyly from the cabin. Deacon reached into his pocket and gave her some notes. The girl hurried down the gangplank and scuttled away in the direction of the cargo sheds. Deacon gave brusque orders in pidgin for his two crew members to continue casting off.

One of the deck hands prepared to untie the final rope binding the cutter to the wharf. He looked silently at the *aofia* for permission to embark upon this new voyage. Kella nodded imperceptibly, hoping that John Deacon had not noticed the subtle transfer of authority on the vessel.

'Take me home, *wantok*,' he said quietly.

He waited until the vessel was chugging out of the harbour before approaching Deacon and asked the question which had been troubling him for some time.

'What happened between you and Sister Conchita when you brought her over from Malaita?' he asked.

Deacon did not pause in his task of rewinding a rope as he glanced up briefly at Kella. Quickly he returned his attention to the swelling coil, working with mechanical expertise, the hemp spinning between his callused hands.

'What did she say happened?' he grunted.

'Nothing, but it was obvious that you're not her favourite plantation manager.' Kella strolled over to the other man at the wheel. 'You didn't threaten her, did you?'

'Why would I do that?'

'You tell me.' Deacon worked on in silence. Kella jerked his head at the two Melanesian seamen, who were watching the scene with open interest. 'You know that if I ask them they'll tell me. Better I heard it from you.'

'Oh, for Christ's sake!' erupted the Australian, throwing the rope down on to the deck. 'It was nothing. The woman got on my nerves. You've had nothing but trouble since you met her. I tried to warn her off, for your sake.'

'No,' said Kella quietly, shaking his head. 'It wasn't that. There's nobody I'd want more by my side in a fight than you, but you're no Good Samaritan. You've never done anything for anybody in your whole self-centred life, unless there was something in it for you.'

Kella left Deacon at the wheel, walked to the stern of the vessel and looked at the dark outline of the slowly receding shoreline of Guadalcanal. The lights of the fishing vessels danced on the port side several miles away. A light breeze whispered across the deck. He tried to work out what had caused the Australian to become so angry with Sister Conchita. He remembered that in all his time with Deacon there had always been one trait guaranteed to drive the white man to the edge.

It had first manifested itself near Sege in the Western Solomons towards the end of 1942. Deacon had been the coastwatcher in the district, reporting back by radio to the Americans on local Japanese movements. By this time he had also formed his own private navy, launching sudden raids on Japanese shore positions, creating the maximum damage and then withdrawing as quickly as they had arrived.

On that December morning Deacon had skippered a captured Japanese 57-foot diesel barge across the Marovo Lagoon as dawn was breaking. Their destination was a Japanese scouting party, which had been landed on one of the small uninhabited islands in the lagoon. The Japanese were plainly engaged in one of their periodic unsuccessful attempts to find Deacon's headquarters. It was a chance too good to be missed by the coastwatcher. He had taken half a dozen with him on his mission, including his second-in-command Pazabosi and the fourteen-year-old Kella.

They had travelled in the half-light, with Mount Mahimba and Mount Hungu rising in the distance above the crocodile-infested swamps. Stopping the engine in a bay, Pazabosi and three other islanders had swum ashore and destroyed the moored Japanese transport vessel, an old whaler, with hand grenades. By this time Deacon and the others, including a thrilled Kella, had concealed themselves in the undergrowth. As the main Japanese force, attracted by the explosions, had rushed out of the jungle into the ambush they had been cut down with fire from a .50-calibre Browning machine gun.

It had been a textbook operation, except in one respect. Among the handful of Japanese survivors Pazabosi had discovered a Roviana youth, not much older than Kella, who had been guiding the soldiers across the island. Deacon's fury had been monumental. He had ordered the terrified, screaming youth to be strapped across an oil drum and had administered a bloody thrashing with a belt to the frightened boy in front of the others.

Afterwards, as the others collected rifles and grenades from the fallen Japanese, Kella had cut the sobbing boy down and did what he could to stem the bleeding from a dozen wounds on his back, until Deacon had called him away roughly and ordered him to return to the barge.

'Betrayal,' said Kella, returning to Deacon. 'That's one thing you can't stand. You never could. You react to it by punishing people. What did Sister Conchita do to you that you construed as betrayal?'

'It was nothing,' said Deacon, staring straight ahead.

'It's not nothing to me,' said Kella. 'She may have broken your code, but Sister Conchita was a *neena*. I promised her my protection and you threatened her. I can't have that.'

It was over a minute before Deacon spoke. The tough former war hero suddenly looked tired and defeated. 'I'm finished on Malaita now, aren't I?' he asked, still not meeting Kella's gaze.

22

TRAILING SPEARS

Pazabosi luxuriated in the heat of the afternoon sun on his old and aching bones and wished fervently that he could lie like this on the mat outside his hut for all the time left to him by the spirits.

He knew there were too many things to do for that to become a possibility. Word had reached him that earlier that day Kella had arrived back on Malaita. The police sergeant's notorious obsession with order and justice meant that he would soon be coming up into the bush to look for Pazabosi and seek an explanation for all that had been going on lately in the mountain area controlled by the old chief.

On the far side of his village compound a bunch of young warriors set out noisily on a pig-hunting expedition. In deference to the presence of the old magic man, most of them carried their spears trailing behind them as a sign of respect. Only one of the men deliberately carried his over his shoulder, glancing defiantly across at Pazabosi, to make sure that the other man had noted his gesture of rebellion.

Pazabosi made no sign that he had even seen the insubordinate villager. He was aware that for some time Hita had been planning a challenge to his authority, and that the young man was only waiting for the right moment to carry it out.

It was only to be expected. Decades before, Pazabosi had made his own reputation by challenging and killing the chiefs in his area. He had set out on his ruthless campaign soon after he had returned from Australia in the early years of the twentieth century.

The labour-recruiting vessel had landed the young Pazabosi and a hundred other islanders in northern Australia. For the next three years he had spent twelve hours a day, six days a week, cutting sugar cane beneath the grilling sun. In all that time he never once saw a town.

Pazabosi was no stranger to hard work, and he had been particularly impressed by the standard of the food supplied to the labourers. The meat, rice, biscuits and tea far exceeded in quality and quantity anything he had known on Malaita, and did much to build up his ever-developing physique and strength.

Early on during his indentured time he had come to the attention of his white field supervisors, after he had won several vicious all-in fights with Melanesians from other islands. As a result he had been appointed a boss-boy, in charge of fifty other labourers.

At the end of his period of service, Pazabosi, who now spoke fluent English, as well as pidgin, was asked to renew his contract. He had refused curtly, as he now had his own agenda. He had taken his accumulated wages of half a crown a week and used part of the total to fill a tool chest with knives and axes, at a cost of a shilling each. Eventually, another labour vessel had taken him back to the same bay from which he had embarked from Malaita.

As he had expected, upon his return Pazabosi found himself a 'big man', someone of wealth and substance. In Queensland he had learned how to plant and cultivate coconut palms, which had been practically unknown until then in the high bush. Within a few years he had established one of the first plantations in the interior of Malaita.

He had also returned, with relish and ambition, to pursue the unrelenting warfare between the bushmen and the saltwater villages. Over the next two decades, he had led many successful and bloody raids on the fertile gardens of the coastal dwellers, taking away many saltwater men and women to work as slaves on his plantation.

He soon became so famous that he was able to marry the daughter of another powerful bush chieftain. As the girl was both a hard worker and a virgin he had been forced to pay a high bride price of twenty-four strings of shell money and a thousand porpoise teeth. The girl had proved to be good value, providing him, in addition, with four sons and two daughters.

Later, when he owned too much land for one woman to maintain, he had taken a second wife. By then Pazabosi was a rich man and was openly contemptuous of the awed family, which allowed the new girl to come to him for a bride price of ten strings of shell money and five gold sovereigns.

By the end of the 1920s, British administrators were beginning to enter Malaita, in the shape of occasional touring officers. These officials had been delighted to discover a respected and influential bushman able to speak English. It had taken little effort on their part to persuade the wily Pazabosi to become a headman.

In this capacity he was charged to maintain law and order in his district. Pazabosi had accepted the position when he heard that it carried with it a wage of two pounds a month, a rifle, and a uniform consisting of a khaki *lap-lap* and a wide red sash, with a purse attached.

If Pazabosi had been important before, now that he had the backing of the white men from faraway Tulagi, the first administrative centre, his new position in the bush was virtually that of a paramount chief. He secured the approbation of his white employers by settling land disputes at local courts, arresting and fining malefactors, and driving a number of professional murderers out of North Malaita.

At the same time he had employed his power and the implicit backing of the absent but feared white men by using his rifle to dispose of the three bushmen most likely to challenge his growing authority.

Those had been good days, thought Pazabosi regretfully. It would be satisfying to dispose of his young rival Hita now with a single shot, but he knew that he would never get away with it as long as Kella was on the island.

Never mind, he thought complacently, stretching out in the calming sun again. There were other ways of dealing with his problems. He might even be able to involve the unwitting police sergeant, now on his way to the high bush, in their solution.

23

BROTHER JOHN

Crowded in with Kella in the back of the jolting Ford truck were a dozen islanders, three pigs and several chickens. The vehicle was making its scheduled daily run along the narrow ribbon of winding road between the trees from the Malaitan district station of Auki to the jetty at the road-head, opposite the artificial island of Sulufou. The road extended for seventy miles. When Kella's father had been a boy it had taken three days by canoe from the district station to the lagoon containing the artificial islands.

Most of the passengers were returning from selling their garden produce at the weekly indoor market in Auki. Kella had been dropped off at the district station in the small hours of the morning by a subdued Deacon. He had picked up a change of clothing, a pack and some supplies at the Chinese store, before starting out on his journey to Ruvabi mission. He had broken his journey in this manner in case anyone had seen him on the Australian's vessel. The bush telegraph would soon spread the news that Kella was back but the sergeant still wanted his forthcoming journey to be as unobtrusive as possible.

He had no idea how the authorities would react to the abrupt way in which he had left Honiara. After all, Grice had told him to take some leave, even if the chief superintendent had been drunk at the time. Kella listened with half an ear to the monsoon rain pounding down on the roof of the truck and wondered if they would even make it to the end of the road. After this weather the rivers they would have to cross would be swollen and overflowing their banks.

The Ford continued on its hazardous, jolting way along the road, stopping to pick up more laden passengers whenever it was flagged down. After little more than an hour it shuddered to a halt at the first river.

All the passengers got out and joined the driver and his youthful assistant in surveying the rushing waters covering the surface of the road. The driver, a grey-haired Kilisakwalo man called Paul, stripped off his shirt and sandals and plunged ahead through the curtain of rain, waist-deep in the water.

Several times the force of the flood almost swept him off his feet, but the driver waded on grimly, flailing with his arms to retain his balance. He reached the far side and then stopped thoughtfully, his chest pumping with his exertions, mentally plotting the best track for the Ford to follow. From experience he knew that if he turned and drove back to Auki, as he should, his passengers would have to pay for their food and lodging at the district centre that night, and few of them could afford that. The driver waved to his suddenly apprehensive-looking assistant to get into the driver's seat and take the Ford across to him.

'Quick time!' he shouted in pidgin.

With a great grinding of gears, the nervous seventeen-year-old edged the truck into the river. Painfully slowly, he steered the vehicle into the path of the flash flood, trying to follow the route being indicated by the frantically gesticulating Paul on the far side. Muddy water swirled around the truck, entering the cab and pouring out of the other side.

Half-way across, the engine cut out. The now stationary vehicle started to rock precariously in the path of the torrent thundering down from the mountains. Kella and the other male passengers pushed their way out through the water and put their shoulders to the back of the truck, straining to force it forward as the youth struggled to restart the engine. Several of the men then darted ahead of the vehicle and attempted to provide a firm bottom to the ford by piling large stones on top of one another, but most of these rocks were soon swept aside by the gushing water.

There was a creak and a groan and a coconut tree, its roots swept away by the flood, toppled into the water. A cheer went up from the passengers, followed by a mad rush to gather the nuts before they were lost from sight. According to custom, the coconuts were now public property, as the tree was no longer attached to the owner's land. Several of the islanders swam across to the remains of the palm tree, caught in the rocks. They tore off the nuts from the branches and threw them to the bank.

It was some time before the driver, aided by Kella, could persuade the passengers to return to the marooned truck. Soaked and buffeted by the current, they pushed as hard as they could, but the vehicle would not budge. Through the driving rain the police sergeant was dimly aware of someone coming up behind him. He was too busy trying to prevent the rocking vehicle from toppling over to pay much attention to the new arrival. Then a massive shoulder was placed against the tailboard next to him, and huge hands grasped the back of the vehicle.

'Heave!' ordered a stentorian voice.

Obediently the assembled passengers pushed. The truck stopped rocking and even began to inch forward. Under the panic-stricken ministrations of the terrified young driver the engine reluctantly whined into life. Kella and the others continued to thrust forward. Slowly the Ford crawled towards the far side and up the bank on to the road.

Kella scrambled after the vehicle. He turned to peer through the rain at the newcomer who had been instrumental in getting the truck restarted. He found that he was looking at a giant of a man. Kella was big, but the other man towered over him and was much broader. He was about thirty, wearing the distinctive attire of a member of the Melanesian Brotherhood, black shirt and *lap-lap*, and a wide black and white belt.

Before the war this had been the uniform of the Solomon Islands Police Force. It had been adapted for the Brotherhood by Ini Kopuria, a former policeman who had founded the evangelistic order. Only Melanesians were allowed to join. Each brother spent a few years dedicated to poverty, celibacy and obedience, touring the islands, preaching and living off the land, before returning to village life.

The big man extended a massive hand. 'I am Brother John,' he said. 'I come from Santa Isabel.'

'Ben Kella,' said Kella, shaking the massive hand.

'Of course! Everyone on Malaita knows you, Sergeant Kella.'

Despite the cascading rain, the other passengers remained where they were, goggling in anticipation at the two big men, as if waiting for something to happen. The mission worker looked at Kella with placid interest. He had the quiet, built-in confidence of a big man who was also well coordinated and knew that he was capable of meeting most physical challenges.

It was the grey-haired driver who broke the silence. 'Let's go!' he shouted, leaping into the cab as his assistant squirmed gratefully across to the other seat.

Brother John took care to sit next to Kella in the back of the Ford as it continued on its jolting journey along the slippery, branch-strewn road.

'Where are you going, sergeant?' he inquired.

'Ruvabi mission and afterwards the high bush.'

'Then we can walk together for a while when we reach the road-head. I'm visiting the next saltwater village. An old man is dying and the family has sent for me.'

The big missionary relapsed into a comfortable silence. Kella was aware of the surreptitious glances being directed at them by the other passengers. Everybody knew that it had been a member of the Melanesian Brotherhood who had been murdered next to the bush waterfall six months before, and that Kella had been accused of negligence leading to the islander's death. The passengers were wondering if Brother John had been sent to extract some sort of payback. The missionary's broad, shining face betrayed nothing as he sat in the noisy, stinking vehicle with them. Kella wondered what lay in store for him that day.

The truck crossed the remaining rivers without mishap. Finally it disgorged its passengers and their animals at the road-head by the wharf. It was still raining. Through the mist covering the lagoon Kella could hardly make out his home village.

Most of the other passengers from the Ford were making their way down to the water's edge to canoes waiting to take them back to their artificial islands. Kella took the track leading from the shore into the bush. Brother John caught up with him and fell into step with the police sergeant, handling a heavy backpack with ease.

'Not going home first then?' he asked pleasantly.

'I have work to do,' said Kella shortly.

'Me, too,' said the other man.

Kella stopped and faced Brother John. 'If you've been sent to have anything out with me,' he said, 'we might as well do it now.'

'You misunderstand me completely, Sergeant Kella,' protested the massive missionary. 'I'm just here to enjoy your company for a brief time; two pilgrims on the road together.'

They said no more until they were deep into the closely packed trees. The track was just wide enough for the two men to walk along it side by side through the vegetation. The interwoven overhanging foliage deflected most of the rain but they could hear it thudding down above them, like the sound of many women pounding taro with cooking sticks.

Brother John reached back into his pack with a long, sinewy arm and produced a hunk of sweet potato wrapped in a banana leaf. He undid the covering and broke the vegetable into two pieces. He offered one portion to Kella. The sergeant took it and muttered his thanks. The two men ate as they walked.

'You know,' said Brother John judiciously after a while, 'you're wrong to blame yourself for the death of Brother Leoni all those months ago.'

'Who says I do blame myself?'

'It's obvious. The Brotherhood had observers at the white man's court of inquiry. You took most of the blame on your own shoulders.'

'So I should have. As a *neena* he was under my protection.'

'I think not,' said Brother John.

Kella stopped. 'What do you know about it?' he asked.

'I knew Brother Leoni,' said the big evangelist. 'He was a good man, but he had one great fault. He liked to interfere. As a result, he was always turning up in places where he had no right to be. That was what was happening when you met him up in the bush that day, wasn't it?'

'Does it matter?' asked Kella, starting to walk again.

Brother John caught up with the police sergeant with two enormous strides. 'It does if you're tearing yourself up inside about it,' he said. 'You may be the *aofia* but you can't hold yourself responsible for every outsider who is killed on Malaita.'

'Who says I do?' asked Kella.

'Do you know what I think happened on that day?' asked Brother John.

'I can't stop you talking.'

'I think', went on the giant, 'that Brother Leoni disobeyed the mission's instructions and went up into the Kwaio high bush, preaching to the islanders. You heard that he was up there and you went after him, trying to get to him before he got into trouble with Pazabosi and his followers. Am I right so far?'

Kella looked straight ahead and said nothing. Brother John nodded and continued, unperturbed.

'I think you found Leoni up at the waterfall by the killing ground. By that time he had infuriated the bushmen with his presence and they wanted to kill him.'

The memory of that dreadful morning, so long pushed to the back of the sergeant's mind, emerged in all its stark terror once again. He had found the Melanesian missionary, bruised and cut, surrounded by a dozen armed bushmen. Kella had managed to persuade them to release their prisoner. It had been obvious that as soon as Leoni left the village they would pursue him and hunt him down like a wild animal.

Kella had ordered Leoni to make his way down to the comparative safety of the coastal strip. He had then remained with the furious bushmen, trying in vain to pacify them before he had gone in search of the Melanesian missionary, but he had been unable to find the stubborn proselytizer.

'From what we've been able to piece together at the Melanesian mission,' went on Brother John, 'at some stage you and Brother Leoni became separated. Knowing him as I did, he probably deliberately gave you the slip and doubled back on you, and returned to the killing ground. Instead of making for the shore, he went the other way, up to the *faatai maea* next to the waterfall.'

Kella suddenly found himself taking up the thread of the story as Brother John relapsed into a sympathetic silence.

'Pazabosi was conducting a custom meeting there,' the sergeant said, haltingly at first but then with increasing rapidity. 'In the old man's eyes Brother Leoni had committed sacrilege by entering the killing ground and attempting to preach there about the Christian God.'

'He had a point,' grunted Brother John. 'So he and his men killed Brother Leoni and left his body as a warning to others. Is that what happened?'

'Just about,' nodded Kella. 'By the time I got there, it was all over.' Now that he had told someone it seemed as if a weight had been lifted from him.

'Why didn't you explain all this at your court of inquiry?' demanded Brother John with exasperation. 'That would have taken all the blame off you. You were a hero even going after Leoni.'

'You know how it is,' said Kella. 'I couldn't talk about custom ways at a white man's court. How could I explain it to them? They know nothing of the islands.'

'No,' agreed Brother John. 'They never have.'

'Anyway,' said Kella, 'I deserved to be punished. I'm supposed to be the island peacemaker. I didn't make much of a job of it with Leoni.'

'That's absolute nonsense!' thundered the big evangelist, suddenly roused. 'You can't impose order over the whole of Malaita by yourself.'

'I can try,' said Kella.

They walked on for another hour until they reached a fork in the track.

'This is where our ways divide,' said Brother John. He placed a hand on the other man's shoulder. 'Take care, my friend.'

There was an air of calm inevitability about the big man. Kella sensed that their meeting today had not been entirely accidental.

'You've been looking for me, haven't you?' he asked. 'You wanted to reassure me that Brother Leoni's death wasn't my fault.'

'Your unfounded assumption of guilt has been worrying some of us in the Brotherhood for some time,' acknowledged the giant. 'I had to come out this way, anyhow. When I heard that you had returned to Malaita, I made it my business to find you. You're a good man, Kella. You mustn't take the guilt of the whole island on your shoulders. Good luck, sergeant, and may your gods go with you, whoever they may be!'

It was still raining heavily when Kella reached the Ruvabi mission complex soon after eleven o'clock that morning. The students were all crammed into their classrooms and the compound was empty as the police sergeant crossed it. When he reached the mission house, Father Pierre was sitting in an old basket chair on the verandah, staring abstractedly at the downpour. Even the sight of Kella caused him only to nod wearily.

'You're supposed to be on your way to Honiara,' Kella told him, stepping on to the partial shelter of the verandah. 'I suppose you're waiting for a slow boat via China?'

'That was the general idea,' admitted the priest. 'Unfortunately the bishop has taken a hand. I'm ordered to fly from Auki to Honiara tomorrow. Anyway, what are you doing back here, Ben?'

'I'm looking for whoever killed Lofty Herman, Senda Iabuli and Peter Oro. It wasn't necessarily the same person who did the three killings. In fact I'm sure of that. But I'm certain the deaths are connected somehow.'

'Why come to me?'

'Because I don't believe for a moment that you had anything to do with Lofty Herman's death. But I'm convinced that you know more about it than you're letting on.'

'What makes you believe that?'

'Remember, I'd been a pupil here before the war, and I know what you were like then. In those days not a parrot farted on this station without you knowing about it.'

'Unlike now, you mean?' Calmly the priest waved aside the police sergeant's embarrassed protestations. 'No, you're right, my boy. I've been here too long, and I've lost touch. I've got a lot more in common with Pazabosi than you might think. Two old men waiting for the end.'

'How do you make that out?' asked Kella. 'He's a crafty villain.'

'He's still given his life to Malaita, just as I've given most of mine. And now, probably, all that he wants to do is to rest, like me. If he is fermenting an uprising, you can be assured that it is against his will. All we both want now is a little time to reflect on the past and prepare for the future. Unfortunately, such a period of autumn rest, the *trochea*, is built into the bushmen's religion, but not into mine.'

His words triggered off a warning at the back of Kella's mind, but he could not think what conclusion they were supposed to lead him to. Doggedly he pressed on with his questioning.

'When did you last see Lofty Herman?' he asked.

'It's all a bit vague in my mind,' shrugged the old priest. 'As I told you, I was ill when the Japanese first came. I had a bad bout of malaria, and I had no idea what was going on at the mission for the best part of a month. By the time I'd recovered, Herman was no longer in the area. I assumed that he'd fled for his life from the Japanese. As it happened, they hardly touched Malaita, but Herman wasn't to know that most of the fighting was going to take place over on Guadalcanal. He wasn't the bravest of men, so I wasn't surprised when he disappeared. After all, he and I and John Deacon were the only white men on the island, and Deacon was making plans to sail his vessel over to Guadalcanal to help with the fighting.'

'Why would Herman be so worried?' asked Kella.

'He wasn't a particularly nice man,' said Father Pierre. 'In fact, he was a drunken lout. He'd made a lot of enemies among the islanders. For years the islands had been controlled by white men like Herman. The invasion changed all that. Now, all over the Solomons, the whites were in a panic and it looked as if the Japanese were going to take their place. It was a very fraught situation; the established order was crumbling and everything was changing.'

'What was Herman doing over here in the first place?'

'Prospecting for gold along the river. He thought he'd found a large deposit at the base of the cliffs. He rigged up a strong hose pipe and trained it on the rocks to dislodge small particles, which he panned in the water as the river brought the rocks down with it.'

'Where did this take place?'

'On the Ulana river, half a mile west of the main track inland from Ruvabi.'

'Did he find any gold?'

Father Pierre shrugged. 'There were rumours that he'd been lucky, but if he was, nobody ever found his cache. Maybe his assistant made off with it. As I said, it was a pretty confused time in May of 1942.'

'His assistant?' asked Kella sharply. 'Who was working with him?'

'It was Mendana Gau, that Santa Cruz man who owns the station trading store.'

'Gau?' repeated Kella. More pieces of the jigsaw were somehow slotting into place. 'Yes, I suppose he has been here a long time.'

'Gau was little more than a labourer until the war. In fact, come to think of it, he disappeared from the district at about the same time that Herman did. But so did a lot of other frightened people, when they first saw the Japanese warships off the coast. Then, after the war, Gau reappeared. He seemed to have done quite well for himself in the interim. He certainly had sufficient money to open his store. But we never saw Lofty Herman again until that earthquake disturbed his grave.'

'It must have been a heck of a tremor to roll back all the heavy rocks which had been over the top of his skeleton.'

'No stronger than many others we've had here over the years,' said Father Pierre dismissively. 'I could tell you about earthquakes—' He stopped himself and looked resignedly at Kella over his half-moon glasses. 'You're not going to let go of any of this, are you?' he asked.

'I've got my job to do,' said Kella.

'Which job – as *aofia* or a policeman?'

'A little of both, I fancy. So Herman and Gau worked the gold mine between them. Just the two of them?'

'No, there were three,' said Father Pierre. 'Didn't you know? Back then Herman was in partnership with John Deacon.'

'Herman got around.'

'He was quite unusual. I got to know him well before the war. He would drop into the mission for a drink and a chat from time to time. He was not a good man but he was a character. He had a fund of good stories and he knew how to tell them. He made me laugh. After he'd gone I missed him. I felt – still feel – responsible for his death.'

'How could that be? Herman was a rolling stone. He was bound to get into trouble one day.'

'I know. For a man of his experience Herman was curiously naive. He was always ready to link up with anyone who promised him a quick dollar. I worried when he went into partnership with Deacon and Gau. They were both much harder men. In any association Herman was always going to be the one who suffered. I should have warned him off.'

'Would he have paid any attention to you?'

Father Pierre sighed and shook his head. 'Probably not. All the same, I should have made more of an effort. But the war came, and then it was too late.'

After a few more words Kella left the old priest sitting hunched on the verandah with his memories, and crossed the mission towards Gau's trading store. As long as he had known the Santa Cruz man the storekeeper had been a crook. If the trader had been associated with Lofty Herman before the war, perhaps he was also a murderer. Herman and Gau could have fallen out over something, thought Kella, hurrying through the rain. The Santa Cruz man might have killed the Australian and buried his body. If Herman had discovered gold in the river, Gau might have murdered him for that. And where did Deacon fit into the equation? Could the Australian have stolen Herman's gold perhaps, and used it later to lease his plantation?

Then there was the matter of the man who had tried to kill Sister Conchita as they had fled across the swamp. The stalker had seemed to make heavy weather of the task, indicating that he was either handicapped or unaccustomed to strenuous activity. The pot-bellied, sedentary trader would certainly come into the second category, and so would the crippled Deacon.

But why would anyone want to kill the young nun? It looked very much as if Sister Conchita was in possession of information that would incriminate Gau, or someone else on the mission, even if she was not aware of what this was.

That was the hard part of the investigation, thought Kella. The fact that a white woman was involved put everything else out of kilter. If his investigation had concerned Melanesians alone, he would have had the custom knowledge to work out what had happened and what was likely to follow. For someone trained from childhood to assess and investigate traditional matters, everything should be assuming a logical pattern now, but it most emphatically was not.

The door of the trading store was open. Kella went inside. Two muscular Santa Cruz men in dirty shorts and singlets were sitting idly on the counter, smoking hand-rolled cigarettes. They recognized Kella without apparent joy.

'Where's Gau?' asked the sergeant.

'We don't know,' said one of the men truculently. 'Fuck off, black whiteman.'

Over the last five days Kella had been reprimanded, insulted, lied to and beaten up. With a certain grim satisfaction he realized that he had had enough. The Santa Cruz man standing before him became the unfortunate recipient of his wrath.

With his left hand Kella grabbed the startled man by the front of his tattered singlet. He brought his other hand across the man's face in a stinging slap.

The Santa Cruz man bellowed with rage, tore lose from Kella's grip, took a couple of paces backwards and then charged head down at the police sergeant. Kella sidestepped adroitly. As the man blundered headlong past him, the sergeant brought the edge of his hand down on the back of the islander's neck.

The Santa Cruz man fell heavily on to his hands and knees and remained there, shaking his head dazedly. Kella chose his spot and drove his foot into the man's side, sending him sprawling over on his back.

Kella glanced at the second man, who had not moved from his perch on the counter and was looking on in open-mouthed amazement.

'You were about to tell me where Mendana Gau is,' suggested Kella.

The second man looked at his companion, who was still on the floor, holding his ribs and moaning softly. 'The boss has taken some crates of tobacco to sell at the villages upriver,' said the second man quickly. 'He left about an hour ago in the canoe with the outboard engine.'

'I do hope you're not lying to me,' said Kella, leaving the hut.

Kella was on his way to the mouth of the river to borrow a canoe from a *wantok*, when he heard his name being called. Impatiently he turned, tensing, half-expecting with relish to see the two Santa Cruz men coming after him. Instead he found himself looking at a very large and very wet Brother John.

'Did you get lost?' asked Kella.

The evangelist shook his head. 'They didn't want me in the village,' he said. 'The old man's dying all right. His daughter's a Christian and she sent for me, hoping that I could convert her father on his deathbed. He insists on dying the custom way. That's why he wants you.'

'Why me?' asked Kella in surprise.

'The old man wants the *tala oto*, the entry to the straight path, intoned over him before he goes. Apparently these days only you and two old custom priests still know how to pray in that way. The other two are a couple of days' walk away, so that leaves you.'

'I'm sorry,' said Kella, brusquely, turning to continue on his way. 'I don't have time. I have to find Gau before he gets too far upriver.'

Brother John walked round until he was standing in front of Kella. 'I don't think you understand,' he said steadily. 'You have been requested to give a dying man the blessing which will enable his spirit to leave the village and make its journey to the ghost island. He won't go my way, so he'll have to go yours. As the *aofia* you have a duty to help the old man on his way.'

'But you don't believe any of that,' said Kella, trying to move round the obdurate form of the evangelist. 'You're a Christian missionary.'

'I am also a Melanesian, like you,' said Brother John, no longer so affable. 'I believe that any man has a right to maintain his faith, and that all others have a responsibility to help him, no matter what their views.'

Kella hesitated. If he made a detour to see the dying man, Mendana Gau might get so far up the river that he would not find him for days, just when he felt that his investigation was approaching some sort of conclusion.

On the other hand, he had been called upon to perform the straight path ceremony, which would light the passage of an old man's soul from this life to the next. It was just another choice that he would have to make between being a policeman and the *aofia*. There had been so many of those over the past few years. He knew which path he would have to tread.

'I'm on my way,' said the *aofia*, changing direction.

'And don't worry about Gau,' called Brother John after him. 'I know where you'll probably find him. He's got a supply of trading goods he keeps in a treehouse in a clearing just outside the village by the killing ground. If he's up in the bush, that's where he'll be. It's getting as crowded as Honiara up there these days.'

'What do you mean?'

The big missionary shrugged. 'The bushmen tell me that someone from Ruvabi mission was hanging around the tree-house a week or so ago.'

'Peter Oro?'

'They didn't know his name. Just fella bilong school.'

'So Oro discovered the treehouse,' said Kella. 'But why would the bush people kill him for that?'

'It's none of my business,' said Brother John firmly. 'I just want the straight path ceremony carried out. Don't forget, it's the first saltwater village along the track. The dying man says he knows you. His name's Andu. He's the ghost-caller!'

24

THE STRAIGHT PATH CEREMONY

In the smoke-filled hut Kella checked that he had all the equipment necessary to prepare Andu the ghost-caller for the straight path. He had assembled a pile of the scarce areca nuts. He had roasted a yam ready to be eaten by Andu's youngest great-grandchild when the old man died. He had borrowed a bush knife and had assembled the dying ghost-caller's fishing nets on the floor of the hut. Outside, a whole pig was being roasted on stones, to be offered as a sacrifice to the spirits and to entice them to the ceremony.

Kella had already purified his mouth with salt water, brought from the beach in a bamboo tube by one of the women. He had rubbed his hands in the sacred red clay found along the bank of the river. He had sung the incantation celebrating the first finding on Malaita of taro in the time before. Now he was ready.

Andu was lying on his bunk, comfort stones steaming beneath him to give comfort and ease to his frail form over the last hours of his life. His eyes were closed and his scrawny, hairless chest hardly moved as the shallow breaths being taken by the ghost-caller struggled to maintain some form of life in his wasted body.

About a dozen of Andu's relatives had crowded into his hut. They were squatting, occupying every spare scrap of available space, except for the sacred rectangle next to the bunk where Kella was standing. They were all watching the *aofia* intently.

More members of the old man's line were waiting outside the hut. In the distance, Kella could hear the shouts of children. Once the ghost-caller had died, no one in the village would be allowed to raise a voice above a whisper for five full days.

Kella took a deep breath and began the straight path chant.

'*Ramo dingana, toli ana aena,*' he intoned. '*Tafui fena igi . . .*'

The assembled men and women looked on in silence as Kella prepared the dying man for the life to come on Momulo. There he would spend long, storm-free days fishing with friends who had gone before him, and he would live effortlessly on wild yams and taro.

To reassure Andu, Kella recited the names of some of the great warrior chiefs who had died in the time before and whose spirits would soon be waiting to greet and protect the ghost-caller in the afterlife. These were Baala, Tabusu, Salaimanu and Angasi. He sang a song honouring the *agalimae*, those war-ghosts who would befriend the spirit of Andu.

In front of the old man's relatives he shredded the ghost-caller's fishing nets with the bush knife, so that no one on earth would take Andu's place in the affections of those he left behind. Gently he placed several areca nuts on the dying man's scrawny chest, to assure him of the protection of the *aofias* from the time before, who were already maintaining peace on the spirit island he was about to visit.

The atmosphere in the packed hut grew steadily more oppressive as Kella made his chants and incantations and offered up prayers for the *ano*, the soul of the man. He begged Andu's *ano* to roam no more fitfully at night, so that it might return and tell the old man in the form of dreams what it had seen on its travels. Now the *ano* must prepare itself for its final journey.

As he drew near the end of the ceremony Kella could sense the sombre presence of death, waiting to bear the old man's soul away. At last there was only one more function for him to perform before the old man could be released from the shackles of life.

Kneeling at the old man's side, Kella whispered in the Lau dialect, 'Andu, you must start your last great journey shriven of your sins. Is there anything you wish to leave behind on earth, to make your voyage to Momulo easier for you?'

At first Kella thought that the dying man had not heard him. Then Andu's claw of a hand reached out and held Kella in a clammy grip.

'Yes,' he gasped with an effort.

'What is it?' asked Kella. He placed his ear close to the ghost-caller's mouth, so that no one else would hear the old man's final confession.

Andu struggled dreadfully to speak. Then the words came out, in little more than an expunged waft of air. 'The tall white man,' he breathed.

'Lofty Herman?' asked Kella. 'What about him?'

Andu fought to get the words out. With a supreme bubbling effort he opened his mouth again.

'I killed him,' he said.

Kella felt numb. As a policeman there were a dozen questions he wanted to ask. However, in the straight path ceremony there was only one more thing he was allowed to put to the dying man, in order to let the spirits decide how peaceful his imminent journey to Momolo would be.

'Is there anyone to share your blame?' he asked urgently. 'Did anyone help you in this act?'

Andu nodded, almost imperceptibly. 'Senda Iabuli,' he croaked, and died.

25

DISTRESSED BRITISH SUBJECT

Sister Conchita waited at the wheel of her van for the trading boat from Malaita to finish tying up at the wharf. A makeshift gangplank was lowered over the side and a thin, bewildered-looking expatriate in his fifties walked down, carrying two suitcases.

He was wearing an old-fashioned, shapeless white linen suit and a straw hat. He put his suitcases down on the wharf and looked about him, as if wondering what he was doing in the capital.

Sister Conchita left the shade of the van and hurried over to the newcomer. 'Mr Wilmot?' she asked. 'Let me take your bags.'

She carried the man's luggage over to the truck and put the suitcases in the back. Wilmot did not move. Sister Conchita returned to him and took him by the arm, propelling him towards the Ford and opening the passenger door for him.

'I'm from the mission,' she told him, taking her place behind the wheel. 'Father Ignatius thought you might prefer to stay there, instead of a hotel, while you're waiting.'

'He's a DBS,' the administrator had told her the previous evening. 'That's short for Distressed British Subject. He's the first one we've had for a few years. Wilmot's run a trading store on the west coast of Malaita for years. Now it's gone bust, and he's bankrupt. The Brits are shipping him home at the government's expense, as they always do in these cases. He's a Catholic, so we'll look after him until a ship comes in to take him away. You may find him a little shell-shocked. These things sometimes hit them hard.'

The administrator had been right, thought Sister Conchita. Wilmot was almost in a catatonic state. She tried to rouse him from his trance.

'How long is it since you were last in Honiara?' she asked, heading from the wharf towards Mendana Avenue.

At first she thought that he was not going to answer her question, but with an effort the trader acknowledged her presence for the first time. 'It must be fifteen years,' he said. 'Just after the war, when I was trying to restart my business.'

His well-modulated voice reminded Sister Conchita of the leading actors in British films of the 1930s. She could have been listening to Leslie Banks or Rex Harrison smoothing their way effortlessly through a drawing-room comedy.

'Fifteen years,' repeated Wilmot savagely. 'I've given my life to this place, and what do I get out of it? Ungrateful, cheating natives and a government that can't get rid of me quickly enough. I won't be sorry to go.'

'It must be very hard,' said Sister Conchita carefully. She was beginning to dislike the bitter, self-absorbed man sitting next to her. Be fair, she told herself. He's been through a lot, and now he's lost his livelihood.

'Very well,' went on Wilmot with a self-satisfied sneer, half to himself. 'I knew that this would happen one day. I've made provision for it. It's time I cashed in on my pension fund. Take me to Johnny Cho's.'

'I beg your pardon?'

'Johnny Cho's,' said Wilmot impatiently. 'Don't you know anything? Chinatown – the Happy Gardens store. I've got to see him at once.'

Sister Conchita drove the Ford towards the bridge and turned left into Chinatown. The stores were beginning to open, she doubted if some of them ever closed, but this early in the morning there were few people around. She had no difficulty in parking outside the Happy Gardens. Wilmot got out of the cab.

'Wait here,' he ordered. 'I've got business to transact.'

Sister Conchita watched him disappear into the store. She wondered what could be so important to make the trader this eager to see Johnny Cho. She had only heard vaguely of the Chinaman, but he and his father were reputed to have their fingers in a lot of pies in Honiara.

Ten minutes passed. A group of curious children gathered around the van. Sister Conchita winked at them. They giggled and ran off down the unmade-up road. Suddenly there was a sound of shouting from within the store. Wilmot emerged, his arms raised to protect his head. He was pursued by four angry Chinese men wielding sticks, which they were bringing down with stinging force on the trader's body. The men were being urged on by a younger Chinese man in well-cut slacks and a silk shirt.

Wilmot staggered out into the road and turned to face his tormentors, who remained threateningly on the verandah outside the store.

'What's the matter with you people?' he demanded despairingly. 'We had an agreement! I've kept my end of the bargain. I've been supplying you for years. Now I need the money. I insist on being paid my money!'

The men on the verandah raised their sticks threateningly. Reluctantly Wilmot heaved himself back into the cab. Unobtrusively Sister Conchita started the engine and sat impassively behind the wheel. The younger man sauntered down and put his head in through the open window. He ignored Sister Conchita.

'Go away, Wilmot, and do not come back,' said the man. 'Chinatown is out of bounds to you.'

'Please, Mr Cho,' Wilmot whimpered. 'You don't understand. I'm leaving the Solomons. For years I've done everything you ask of me. I've kept a steady supply coming to you, on the understanding that you would look after the money you owed me. Now I've got to have it.'

'What money?' asked Johnny Cho contemptuously. 'Have you a contract?'

'Of course not! Not for what I've been providing you with. It would have been too dangerous. How could there be any paperwork?'

Cho spread his hands in an expansive gesture. 'Sorry! No contract, no deal. Goodbye, Mr Wilmot.'

'Please,' begged the trader, almost in tears.

'Of course,' said Cho, smirking, 'if you think you have cause for complaint, you could always go to the police. Good morning.'

Suddenly he raised his fist to hit Wilmot through the open window. Sister Conchita had been waiting for such a move. She accelerated suddenly. The van lurched into motion. Propelled by the weight of his blow John Cho staggered forward. He lost his balance and fell forward into the dusty road. His men rushed down to assist him to his feet. Sister Conchita spun the van round and headed back towards the mission, brushing the infuriated Chinese men aside as the Ford gathered speed.

'Sorry!' shouted the nun unconvincingly as her vehicle bounced erratically away.

Wilmot sat slumped in the seat beside her, staring dully ahead. What had all that been about? thought the nun as she headed for Mendana Avenue. Wilmot had plainly been involved in some sort of shady deal with Johnny Cho, and the Chinese man had reneged on his end of the bargain leaving the Distressed British Subject with nothing, and palpably even more distressed than ever.

Not for the first time Sister Conchita realized that there was so much about life in the Solomons about which she knew nothing. She wished that Sergeant Kella was there to explain matters to her.

26

HIGH BUSH

'We can't put it off any longer,' conceded Chief Superintendent Grice. 'We've got to go over to Malaita and find Professor Mallory. There's been no sign of the man for a couple of weeks. The American authorities are starting to kick up a stink.'

And that would mean an imminent unpleasant interview with the chief secretary, he thought gloomily. Either that, or an official visit from the touring inspector of the Commonwealth Police, and another nail in his professional coffin.

'We don't have nearly enough men for a systematic search of the Kwaio high bush,' Inspector Lorrimer pointed out. 'Even if we did, half of them would refuse to go over to Malaita anyway. They know they'd get picked off like sitting ducks by Pazabosi's men.'

'And then there's the matter of Peter Oro's death,' Grice ploughed on, ignoring his subordinate as usual. 'We can't write that off as just another bush killing. Oro was a senior student at a mission school, for God's sake!'

'Practically an honorary white,' murmured Lorrimer. He paused and then went on, 'If we must interfere, Sergeant Kella's the only man for the job. You know that, sir.'

'Kella isn't available,' said Grice quickly. He ransacked his mind, trying to remember exactly what he had said to the stubborn Melanesian outside his office only a few days ago. His memories of the encounter were vague, but he thought he had tried to get rid of the polite but importunate sergeant in the time-honoured way.

'He's taken some leave,' he said vaguely.

'That almost certainly means he's gone back to Malaita,' pointed out Lorrimer. 'He'll already be over there, probably in the bush.'

'That's immaterial. I don't want Sergeant Kella involved in this. I don't even want to know where he is,' said Grice. He drummed on his desk with his fingers as he searched for the right phrase. 'He's too emotionally involved with events on the island,' he said triumphantly. 'Leave him out of it. Anybody would think we couldn't handle this ourselves.'

He looked hopefully at the younger officer. Lorrimer's roots might lie in the Metropolitan Police area, and his culture and loyalties were as alien to the chief superintendent's as those of a Tikopian pearl-diver, but the pragmatic Grice was aware that he could always manipulate Lorrimer by playing on the inspector's conscientiousness.

Lorrimer sighed and stood up. He knew, as well as his superior officer did, that Kella would go where he wanted to go and do what he wanted to do. He just hoped that the Melanesian sergeant's *mana* had taken him to the Kwaio area. Over on Malaita, the success or failure of any police mission would depend on Kella's response to it.

'How many men can I take, sir?' he asked.

27

ROCKFALL

Kella walked down the track from the mission school to the river bank. He had spent the night at the school after performing the straight path ceremony for the ghost-caller. He walked through the trees to the site of Lofty Herman's former grave at the foot of the cliff.

A protesting Solomon Bulko lumbered mutinously after the police sergeant, complaining that he had to start teaching in half an hour's time. The headmaster was wearing long black trousers and a white shirt. He was reacting with petulance to the branches whipping into his sweating face.

'I went into teaching to get away from this nature shit, man,' he complained loudly as he plodded after the police sergeant. 'What are you trying to do, return me to my fucking roots?'

The early morning sunshine seeped through the branches and dappled the ground. Kella reached the rockfall where the skeleton had been found. He examined the scattered stones there carefully. He had noticed when Sister Conchita had first brought him to the scene of the earthquake that some of the rocks were freshly scratched and scarred, but he had been too busy getting out of range of the rifle shots with the sister to pay much attention to them at the time.

Now, bearing in mind the ghost-caller's confession that he

and Senda Iabuli had been responsible for the death of the tall beachcomber in 1942, the disturbed grave assumed a much more important aspect of his investigation.

'Take a look at those,' he told Bulko, indicating the marks on the boulders.

'What am I supposed to be looking for?' demanded Bulko, disdainfully, peering from a distance and fastidiously keeping to the path, away from the jagged stones.

'Examine the rocks that were on top of Herman's grave.'

'So, they're rocks,' said Bulko, reluctantly advancing a wincing pace or two in his highly polished shoes before stopping. 'Seen one, you've seen them all.'

'The marks on the rocks,' Kella persisted patiently.

With an effort Bulko folded slightly at his swollen midriff. He stared with distaste at the debris heaped before him. He resembled a bulky ebony carving teetering on an insecure base. When the mission school headmaster straightened up, he was no longer indifferent.

'Someone's been hitting the rocks with a tool,' he acknowledged.

'Be bold,' Kella urged. 'Take it one logical step farther. Someone's been digging these particular rocks up with a pickaxe. That's the only explanation for these recent scratches and indentations. I noticed them the first time I saw them, but I didn't pay much attention, until I found out last night who killed Lofty Herman.'

'How the hell did you do that?' asked Bulko, blinking. 'Who was it?'

Kella hesitated. Both as the *aofia* and as a policeman he should not disclose Andu's deathbed confession. But at this moment he needed a sounding board for his theories. Solomon Bulko possessed the twin attributes of being both highly intelligent and completely apathetic about island life. He would pass Kella's ideas on to no one, mainly because he did not have the slightest interest in them, unless they affected his comfort or well-being.

'I heard about it yesterday,' Kella said, not going into details. 'Lofty Herman was probably killed and buried by two men from the nearest saltwater village. Their names were Andu and Senda Iabuli. Now they're both dead.'

Bulko shook his head. 'Surely the grave was unearthed as a result of the earthquake?' he asked. 'At least that's what I was told.'

'No way,' said Kella decisively. 'That's what we were meant to think. Those rocks were deliberately dug up by hand by someone, no doubt about it. Lofty Herman's grave was disinterred on purpose.'

'Why on earth would anyone want to do that?' asked Bulko. 'Graves are supposed to be sacred in these parts.'

'You'd have to be pretty desperate,' admitted Kella. 'Either that, or resigned to your fate.'

'What's the weather like on your planet?' sighed the headmaster. 'Do you mind telling me what you're talking about?'

'I think', said Kella, 'that Herman was killed by Andu and Iabuli on behalf of the local people.'

'For what possible reason?' asked Bulko in exasperation.

'Fear,' said Kella. He elaborated on the theme he had been considering all night. 'In 1942, the British were abandoning the Solomons in droves, and the Japanese were coming in to take over. The locals were worried in case the Japanese thought they were harbouring a white man.'

'So they murdered Herman, you mean?' asked Bulko, jolted out of his customary complacency. 'That's creepy!'

'If I've got it right, yes; Iabuli and Andu were deputed by the rest of their village to murder the unpopular Herman, in case his presence got them in bad with the Japanese when they arrived. Custom states that *ramos* who kill for the good of their clan must keep all knowledge of their activities to themselves, and take any consequences upon their own heads. It's a part of their *mana*.'

'If you say so,' sighed Bulko. 'On Choiseul we don't run around killing people – hardly ever, anyway. As a rule we've got enough intelligence to lie ourselves out of trouble.' A thought occurred to the headmaster. 'Where would those two have got a rifle from to shoot Herman with?'

'They probably used Herman's own weapon. No white man travelled on Malaita without a rifle in those days. He was almost certainly sifting for gold in the river, and left his rifle on the bank.'

'So these two old men dug up Herman's grave a week or two ago?'

'Not both of them, no,' said Kella. 'I don't think Andu was involved in that. He was a ghost-caller. He wouldn't risk upsetting the spirits by meddling with the dead. With Iabuli it would be different.'

'How come?'

'Iabuli knew that he only had a short time to live. Because of his astounding escape from his fall from the ridge, the other villagers believed that he was in league with the devil. He had already received a curse from the village headman, placed among his comfort stones. Iabuli knew that before long his own people would murder him to drive away the devil from the area.'

'You Malaita men sure are primitive bastards,' complained Bulko, with a genuine shiver.

'You mean we have a proper and fitting respect for our ancestors,' corrected Kella. 'The only reason Iabuli would risk offending the ghosts would be because he wanted to do something for his grandson Peter Oro before he died.'

Bulko groaned. 'I might have known that one of my students would be involved,' he said self-pityingly. 'I think they do it just to annoy me. But how do you know all this?'

'By putting different pieces of information together,' said the police sergeant. 'Last week Michael Rapasia, one of your teachers, saw Senda Iabuli talking to Peter Oro at the school. And then there were the tools.'

'What tools?' asked Solomon Bulko.

'Don't you remember? You told me that the shed containing the school's garden tools had been broken into, and the implements scattered all over the area. You thought at the time that it had been done by students who wanted to get out of gardening chores.'

'I remember,' said Bulko.

'Well, that was what you were supposed to think. I believe that Senda Iabuli had persuaded his grandson Peter Oro to steal a pickaxe and a spade. To conceal their loss he spread all the tools over the bush. Was Oro one of the pupils who later recovered some of the tools?'

'As a matter of fact, I think he was,' said Bulko miserably.

'Including a pickaxe?'

'I can't remember,' said the headmaster dismally. 'Probably.' He looked imploringly at Kella. 'So Iabuli persuaded Peter Oro to steal a pickaxe and dig up Herman's grave with him. Why on earth would he do that?'

'Maybe there was something buried along with Lofty Herman's body all those years ago,' Kella suggested, 'something that might have been worth retrieving, to leave Peter Oro as a legacy. I've just heard that Oro was seen hanging around a treehouse in the bush containing trading goods.'

'Why would he do that?'

'Do you expect me to know everything?' asked Kella.

28

MARCHING RULE

The Friday night swill was in full flow at the Auki Club. John Deacon and Hans Gunter, a German logger, were playing the label game, watched by Lorrimer and the forty or so other expatriate men and women present.

Twenty bottles of beer were cooling in a large metal cask of water in the centre of the room. It was Deacon's turn. Deliberately the Australian selected a bottle from the tub. He whirled it in his hands and then peeled the soaked label from the bottle. Then he replaced the label, with the logo facing inwards.

Taking careful aim, Deacon spun the bottle up into the air. It struck the ceiling with force. The label came off and stuck to the ceiling, the logo and description now facing outwards, joining the other labels already there. As the bottle fell back, Deacon caught it, removed the top with his callused thumb and swallowed half the contents with one gulp.

'Your turn, Hans,' he invited his opponent.

The blond, good-looking German staggered forward unsteadily. He had been drinking ever since he had arrived at the club. He groped for one of the bottles. With trembling hands he reversed the label and threw the bottle up into the air. He misjudged the distance and the bottle fell back to the floor and shattered, its contents oozing into the large lake of beer already there.

'One more for me,' claimed Deacon. The Australian drained the bottle in his hand and made his way towards the waiting cask. Changing his mind, he veered away and weaved over to Hans Gunter, and stood swaying in front of the German, grinning inanely.

'It was 1946, see,' he slurred. 'This British ship is sailing along, when up pops an old German U-boat. The German skipper comes up on to his conning-tower and shouts, "How is the war going?" The British captain shouts back, "It's over. Your lot surrendered last year." "Ach!" snaps the German skipper, going below. "Damn the Kaiser!"'

Some of the onlookers laughed. Others looked uneasily at the German logger. Hans Gunter frowned.

'I don't get it,' he said.

Deacon leaned forward and waggled two fingers under Gunter's nose. 'Two, Hans,' he said pityingly. 'Your lot lost two wars, you cunt.'

'Nutter,' snarled the German, stalking towards the bar. 'That's all you are, Deacon, a bloody nutter.'

'It takes one to know one,' said the Australian. He gazed up at the ceiling and counted the labels. 'Twenty-two,' he boasted loudly. 'The winner by default! Not bad. Before the war, I saw that Tazzy who became a film star, what's-his-name, Errol Flynn, I saw him get thirty-six labels to stick to the ceiling in a Port Moresby bar, when he was managing a plantation in New Guinea. Now there was a real piss-artist!'

Lorrimer sat at a table in the corner and surveyed the others. Most of the expatriate inhabitants of the district station were present, government officers, doctors and nurses from the hospital, store-owners, technicians from the boat-building yard, and several Voluntary Service Overseas youngsters. There were also a number of planters and traders like Deacon and Gunter, who worked farther along the coast and had made the journey in by boat for a weekend's drinking. The Auki Club was notorious for its wild parties and this one looked to be getting under way nicely.

Lorrimer stood up and edged through the crowd to the bar where he ordered a bottled beer from the Melanesian steward. Without apology Deacon pushed his way through the throng and stood by the inspector's side. Although he had been drinking heavily for several hours the Australian seemed lucid enough. He extended a hand.

'John Deacon,' he said expansively. 'You'll be Inspector Lorrimer. You flew over from Honiara this morning.' Lorrimer's beer arrived. Deacon gestured for it to be put on his tab. 'I hear you're waiting for a boatload of police to arrive and then you're going to look for the missing Yank in the high bush.'

'Something like that,' said Lorrimer non-committally, sipping his beer from the bottle. He had grown accustomed to the fact that there were few secrets in the Solomons.

'Well, you take care of yourself, mate,' said Deacon. 'Old Pazabosi might be a bit past it, but he's still capable of pulling a few strokes in the Kwaio country. The Brits wanted to pull him in after Marching Rule collapsed ten years ago, but they didn't dare go up after him. And that was when they still had an empire and delusions of grandeur. You mark my words, if you go up into the interior with just a dozen Roviana coppers, you'll be asking for trouble.'

'I'll just have to take my chances then, won't I?' said Lorrimer.

'You'd be bit more worried than that if you'd seen what happened when the Marching Rule rebellion started. I know. I was here, mate. As soon as the locals saw the black Yanks, who'd been so good to them, sailing away, they took it as a sign to start trying to chuck the Brits out. They reckoned that the Yanks had gone to paradise, and would come back to fight along with them once the uprising started.'

'What do you suggest I do?' asked Lorrimer.

'Leave it to Kella,' said the plantation manager emphatically. 'This is his island. He'll sort things.'

Someone had put an LP on the Dansette record player. Men and women were beginning to dance to the sound of Dick Haymes singing 'Little White Lies'. The music seemed to rejuvenate Deacon. Impulsively he burst away from the bar, gathered one of the Forestry Department's typists in his arms and swept her away across the floor, his arms pumping vigorously.

'Mastah,' said the club steward warningly to Lorrimer, jerking his head towards the door. A uniformed police constable was standing in the entrance, beckoning urgently to the inspector. When Lorrimer walked over to him, the constable turned and led him outside.

'What is it?' asked Lorrimer.

'Come long hospital quick time,' urged the policeman. 'Plenty big trouble!'

The police constable hurried Lorrimer along Loboi Avenue, the main street of the district station, to the concrete hospital. They went inside. In the reception area two scruffy islanders in dirty shorts and singlets were sitting sullenly on a bench, supervised by several constables.

'What's going on?' asked Lorrimer.

The constable who had brought him from the club pointed to one of the doors leading from the hall. A cardboard sign attached to the wall read *Operating Theatre*.

The two men sitting on the bench refused to meet Lorrimer's gaze. The door of the theatre opened and a balding, middle-aged white doctor came out. He nodded when he saw the police inspector.

'You must be Lorrimer,' he said. 'I heard there was a top cop on the station. We haven't had a policeman with any authority on Malaita since you took Ben Kella away from us. My name's Morgan, by the way.'

'Dr Morgan,' nodded Lorrimer. 'What's the problem?'

The doctor turned to the islanders on the bench and questioned them in a pidgin that was too fluent for Lorrimer's grasp of the lingua franca. One of the islanders replied in guttural monosyllables. He and his companion still seemed to be in deep shock.

'They're still telling the same story, so it's probably true,' Morgan told Lorrimer. 'They say they went into the Kwaio bush country to recover a box of artifacts they'd left up there.'

'What sort of artifacts?' asked Lorrimer.

The doctor questioned the two men again. The spokesman responded briefly.

'Custom carvings,' translated Dr Morgan. 'Very old, by the sound of it. Their boss used to go round the villages buying them up in return for tobacco. Sometimes there would be too many carvings to get into their canoe to bring back down to Ruvabi. When that happened they would store the surplus carvings in a treehouse they had hired from a local man, and go back for them later. This time they had a large cache hidden away, and had returned for the box.'

'Presumably to export from the Protectorate,' said Lorrimer. 'Very lucrative, and highly illegal. Sorry, doctor. Go on.'

'They were attacked by a gang of bushmen. Their boss was hacked down. These two guys ran away into the bush and hid. When they came back later, their boss was still alive, but only just. They carried him to their canoe, which is equipped with an outboard engine, and brought him downriver and then along the coast here to the hospital.'

'A nasty business,' said Lorrimer.

'It'll be more than that when the expats here get to hear of it,' predicted Dr Morgan grimly. 'That's how the Marching Rule uprising started on Malaita after the war. Groups of islanders started attacking traders and government district officers in the bush. It looks as if Pazabosi's back on the warpath. When the news of this latest attack gets around, there'll be a bloody panic among the whites in the Protectorate.'

'What's the name of the man who was attacked?' asked Lorrimer.

'Gau,' said Morgan. 'He's a half-caste who owns the store at Ruvabi. His name is Mendana Gau.'

29

GOLD RIDGE

'We may be on the way to eradicating malaria,' sighed Father Benedini, 'but hookworm, that's a different deal altogether.'

He was standing with Sister Conchita in the square at Tinomeat on Gold Ridge, preparing to distribute measured doses of tetrachloroethylene to the children of the village. Earlier in the year a World Health Organization survey team had diagnosed a particularly virulent strain of the parasitical *Ancylostoma duodenale* roundworms in the area. To her surprise the medical priest had asked Sister Conchita to accompany him on his tour to the interior, twenty miles south-east of Honiara.

The trek through the steep incline of the rain forest once they had left the road on foot had been the usual gruelling one. The nun had forced herself to concentrate on the narrow path ahead, knowing that if she looked to either side she could easily slip and fall down one of the steep slopes. She saw deadly snakes, centipedes, scorpions and regiments of ants moving quickly into the undergrowth in the gloom caused by the densely packed trees. She tried, sometimes in vain, to avoid the knee-high stinging nettles infesting the path.

Some hours after they had started their climb suddenly the landscape was transformed. The ground levelled out and there were large gaps where trees had been felled. Gaping pits had been dug and abandoned in the ground. Handmade water races meandered aimlessly from streams. The sides of a cliff were scarred and pitted. Sister Conchita wondered if the surface of the moon could look as ghastly as this.

'Gold Ridge,' explained Father Benedini. He was from Chicago, rotund, dishevelled and benign, wearing slacks and a tattered white shirt, with a crucifix around his neck. 'There was a pretty slick alluvial mining operation here, until the Japanese invaded Guadalcanal. Half a dozen Europeans and around a hundred islanders from other parts of the Solomons extracted quite a lot of gold around this part of the island.'

'What happened when the war broke out?'

'They hightailed it away rapidly.'

'Frightened of the Japanese?'

'Scared of the locals, more likely. Relations between the miners and the villagers were strained, to put it mildly. This is a custom area. The villagers resented the presence of the miners, but the expats were too heavily armed. Once they fled to the coast to be evacuated, the locals destroyed the mine workings and made sure that the foreigners never came back after the war. The only thing left of the mining set-up is the names the miners gave to some of the local villages – Tinomeat, Old Case, Bagorice. For some reason those names stuck.'

His words struck a chord with the sister. Lofty Herman had been prospecting for gold when the Japanese had invaded the Solomons. Perhaps he had offended against local traditions as well. Could the local villagers have been emboldened by the thought of the government being in disarray? Perhaps they had exacted vengeance on the beachcomber before he could flee?

Sister Conchita tried to put the thought out of her mind. There would be time enough to ponder over that later. In the meantime they were approaching the outskirts of the village.

Children were running out of the huts to meet them. She would need to concentrate on the task in hand.

'Thank you for picking me to help you,' said Sister Conchita. 'I appreciate it.'

'It was no contest. You were the only one suitable for the job. Especially after you commandeered the clinic at Sulufou and dispensed the medicines there.'

'I got into trouble for that.'

'Quite right too,' said Father Benedini, straight-faced. 'Can't have new sisters showing initiative and guts. I only hope I don't suffer from guilt by association.'

Sister Conchita wondered if the priest was in earnest. Then she saw a grin playing around the corners of his mouth. She hurried after him as they entered the village. Her heart leapt at the thought that not everyone in the Church regarded her as an unmitigated nuisance. Somehow she thought that she was going to enjoy working with Father Benedini.

30

THE CANARIUM TREE

Kella found the remains of Lofty Herman's leaf house on the river bank early the next morning. Time had erased all signs of any gold workings. The river ran smooth and sluggish through the trees under the cliff. He remembered from his time as a student at Ruvabi that Lofty Herman had installed a series of wooden barriers in the headwaters of the river, to cause the water to flow faster into the wooden aqueducts he had constructed. The resulting torrent had been connected to a fire hose that he had trained on to the cliff, sluicing soil and occasionally nuggets of gold into boxes at the bottom of the slope.

Only a white man would have built a house in such an unprepossessing place. It had once been a simple leaf hut, but over the years the undergrowth had secured a stranglehold over it, constricting and torturing the simple structure out of position. The roof had fallen in and the support posts had buckled, causing the remaining woven leaf sides to slip drunkenly out of shape. The police sergeant entered what was left of the leaf structure's single room.

There was little to mark the fact that the place had once been inhabited. Vigorously Kella trampled on the undergrowth covering what once had been the wooden floor of the hut. His boot clinked against something. The police sergeant stooped and groped along the ground. After a minute or so, his hands closed over a rusty old cocoa tin. He wrenched off the lid. The tin was empty but a few traces of yellow dust remained at the bottom.

Carefully Kella scraped the dust out of the tin. He took a small cellophane bag from his pack and tipped the dust into it. He sealed the bag and replaced it in a pocket of his pack. It looked as if Lofty Herman had found the gold he had been searching for in the last days of his life.

The question was, what had happened to the rest of it? Could Andu the ghost-caller and Iabuli have buried it with the beachcomber's body, after they had murdered Herman? They might have believed that the yellow dust had some religious significance for the dead Australian.

In the early 1940s, not many Malaitans would have had any concept of the value of gold. Eighteen years later, Iabuli might have realized the significance of the yellow dust he had interred with the beachcomber's body. Could it have been the gold, not Herman's skeleton, that the islander had retrieved?

On the other hand, Mendana Gau had been Herman's assistant at the time. Perhaps he had stumbled across Herman's body before it had been buried. He would not have been deterred by the *tabu* that bound the Lau people, and he would have had no scruples about entering Herman's hut and stealing any gold he found there. That would certainly account for the islander's sudden relative affluence at the end of the war.

Kella looked at his watch. It was time he started climbing the mountain to Gau's treehouse, to see what was going on there. He also had to find out what Peter Oro had been doing up there. It looked as if he had played a larger part in the mystery than Kella had at first thought, and that the schoolboy had not been as innocent as he had seemed.

* * *

It took Kella four hours to climb the narrow, winding mountain path to the waterfall. For much of the way the path followed the course of the wide and now fast-moving river. He passed crocodiles basking on mud flats in the sultry heat, and watched kingfishers swooping for fish where the water grew deeper. He saw no bush people. Most of them could not swim and kept well away from the river, except to draw water from the easier-running sections.

As he got higher, the police sergeant began to pass a few bush people on the way down to the weekly market, where the Kwaio farmers exchanged taro and yams for the fish caught by the saltwater villagers.

The unmarried Kwaio girls, balancing wicker baskets of vegetables on their heads, who normally went naked, had donned faded grass skirts for the occasion. Kella greeted them politely but they ignored the presence of the stranger in their midst. The police sergeant took care not to address by name any of the bush people he knew. It was the Kwaio custom for people to change their names to prevent the spirits of dead enemies from finding them.

It all seemed very normal, thought Kella as he walked unhurriedly up the track. If Pazabosi was planning some sort of uprising, he was concealing his preparations well.

He found the canarium tree and the house in its fork soon after noon on the track between the waterfall and the bush village where he had spent the night with Elizabeth, the Sikaiana girl.

Kella stared up at the tree. This type was much favoured for the building of treehouses. The distance of the branches from the ground made it impossible for enemies to climb it unaided, while the wide spread of the branches in the upper reaches of the mighty canarium almond provided a strong foundation for the base of a treehouse. The man who owned the tree would possess a suitable ladder made of fine creepers, which he would have hired out to Gau when he visited his store there.

Kella examined the ground around the spreading prehensile roots of the tree. The fallen leaves, trunk and soil were spattered with freshly dried blood. Someone had certainly been attacked and, judging by the amount of blood, badly hurt here. But the blood was new. Any assault must have taken place over the last couple of days.

But Peter Oro had been murdered more than a week ago.

31

CUSTOM SIGN

Kella looked at the pile of boxes and packages that Inspector Lorrimer had assembled on the floor of the mission hut, ready to take on his tour of the bush region with him. There were containers of tinned meat and sacks of rice from the Auki general store, a Tilley lamp, a camp bed, a mosquito net, a small portable radio, a pillow, a primus stove and several changes of uniform.

'I fought in a war with less equipment than this,' he told the inspector.

'So did I, come to that,' replied an unruffled Lorrimer, 'but that was then, this is now.'

'No trusses?' asked Kella, mentally doubling the number of porters the inspector's patrol would need the next day.

'What?'

'For your carriers. Half of them are going to end up with ruptures.'

'Don't let this fool you,' said Lorrimer equably, his airy gesture embracing his ever-growing pile of provisions. 'These few basic essentials apart, I am essentially your lean, mean fighting machine.'

'Really?' asked Kella. 'We had one of those, but it died.'

'This leave period you're supposed to be on,' said Lorrimer, trying to sound casual. 'Bit of a busman's holiday, is it?'

'Something like that,' agreed Kella.

The two policemen were sharing a spare hut on the school compound at Ruvabi mission station. The twelve uniformed officers from Roviana had arrived from Honiara by boat earlier that day and were sleeping in two of the classrooms.

Kella had made his way down from the treehouse that afternoon to find Lorrimer preparing for his expedition into the mountains to find Professor Mallory. The inspector had brought him up to date with news of the attack on Mendana Gau in Kwaio country, when the trader had tried to retrieve his box of custom carvings. That explained the bloodstains on the ground by the treehouse.

Kella was tired. He had walked in the tropical heat for almost eight hours that day. Now he wanted no more than a shower and a convivial meal with his friend Solomon Bulko. But still there were things to be done. The work that he was doing had become so complicated that Kella wanted to sort out aspects of it in his mind.

The sergeant knew that he had reached the stage in his investigation where he needed to share his information with someone. Kella did not normally trust white men, especially old colonials, but he suspected that Lorrimer was different. The Metropolitan policeman did not talk much about his work in London, but Kella gussed that Lorrimer had been as devoted to his patch there as Kella was to his island beat.

'Fancy a stroll?' he asked.

Lorrimer looked up in surprise from his packing, but nodded at once and stood up, dusting his hands on his trousers.

'Sure thing,' he said.

They walked casually across the compound and along the bluff over the wide ribbon of river approaching the sea, and the dark mass of surrounding trees huddled on either side of the water.

Most of the schoolboys were sitting in the grassy square

outside their classrooms, watching the film that their headmaster was showing them, using an antiquated projector attached to the generator. The black images of the old Hollywood movie flickered on a white sheet in the darkness.

Kella led the inspector down the cliff path towards the river at its foot. They strolled along the grassy bank in the moonlight. At first they discussed aspects of the case in a desultory manner. Kella decided that it was time to find out how much Lorrimer was beginning to understand about the Solomons and its people.

'Right,' he invited. 'Let's see what we've got.' He ticked off the items on his fingers. 'The sacred *havu* carving is missing from the Kwaio cave-temple by the waterfall. Professor Mallory has disappeared up in the Kwaio bush. I've talked to the local people, and he was seen being guided up to the killing ground by two bushmen. That means that Pazabosi has kidnapped him, or that whoever has taken him has done so with Pazabosi's knowledge and permission. Why is Mallory being held?'

'As a retribution for stealing the *havu*?' suggested Lorrimer.

'Possibly. Anything else?'

'As some sort of preamble to an armed uprising that Pazabosi's been plotting on the island?'

'That's what I thought at first,' nodded Kella. 'But now I'm not so sure.'

'Why not?'

'For one thing, practically everyone who knows Pazabosi seems convinced that he's simply too old and tired to take part in another uprising like Marching Rule. All right, so he's keen to maintain his authority up in the Kwaio country as long as he's still alive, but no one except you Brits, pardon me, seems to think he's plotting insurgency.'

'Then what's going on?' asked Lorrimer.

'I don't know, but believe me, there are no signs of an

uprising in Kwaio country. I've been up there two or three times lately, and it's all looked normal enough.'

'I wonder—' said Lorrimer, and stopped.

'Go on,' encouraged Kella.

'Mendana Gau was trying to retrieve a box of custom carvings when he was hacked down by bushmen a couple of days ago. Gau's two men implied that he made a practice of touring the bush villages, buying artifacts at a fraction of their true value. Presumably he's been smuggling the carvings out of the Solomons, to sell them to collectors abroad. Perhaps he got greedy and overreached himself and stole the *havu* while he was up in the bush. That's why the bushmen were waiting for Gau when he returned this week.'

'Something like that certainly happened,' agreed Kella. 'I think that Peter Oro comes into the equation somewhere. Perhaps he was involved in picking up the carvings left by Gau at the treehouse. And Peter Oro was also attacked by bushmen, remember. Only his body was moved to the killing ground, where I would find it. Why?'

'If you ask me,' complained Lorrimer morosely, 'that boy Oro comes into it all over the place. He was involved in digging up Lofty Herman's grave. He drew attention to Senda Iabuli's death by asking for the ghost-caller to investigate the death, and now you tell me that he was mixed up in an organized and dangerous smuggling racket.'

'It's all this modern education,' said Kella. 'I blame the teachers myself.'

'Well, I hope you're right about Pazabosi not starting an uprising,' said Lorrimer fervently. 'I'm not so sure. Maybe he's just waiting for a sign, like last time.'

'What did you say?' asked Kella, something suddenly triggered at the back of his mind.

'John Deacon, the Australian, told me about it at the Auki Club on Saturday night. Apparently the Marching Rule uprising in 1945 was started by the sight of black American troops leaving the Solomons. The locals took it as a sign that they were going to a special heaven to wait for the islanders and then come back to help them defeat the Brits. Perhaps Pazabosi is waiting for a similar sign now.'

'Tell me,' said Kella, all his attention on the other man, 'what have you been taking lately, because I want some of it.'

'Have I said something right?' asked the inspector.

'Let me put it together in my mind first, will you?' asked Kella.

'All right,' said Lorrimer. 'In the meantime, where do I start looking for Professor Mallory tomorrow?'

'Your guess is as good as mine,' said Kella, his brain working busily. 'Well, almost as good.' He took out a notebook and started sketching an outline map on a page. He tore it out and handed it to the inspector. The route he had indicated should keep Lorrimer and his men out of trouble.

'Follow that trail and stop each night at the spot I've indicated,' he said. 'I'll be making my own inquiries up in the mountains. I'll keep in touch from time to time.'

'Thanks,' said the inspector, folding the map into the breast pocket of his shirt. 'Did you mean what you said just then, about me helping you out?' he asked.

'I did,' said Kella. 'Believe me, I'm grateful. I'll tell you all about it, just as soon as I've made a few more inquiries.'

'I'll get on with my packing then,' said Lorrimer, turning away. 'Are you coming?'

'In a minute. I'll just stay here for a while. Goodnight.'

'Goodnight, Ben,' said Lorrimer, walking back along the side of the river, towards the track leading to the mission school.

Left on his own, Kella stared across the smooth surface of the river. Misshapen branches from trees on the far side trailed listlessly into the water, like long arthritic fingers.

Lorrimer had done well, he thought. The inspector had

appreciated the significance of the *havu* and had related Gau's visit to the high bush to its disappearance. But it had been the inspector's remarks about the bush people waiting for a custom sign that had really impinged on Kella's mind.

Then he realized what it was. He stood very still as events and times all tumbled surely into place. The names connected with the case achieved a new significance in his mind: Herman, Oro, Gau, Iabuli and Mallory. They all stopped being unrelated entities and swam steadily into a fixed new orbit.

With absolute conviction Kella now knew what had been happening and what was going to happen. He also knew what he would have to do to bring matters to a conclusion.

He only hoped that he was not too late.

32

HUMILITY AND OBEDIENCE

Sister Conchita steered the Bedford carefully down the hill road from the Catholic mission headquarters building to Mendana Avenue.

'Are we going to visit the cruise ship again?' asked Sister Philomena hopefully at her side.

'I'm afraid not,' said Sister Conchita, flinching at the memory. She had already been reprimanded for her detour to the docks several nights before and her consequent invasion of the cruise ship with her contingent of elderly nuns. Neither had her superiors been over-enamoured when the party had returned later that night accompanied by several noisy police cars.

Sister Conchita feared that she was being confirmed as a nuisance by the local church hierarchy. Again she resolved genuinely to work harder on the twin virtues of humility and obedience.

'That's a pity,' said Sister Philomena wistfully. She was small and wizened. 'It was a lovely evening.'

'It wasn't bad, was it?' grinned Sister Conchita.

'I particularly liked the bit when you ordered the police cars to sound their sirens as we approached the mission house. Such a pity the bishop had just gone to sleep.'

'Ah well,' said Sister Conchita philosophically, her good

intentions receding like the tide. 'Into each life a little rain must fall.'

Unexpectedly Sister Philomena began to cackle with maniacal laughter. After a moment the other sister joined in. They were both still giggling when they turned into Mendana Avenue and headed towards the wharf in the centre of the capital.

It was only a little after six o'clock in the morning. The streets of Honiara were almost deserted. Canoes from the fishing village were drifting out to sea. A contingent of prisoners on remand at police headquarters were cutting grass on the roadside verges, watched by a couple of bored policemen. Newly hatched megapode birds flew uncertainly over from their nests in the warm sands of the island of Savo, able to fly within hours of their birth. Sister Conchita concentrated on the road, determined to carry out her present mission efficiently and in a low-key manner.

Back at the mission house the previous evening Father Ignatius, the administrator, had sounded less optimistic. 'A box of carvings made by the students will arrive from Ruvabi mission station early tomorrow morning,' he had told her drily. 'I want you and Sister Philomena to supervise its unloading, see it through Customs and make sure that the crate is stored in the Customs warehouse to await the next cargo vessel to Australia. Do you think you can accomplish that without any unnecessary detours, sister?'

Sister Conchita had assured the administrator that she could. After all, what could possibly go wrong? she thought as she drove the van on to the wharf. This should be a suitably low-key chore and a fitting starting point on her long overdue road towards her acceptance and redemption.

'Do you know,' said Sister Philomena, 'the other day the radio said that they've discovered a Japanese soldier still surviving in the bush on Rendova island. Apparently he's been there for fifteen years, unaware that the war was over. He's been hiding on a little plot of land barely more than acre square, seeing nobody and doing nothing.' The elderly sister sighed. 'And I will bet you anything that he's still had a much more interesting life than I have since they brought me back to Honiara!'

'Is it that bad?' asked Sister Conchita.

'I will say just one thing,' replied the old sister. 'For the sake of your immortal soul, keep on doing the wild things they tell me you've been doing lately for as long as you can. Don't let them grind you down, sister!'

The large visiting vessels of a few nights ago were no longer in the harbour. The cruise liner had departed during the night for Port Moresby, while the two cargo vessels had set out on their return voyages the previous day. Only a solitary battered Chinese trading vessel was moored askew in the harbour. Half a dozen Melanesian labourers were unloading the cargo it had picked up on its labyrinthine voyage back from Malaita.

The two sisters descended from the cab and approached the trading ship. One of the labourers saw them coming and manhandled a wooden crate on to a trolley, which he proceeded to wheel towards the Customs shed. The two nuns fell into step beside him and entered the building.

The shed was long and low, with a counter running its length. Standing behind the counter were three Melanesian Customs inspectors wearing uniform grey shorts and shirts and red berets. The labourer came to a halt, waiting for one of the inspectors to check the contents of the crate. Idly Sister Conchita examined the label on the box. It had been dispatched from Ruvabi some time before she had first arrived at the mission station. Heaven only knew how long it had been carried up and down the coast of Malaita before the trading ship had decided to return to Honiara.

One of the Customs inspectors, middle-aged and bespectacled, detached himself from the group and came over to the box. Yawning, he scribbled his initials on the lid with a piece of chalk. Automatically the labourer started to wheel the box towards the warehouse door at the far end of the shed.

'Aren't you going to examine the contents?' Sister Conchita asked the inspector.

'Oh, they never do,' said Sister Philomena. 'What's the point?'

'No examine, no examine,' said the inspector quickly, waving the labourer on. 'Everything all right. Plenty good too much.'

Something in the urgency of the official's tone alerted the nun. The man was looking at her with something almost akin to fear in his eyes at her unexpected attention to detail. In spite of all her good intentions Sister Conchita heard herself ordering the labourer to wheel the crate back to the desk.

'I'd feel happier if you were to open the crate and see what's inside,' she said firmly. 'After all, I am responsible for the contents, and I wasn't at Ruvabi when they were packed.'

The inspector hopped from one foot to another in an agony of indecision. His two companions, alerted by the sudden noise, walked over. As they neared, the first inspector looked as if he wished he were somewhere far away.

'I would like this crate opened and its contents checked, please,' Sister Conchita told the other two inspectors, who were looking on without much interest. She did not know why she was being so persistent but the first Customs man's undisguised air of apprehension alerted her to the fact that something might be wrong.

'Oh, sister,' wailed Sister Philomena. 'We'll be late for breakfast!'

Sister Conchita continued to stare down the other two Customs officials. They were looking puzzled. One of them yawned and nodded and said something to the labourer. The Melanesian took a crowbar from a pile of tools in a basket in front of the desk and started to prise open the lid. It took him less than a minute to reveal the contents of the box. Sister Conchita and the others gathered round. She took out several of the carvings and examined them in silence. Then she removed another two carvings and looked at them carefully as well. Finally she replaced them.

'Sister Philomena,' she said quietly, 'I want you to wait here until I return. Make sure that no one touches this box or its contents. Is that clear?'

The elderly nun blinked in surprise. Then suddenly she looked twenty years younger. After all, she had served in the Sinerango district in 1927, when there had been a tax revolt and District Officer Bell had been murdered. She glanced at the patently sedentary and uneasy Customs officials before her with an expression making it all too clear that if she had outfaced Malaitan rebels these three would present no problems.

'Certainly, Sister Conchita,' she said, throwing back her head with an expression of sheer pleasure. 'Nothing will be moved, I promise you. Where are you going?'

'To police headquarters,' said Sister Conchita, hurrying out of the shed.

33

PARAMOUNT CHIEFTAIN

Just before noon Kella approached the bush village of Nikona, high in the mountains. This was where Sam Beni, fatalistically disposing of ammunition from his barge, had told him he would find Pazabosi.

It was one of the most inaccessible regions of the whole island of Malaita. The highest peak here was marked as Mount Kolovrat, over four thousand feet above sea level. To the bushmen it was known as Tolosoi. Few if any of the names on the white men's maps were used by the islanders.

Even Kella had found the climbing hard. He stopped gratefully to rest on the trunk of a felled tree in a clearing containing gardens reclaimed from the jungle outside the bush village. The collection of huts was on the far side of a wall of trees left standing by the villagers to shield the gardens from the constant winds blowing at this altitude. A number of women, wearing skirts to denote that they were married, were digging in the gardens.

The Tali Kali dialect of this part of the bush area contained enough similarities with the Lau language for Kella to be able to make himself understood. He called across to the women that he was from the artificial island of Sulufou, and that he wanted to see their leader Pazabosi.

At first the women seemed to pay no attention, but after a few minutes, one by one, they put down their wooden digging sticks and drifted unhurriedly away in the direction of the village on the far side of the line of waving trees.

Kella had to wait another quarter of an hour before there was any response. Then three young men came from the village through the trees and swaggered truculently in his direction. They were hard-looking, marked across their faces with savage warrior slashes. They all carried stone-tipped hunting spears.

One walked ahead of the others and addressed Kella curtly. The islander wore a bone through his nose, and in his ears were sticks of cane, dyed red and plaited with yellow fern. In his hair he wore a decorative comb of fine strips of black palm bound together with creepers.

'I am Hita,' he announced bombastically, as if that explained everything.

'It is Pazabosi I have come to see, not you,' said Kella.

'There is no point in talking to him. Pazabosi is old and useless. If you seek anything from the Kwaio people talk to me. I am their leader.'

An ambitious young buck on the make, thought Kella. There was often one in a clan, waiting for a propitious moment to take over the leadership. It looked as if Pazabosi had his problems. If so, that would explain a great deal.

'As long as Pazabosi lives, he is the paramount chieftain of the Kwaio,' said Kella, as if explaining something to a child. 'He has earned his position through deeds, not words.'

He spoke loudly and clearly, so that the other two warriors would hear him. The affronted Hita clutched his spear more firmly. His companions looked surprised at the police sergeant's forthright attitude.

Before Hita could reply, Pazabosi came out of the trees and walked across the garden track to them. The old clan leader was wearing a long *lap-lap*. He surveyed the group calmly. The two warriors seemed uneasy at his presence and looked to Hita for a lead.

'The white blackman has come into our territory,' growled Hita. 'I was about to send him away.'

'I choose who stays and goes in the Kwaio country,' rebuked Pazabosi. 'Kella and I fought together against the Japani in the war. We were real warriors, not barking young hounds who have never seen battle.'

Hita surged forward furiously, but his two companions held him back. Pazabosi looked on disdainfully. Finally Hita subsided. He turned and stamped away into the trees, followed after a confused moment by the two warriors. Pazabosi stared thoughtfully after the three men.

'I may have to do something about Hita soon,' he said in English.

'Or get someone to do it for you,' suggested Kella.

'Is that what you think I'm doing?' asked the old bushman, a smile dusting his mouth. 'Do you imagine, *aofia*, that I am setting up a conflict between Hita and yourself?'

'The thought had crossed my mind,' said Kella. 'You always were a good plotter. Hita and I are both threats to you in our different ways. Why not get us both to eliminate one another?'

Pazabosi nodded approvingly. 'You always caught on quickly when we were fighting the Japani,' he commented.

'Of course,' Kella told the old man, 'you could always retire and make Hita chief in your place.'

'I took the leadership from Alibaua of the Golobi clan when I was about the same age that Hita is now,' said Pazabosi. 'Luckily, I was more intelligent than Hita.'

'Not to mention being a greater warrior,' said Kella.

Pazabosi smiled again. 'Have you come all this way from the salt water just to spread your honey, Kella?' he asked.

'No. I have come to fetch the white man Mallory back.'

'I know nothing of this,' said Pazabosi, no longer smiling.

'Over the last week I have learned things about you and Mallory,' said Kella. 'I would like to tell them to you now. Just so that you can correct me if I am wrong.'

Pazabosi sighed. 'When I first heard that you were back on Malaita, I did my best to make sure that you kept out of the Kwaio high bush,' he said. 'I even walked down to the saltwater village to put my bones curse on you, as a sign that you would not be welcome up here.'

'Is that why you did that?' asked the sergeant. 'I thought you were warning me off investigating the death of Senda Iabuli.'

'Why would I be interested in a saltwater man like him?' asked the clan leader indifferently. 'No, I just didn't want you coming up here. It is a difficult time for the Kwaio people at present, and you have a reputation for interfering where you're not wanted, Sergeant Kella.'

'You saved my life during the war,' Kella told the other man. 'Because of that, bush custom says that you have an obligation to me. How I use the life you gave me must always be of interest to you.'

'And sometimes a source of annoyance,' said Pazabosi. 'Go on.'

'It all started when Mendana Gau, or someone connected with the trader, stole the sacred *havu* from the custom temple at the waterfall. Am I right?'

Pazabosi said nothing. Kella went on. 'The *havu* is the most sacred of all the Kwaio relics. Your people were very angry when it was taken. They looked to you to get it back for them.'

'Of course,' said Pazabosi wearily. 'They expect me to do everything.'

'They thought you would raise a force, track the thieves down and kill them,' said Kella. 'Only you couldn't do that. You had entered your *trochea*, the secret period of contemplation that an old man goes through before his death.'

'You know about the *trochea*?' asked Pazabosi without emotion. 'Yes, I suppose you would. You follow the custom ways more than any other young man on Malaita.'

'It was more than that,' said Kella. 'I was meeting more and more people who knew that something had gone wrong up in the high bush, and who were surprised that you had done nothing to remedy it. They thought that you were waiting for a custom sign, but I wondered if perhaps you *couldn't* do anything about it. If you had entered the *trochea* you were bound by custom to spend your time thinking about the past and preparing to meet the spirits in the future.'

'It would have been an offence against the ghosts if I had taken my mind off them at this time,' acknowledged the old chief. 'Once I had started to prepare for death, I could not fight again. That's why I tried to frighten you away, Kella. I knew that you were the only man on the island who would be likely to guess why I could not respond to the theft of the *havu* with force.'

'Why didn't you explain that to your people? They would have understood.'

'The *trochea* had nothing to do with them. It was a matter between me and the ghosts.'

'Of course,' said Kella, understanding. 'But all the same, people were wondering why you had not raised a war party to hunt down Gau and his fellow thieves. I thought about it myself. But when I came up here on several occasions there were no signs of preparations for violence. That got me thinking.'

'You always were curious,' observed Pazabosi. 'It almost got you killed several times during the war.'

'Actually, it was a white man who put me on the track,' Kella said. 'A fellow police officer called Lorrimer reminded me that the last uprising on the island, Marching Rule, did not start until there had been the custom sign of black American soldiers sailing away. Once I began thinking about that, things started falling into place.'

'There are some who believe that you think too much, Sergeant Kella.'

'After the *havu* had gone, a story started spreading that the mighty Pazabosi was waiting only for a custom sign from the spirits to go after the men who had stolen the *havu* and then lead a great uprising against the Brits on Malaita.'

'You should have been a bushman,' said Pazabosi. 'You have the right sort of cunning mind. I would not have minded handing the leadership over to you.'

'No, thanks, I've already got enough problems,' said Kella. 'But that's where the old saltwater man Senda Iabuli and his grandson Peter Oro came into the matter. Iabuli knew that his days on earth were numbered. He was under sentence of death in his village because the people there believed that he was in league with the devil. He had no money, but he wanted to leave his grandson something when his death came.'

'Iabuli was a greedy fool,' said Pazabosi flatly.

'Years before, in 1942, with the imminent arrival of the Japanese, Iabuli and his friend Andu, the ghost-caller, had been deputed by the villagers to murder Lofty Herman, the beach-comber, in case the Japanese troops punished the whole area for harbouring a white man. Iabuli thought you were waiting for a custom sign to start your uprising. He decided to provide you with one. Am I right so far?'

'He dug up Herman's grave after the earthquake,' agreed the old bushman. 'Peter Oro stole some tools from the school and helped his grandfather bring up the white man's skeleton one night.'

'Then Iabuli made sure that everyone thought the body had been brought to the surface by the earthquake,' said Kella. 'That would be regarded as a custom sign, if ever there was one.'

'Senda Iabuli came to me one night and told me what he had done,' said Pazabosi. 'He thought I would be pleased. He told me that he was expecting to be poisoned by his own. He asked me to give him some gold sovereigns for him to hand over to Peter Oro as his last bequest.'

'But really that was the last thing you wanted.'

'I had to put Iabuli off while I decided what to do. I told him that it would take me some time to gather the gold coins together,' nodded Pazabosi.

'But why did you kill Senda Iabuli and Peter Oro?'

'I didn't,' said the old man simply. 'I had entered my period of contemplation, if you remember. I could harm no one. I sent the bones *tabu* sign to Senda Iabuli, to warn him to keep quiet while I thought the matter through. It was not necessary. By that time his own people had murdered him.'

'And Hita then killed Peter Oro?'

'Hita was perfectly prepared to use the custom sign of Lofty Herman's body as a signal to lead an uprising and make a name for himself,' said Pazabosi. 'I had to tell him that the sign was a false one.'

'So Hita heard that Peter Oro was hiding in the bush, after you frightened the boy when you pointed the bones *tabu* at me,' mused Kella. 'Hita and his warriors set out to find him. They murdered Peter Oro, because they knew that he was the only one left who realized that the uprising sign of Herman's skeleton was false. It wasn't a real custom sign. So Oro had to be disposed of.'

'Hita left the body by the killing ground to warn you off,' said Pazabosi. 'Next he attacked Mendana Gau, to gain face among the bush people as a warrior. He is trying to show the Kwaio people that he is a true leader. As soon as I have gone, he will start the uprising against the whites on the island.'

'He won't wait for ever,' warned Kella. 'If you look like

lasting much longer he'll have to kill you before he can take over the leadership.'

'Do you think I don't know that?' asked Pazabosi.

'That just leaves Professor Mallory.'

'What about him?'

'Oh, come on,' said Kella impatiently. 'You know where he is and Hita probably doesn't – yet. This is all a part of your delaying plan, to enable you to see your *trochea* through in peace. You lured Mallory up here by pretending you were prepared to show him the *havu*. When he arrived, you and your men kidnapped him. You've got that American hidden away somewhere, so that you have some sort of insurance in case you have to start negotiating with the authorities one day. It won't work. I have to take Mallory back now.'

'If I have him,' said Pazabosi steadily, 'I will still need him.'

'The authorities won't bring any charges against you,' argued Kella. 'They'll be so relieved to have Mallory back, if he hasn't been harmed, that they'll leave you alone. I'm going to arrest Hita for the murder of Peter Oro, so you won't have to bother about his challenge to your leadership either. It's all going to come out well for you, just like you've planned.'

Again Pazabosi shook his head. The police sergeant wondered why the old clan leader was being so unwilling to make any concessions when he was in such a strong position. Then he realized why.

'I get it,' he said. 'Hita doesn't know where Professor Mallory is either. But he's looking for the American. If he can find him and butcher him, it will make Hita an even bigger hero in the eyes of his people.'

'That is possible,' nodded Pazabosi, and waited.

'But you're hoping that I'll find Mallory as well,' went on Kella, thinking aloud. 'That could bring Hita and me into conflict. You don't care which one of us wins. If Hita and I come up against each other, one of us is almost certainly going to die, and that's fine with you.'

Pazabosi looked at Kella with the benign air of a schoolmaster whose pupil was doing unexpectedly well.

'That's how I see it, too,' concurred the chief.

34

DREAM-MAKER

'You're absolutely sure?' asked Sergeant Ha'a, looking dubiously at the line of carvings arrayed on his desk. 'These are genuine custom carvings, not replicas produced by the schoolboys at Ruvabi?'

'There's no doubt about it,' Sister Conchita assured him. 'I recognized them as soon as the crate was opened on the wharf. Most of the carvings were made by the boys, but these six are definitely the genuine article. They're all listed in Melanesian ethnographies. Look at this shark hook! It's at least a century old and made of turtle shell, which has to be heated before it can be shaped. No schoolboy could produce work of this quality.'

She regarded the short, plump policeman with triumph. Several days had passed since she had discovered the artifacts in the case at the Customs shed. She had encountered Sergeant Ha'a in the entrance hall of police headquarters after her rapid departure from the shed. When she had gabbled a breathless explanation of what had happened on the wharf he had gone back with her to the harbour immediately and commandeered the box, returning with it to the headquarters building, She had heard nothing else until this morning, when she had received a message from Sergeant Ha'a, summoning her to police headquarters.

'Hmm,' said Sergeant Ha'a.

'Have you arrested the Customs inspector?' Sister Conchita asked eagerly.

'Whatever for?' asked Ha'a, sounding shocked by her enthusiasm.

'Well, for being involved in abstracting the genuine artifacts from the box, of course.'

Ha'a raised a bushy eyebrow. 'Have you any proof of this?' he asked.

'Isn't it obvious?' asked the nun, beginning to get annoyed at the islander's apparent indifference. 'Someone is putting valuable old carvings into the crates at Ruvabi, among the boys' efforts, and then removing them when they reach Customs at Honiara, and smuggling them out of the Solomons.'

She remembered the words of Jimmy, the malaria sprayer on Sulufou. He had warned her about getting involved with smuggling. She had thought that he was referring to Deacon's shell racket, but obviously he had heard rumours of what was happening at Ruvabi mission.

'Again, I ask you, do you have any evidence?' asked the sergeant placidly.

'Well, not as such, but it was obvious from the way that the Customs inspector behaved that something was wrong. He was far too keen to accept the crate without checking the contents, and then when I asked for it to be opened he looked terrified.'

'Perhaps you had frightened him. Could that be possible?' suggested Ha'a gently. Sister Conchita opened her mouth to reply, but the sergeant was talking again. 'Sister, this is a British Protectorate, policed by British-trained officers. The British rule of law applies here. We do not arrest people because they look worried when hectored by an expatriate member of a religious order with a strong personality and a pronounced sense of justice. However, you may take it from me that the matter is under investigation.'

'Look, I know you don't know me, Sergeant Ha'a—' began the nun.

'You underestimate yourself, sister,' interrupted the policeman. 'Your fame precedes you from Ruvabi.'

'It does?' asked Sister Conchita, for once at a loss for words.

'Indeed. You are known for getting out to the Lau Catholic villages and leading the prayer sessions there. You conduct their worship with such verve and gusto that the islanders have even given you a name – mary talk-talk long God.'

'What does that mean?' asked Sister Conchita.

'Roughly – the Praying Woman.' Sergeant Ha'a rose and glanced at his watch. 'And now I believe that it is time for you to leave. Aren't you meeting Father Pierre's aircraft at Henderson Field at nine o'clock this morning?'

'How on earth did you know that?' asked Sister Conchita, finding herself on her feet despite her firm intention to stay.

Ha'a escorted her urbanely to his office door. 'I would like to claim that it was due to unremitting toil and and instinctive detective work,' he admitted innocently. 'In fact, I have a *wantok* who works as a cleaner at the mission headquarters and keeps her ears and eyes open! Good morning, Sister Conchita.'

Sister Conchita was still fuming at the sergeant's smooth dismissal of her protests as she drove the mission jeep over the Matanikau Bridge out of Honiara along the eight-mile stretch of road flanking the sea to Henderson Field, the airport serving the capital. If only Sergeant Kella was still on Guadalcanal, she thought bitterly, he would have paid proper attention to her theories. Then, with a pang of remorse, she remembered how earlier she had impulsively accused the Malaitan of deliberately implicating Father Pierre in his inquiries.

Sister Conchita usually managed to see the bright side of most situations, but this morning she was undeniably depressed. Father Ignatius had been decidedly cool in his attitude towards her lately. The fact that she had unwittingly implicated Ruvabi mission station in the alleged smuggling of carvings out of the Protectorate had done nothing to increase her popularity with the precise administrator. As a result Sister Conchita had been banished lately to the headquarters motor pool, with long hot days of grappling with wrenches and ill-fitting and antiquated engine spare parts.

She drove over the speed limit past the Kukum golf course and King George VI Secondary School. Soon there were no more buildings, only the foothills to her right and green plains skirting the sea on her left. Father Ignatius had allowed her to meet Father Pierre's flight only because no one else had wanted to waste a morning waiting for the erratic Baron Beechcraft service to arrive from Auki.

'Father Pierre is an old man who has spent rather too long in the bush,' the administrator had told her with hauteur. 'In fact it is feared in some quarters that over the years he has allowed his message to become diluted with pagan practices. In short, sister, we fear that he has suffered the fate of more than one long-serving missionary, and gone native!'

Sister Conchita had suppressed the angry retort trembling on her lips. If she antagonized this complacent and ignorant headquarters pussy-cat further the man might rescind his decision to send her to meet the priest, and she needed to see Father Pierre again more than anything.

It would also be nice to see Sergeant Kella once more, she admitted wistfully to herself. Not only did she want to apologize for maligning him, but she realized how much she had taken comfort in the big man's taciturn but solid presence. If anyone was going to solve the mysteries surrounding Ruvabi mission, she was sure that it was going to be the *aofia*.

She parked outside the unfurnished single-storeyed brick building, which doubled as reception lounge and Customs and

Immigration area for the bi-weekly international flights from Papua New Guinea and Fiji. Inside, a large ceiling fan lethargically pushed aside layers of hot air.

Sister Conchita passed through the building and emerged on the far side, stopping behind a small fence running parallel to the airstrip. Only a handful of expatriates and islanders waited in the morning heat to meet the scheduled inter-islands flight from Malaita. For once the Baron Beechcraft was on time. Sister Conchita could see it flying across the bay, banking over the heavily forested island of Nggela. Within minutes the trim aircraft was shuddering to a halt outside the airport building. Half a dozen passengers emerged from the plane, among them the unmistakable form of Father Pierre, bowed, shuffling, clad in a long black habit and carrying his belongings in a Gladstone bag.

Sister Conchita shook the old man's hand vigorously, shocked at the change in him. The sprightly air that usually distinguished the old priest was gone. If she did not know him better Sister Conchita would have believed that he was defeated. She dismissed the thought; her mentor was merely tired, she assured herself.

Forcing herself to chatter inconsequentially, the nun conducted Father Pierre to the makeshift car park. The old man's eyes widened in mock wonder as he saw the waiting vehicle. 'The mission jeep!' he exclaimed reverently. 'I was expecting something much less grand; a bicycle, perhaps. Don't tell me Father Ignatius said you could use it?'

'He didn't say I couldn't,' said Sister Conchita.

A chuckle escaped the priest's lips. For a moment he looked like his former mischievous self. 'Oh, sister,' he said solemnly, 'unless we are both very lucky we shall spend so much time in purgatory together!'

They sat in the jeep. Sister Conchita made as if to start the vehicle. Father Pierre lifted a restraining hand.

'First, tell me everything,' he invited.

It was as if a dam within her had been breached. Sister Conchita found herself telling her expressionless listener all that had happened since she had arrived in Honiara, of her run-ins with the headquarters administrator, her encounters with Kella and her increasing unease at the danger the police sergeant seemed to be heading into.

'Ben Kella's all right,' said Father Pierre after Sister Conchita had finished, half-ashamed at revealing so much about her feelings. 'I saw him recently at the mission station. He's probably heading for trouble in the high bush, but if anyone can look after himself it's Ben.' He paused. 'You like our sergeant, don't you?'

'I don't know what I feel about him!' said the nun.

'How so?'

'Well . . .' Sister Conchita struggled to express her feelings and to put into words what had been bothering her ever since she had first met the police sergeant. 'Yes, I like him fine,' she conceded. 'He's a great guy, he's brave and he knows so much about Malaita. But . . .'

'Yes?' prompted the priest. 'You find it difficult to come to terms with his background, is that it?'

'Exactly,' said Sister Conchita miserably. 'Father, Ben's a pagan. He worships his own gods. His beliefs go against everything I've been taught. Yet he's putting his faith and his ideology to use to help the mission.'

'He's not doing it for the mission,' Father Pierre corrected her. 'He's doing it for his people, because he's the *aofia*.'

'It still worries me.'

Father Pierre was silent for a few seconds. When he spoke it was almost with reluctance. 'I knew that we would have this conversation one day,' he said. 'I just hoped that you would have learned a little more about the islands before you had to make a decision.'

'What decision?' asked the nun.

'You've agreed to dedicate your life to God in the Solomon Islands, and I'm glad that you've done so, because you have so much to offer, Sister Conchita. But to be effective you've got to immerse yourself in the customs and traditions of the islands.'

'I'm trying to do that!'

'I know, I know. But you won't get it all from books. Over the years to come you've got to mix with plenty of islanders like Ben Kella – highly intelligent and just as dedicated to their gods as we our to Our Lord. And you've got to understand their beliefs and appreciate that sometimes they can bring about miracles too, if people believe in them strongly enough.'

'Are you asking me to—'

'I'm putting a choice before you. You can follow in the way of Father Ignatius and go by the book. Many do and lead useful and productive lives within the Church. Or you can do what a number of priests and nuns who have spent much of their time in the bush do, and appreciate that there are two worlds of the spirit in the Solomons, and that sometimes they intermingle. It's a big decision for someone as young as yourself to make, and perhaps I'm being unfair in urging you to take it so early in your career. But I think you're ready to make up your mind. To do that you've got to experience both sides.'

'How do I do that?'

'I'll show you,' said Father Pierre.

Sister Conchita toiled up the narrow track leading to the top of Mount Austen, a few miles outside Honiara. Leaving the airport, she had driven inland up the unmade road as far as she could persuade the jeep to jolt along. Then Father Pierre had told her that she would have to go the rest of the way on foot by herself. He would wait for her for as long as it took.

'But I don't know where I'm going or what I'm looking for,' she had objected.

The priest had shrugged. 'Maybe nothing,' he had said. 'But if you want to begin to understand Kella and what he stands for, you will have to put yourself in a position to learn about his faith.' He had seen the look of incomprehension on the nun's face and reluctantly had explained a little further.

'On the hilltop there's a Malaitan community,' he said. 'They're men and women who have come over from the Lau Lagoon to Guadalcanal. They don't own land on this island, so they're squatting in an area the local people don't want. Make no mistake, it's a long hike up to the summit and it's pretty rugged when you get there too.'

'But what am I looking for?'

'You'll know when you arrive – if you're lucky. The Lau people have transferred their culture to this area, remember that, and they'll be reluctant to disclose it to strangers. But this is the only place on Guadalcanal where you can get in touch with Kella, and maybe begin to understand him. On the other hand, you may just have a long and unpleasant walk for nothing. It's up to you!'

'I'll do my best, father.'

'I know you will. Just one word of advice – if you do get lost, don't follow any water-course up there. An apparently harmless stream could lead you straight into a swamp or a gorge. Don't worry; you ought to be safe enough. If I'm right you should be looked after all the way.'

The old priest would be drawn no further and, despite the voices screaming inside her not to go, the bewildered young sister had set off up the steep incline. Before she had gone more than a few paces Father Pierre had called her back. The old man's face was lined and strained.

'There's one more thing,' he had said. 'It's only something I've heard, and I may be wrong. But I believe that what you are looking for is in a cave. And that cave will be distinguished by the sign of the local dream-maker carved outside.'

'What sign?' asked Sister Conchita.

'A snake,' said the priest. '*Baekwa I Tolo*. Be careful in your dealings with it. It has very powerful *mana*.'

Now, three hours later, she was still plodding up the narrow track. Farther down, the hillside had been forested but now there was nothing but brown, spiralling vegetation on either side of the track. The mountainside bush was nothing like the lush damp greenery to which she was accustomed on Malaita. Here it was just as thick and impenetrable, but brown and wire-like in appearance, with great threatening thorns stirred into sudden sallies by the breeze. Sister Conchita could understand why the local Guadalcanal people did not want to live in such a remote and infertile place.

She turned a corner and saw the plateau of the summit ahead of her. It was covered with ramshackle buildings made of planks and boxes. Presumably there was no suitable wood for building houses in the area, resulting in the sprawling shanty-town lying before her. The inhabitants must have carried every scrap of material five miles up the mountain track from the main road. She could see no stream, just a series of man-made rock pools designed to catch rainwater.

There were the usual teeming groups of half-naked women and children outside the makeshift homes. As soon as they saw the nun they disappeared rapidly inside the dwellings, although Sister Conchita was aware of dozens of pairs of eyes peering out at her through the open doorways. She stopped, at a loss. This was so unlike the effusive welcome she would have received as a matter of course on Malaita.

Eventually a man appeared from the far end of the settlement.

He was of medium height but tightly muscled. He wore a pair of tattered shorts.

'I am Sam Beni,' he said abruptly in English.

'Sister Conchita,' faltered the nun, extending a hand.

The man did not take it. 'What can I do for you, sister?' he asked.

'I'm not sure,' said the sister, trying to conceal her embarrassment at her total sense of misplacement. 'Father Pierre from Ruvabi sent me up here – to look for something, I think.'

If her words made any sense to the islander he showed no sign of it. He shrugged scornfully 'We cannot help you up here. Like you, we are exiles.'

'Tell me, is there a path leading anywhere?' begged Sister Conchita. She was tired and thirsty, but determined not to turn back.

Beni shrugged briefly. 'One track,' he said, indicating the direction from which he had appeared. 'It soon disappears into the bush and cliffs. There is nothing for a white sister there.'

Sister Conchita thanked the man but nevertheless took the direction he had indicated. She soon left the settlement behind her and was aware that the ground was sloping gradually beneath her feet. The sun-browned vegetation grew thickly all around her and there were great outcrops of rock, some towering into the sky and many yards long. Presumably the cave Father Pierre had mentioned would be a fissure in one of the grey, looming outcrops.

Again and again as she struggled onwards Sister Conchita wished that she had never embarked upon such a quixotic and apparently unnecessary journey. She found herself resenting Father Pierre and the cryptic manner in which he had dismissed her with a mere passing reference to someone called a dream-maker. All right, so presumably he had wanted her to embark upon a voyage of self-discovery, but at least he could have given her some sort of clue as to what she was supposed to be looking for.

Then she remembered that he had. The old man had told her to look for a snake carved on the exterior of a cave. Doggedly Sister Conchita forced herself off the path in the direction of the great stone outcrops growing out of the undergrowth.

Cruel looping hooks of thorns tore at her flesh and habit but the nun forced herself to keep pressing towards the rocks. The sweat stung her eyes into paroxysms of blinking. Almost blindly she skirted piles of dead brushwood and crumbled stones at her feet, her bleeding hands fending off the creepers and canes lurking before her. Eventually she reached the first of the outcrops. Here it was cooler, sheltered from the sun, but greyer, casting macabre shadows to form a harsh, separate, unforgiving world of its own. Sister Conchita slumped breathlessly against the stone wall, grateful for the temporary respite it bestowed upon her tortured limbs. Then, almost sobbing with agony, she forced herself onwards in desperate search of the cave marked with the snake carving.

Small creatures making their homes among the rocks and undergrowth scuttled beneath her feet; lizards and bush mice paused in their activities to survey her before disappearing urgently. Somewhere muffled by the undergrowth she could hear the snorting of an angry pig.

Sister Conchita moved as fast as she could between the cliff faces. There were apertures enough worked into the face of the rock, of differing shapes and sizes, but none with any visible marking signs outside. She dragged her protesting body exhaustedly from outcrop to outcrop, pulling herself along the uneven sides of the rocks by her frayed fingertips when the creepers threatened to scale the walls to a height above her head.

Finally she almost literally stumbled across it. The outcrop was relatively small, granite-grey in colour, separated from the main range by a sea of knee-high springy rough grass. Sister Conchita reached the wall of rock by the exercise of main force and headed with little hope for the entrance to a cave she had noticed about a third of the way along the length of the rock growth. She pulled herself to the hole and stopped, wiping the perspiration from her eyes with initial disbelief and then a flood of triumph.

The snake was etched into the wall to a depth of several inches, long, curling, with large, angry eyes and a head reared back ready to strike. Sister Conchita took a deep breath and entered the cave.

After her initial misgivings the interior of the cave proved almost to be an anticlimax. It was small, remarkably light and simply furnished with various flat stones strewn about the floor. What caused Sister Conchita to pause abruptly was the sight of the occupant. Standing just inside the doorway, smiling approvingly, was a young girl. She could not have been more than twelve years of age, clad in a grass skirt, with her cropped hair bleached blonde. She was holding out half a coconut shell filled with some liquid.

'Why, hello there,' smiled Sister Conchita, taking care to speak quietly, aware of the fearsome sight she must present after her recent battle with the undergrowth. Her habit was tattered and hanging in shreds, her face stained and sweating, her knees buckling with fatigue as she panted for breath, her hands bleeding profusely.

'Is your mother here?' she asked hopefully. The girl continued to smile serenely but made no answer. Awkwardly the nun tried to repeat the question in a rough approximation of pidgin. 'Mama bilong you?'

The girl giggled. Probably at her visitor's inexpert attempt at pidgin, thought Sister Conchita. Again the girl lifted her thin arms and proffered the coconut shell. The nun realized how thirsty she was. She nodded gratefully and drained the contents. The girl indicated one of the flat stones. Wearily Sister Conchita sat down on it.

Almost immediately she was drifting away. She was aware of her head slumping on her chest and then suddenly, through a haze that cleared slowly, she was in the company of her family in Boston once again. Her father was mowing the lawn while her mother was bringing a pitcher of lemonade out of the house. It was an idyllic scene and one that eased her heart to an amazing degree. But then as she watched it all started to go wrong. Her father deliberately steered the lawnmower off the grass and across a flowerbed, smashing it with force into the garden fence. Bewildered and horrified at such an act of random violence Sister Conchita turned to face her mother just as she turned the pitcher upside down and disgorged its contents on to the patio, laughing vindictively at her daughter. Sister Conchita goggled at the sight. She became aware of Ben Kella standing at her side in the suburban street. Both of her parents were staring meaning-fully at the police sergeant.

The scene changed. Sister Conchita was in the cellar of her house now with her fifteen-year-old brother Jack. The basement was dusty, used as a storeroom. They were playing checkers on a board supported by an upturned box. Sister Conchita, or rather a ten-year-old version of the nun, was winning game after game. Jack stopped smiling. Suddenly he lunged across the board at his sister. He seized her by the throat and started choking her. Sister Conchita fell to the floor, screaming. The inexorable pressure on her neck did not cease. She could hardly breathe. In another moment she knew that she would be dead.

Sister Conchita woke up, her arms flailing. Curiously she no longer felt tired, although she was sure that she could not have slept for long. The child with the bleached hair was no longer in the cave.

The nun recalled her dream and shuddered. She had never received anything but love and care from her parents and brother. The sight of the three of them in the dream behaving in such an irrational and cruel manner was discomfiting. She tried to dismiss the affair from her mind. She told herself that she had been distraught after her exhausting search for the cave; the experience would have been enough to give anyone bad dreams.

She had no trouble finding her way back to the Lau settlement on the plateau. She walked with such certainty that it was almost as if an unseen force was guiding her footsteps. Sam Beni was waiting for her between the huts. He raised an eyebrow at the nun's abstracted approach.

'Is everything all right?' he asked.

'Fine,' replied Sister Conchita. 'Except . . .' She hesitated and then continued, 'There was a young girl playing in one of the caves. Is it safe for her to be so far from the settlement on her own?'

'You met her?' asked Beni, appearing startled.

'Why yes. Only I'm afraid I was so tired I fell asleep. Who is she, do you know?'

Beni muttered an apology and reached for the sister's wrist. Sister Conchita looked down. The outline of a snake had been painted with lime on her flesh while she slept.

'You have seen the dream-maker,' said the islander, visibly shocked and impressed. 'Did she summon up a dream for you?'

'Yes, as a matter of fact she—'

'I don't want to know about it,' said Beni sharply. 'It is between you and the ghosts. You must have powerful *mana* to be accepted by them so quickly.'

'I only stumbled across her by chance.'

'No one meets a dream-maker by chance. They summon people when they have messages for them.' The now concerned Sister Conchita tried to say something but Beni waved her away. 'It will soon be night,' he told her, clearly anxious to be rid of the white woman who had invaded his culture. 'It is time you began your descent. Don't worry. Your footsteps will be guided all the way, I promise you. I will ask one of the magic men to tie a knot in a piece of custom grass. That will slow down time and allow you to get back.'

Sister Conchita stumbled down the track back towards the waiting jeep. What had been in the coconut shell she had accepted from the girl? Could her dream have been some sort of message? Perhaps there had been a drug in the drink and her dream had been the result of an induced hallucinatory trance. Was she meant to deduce something from the antagonistic nature of her parents and brother in her recent and so vivid dream?

It must have taken her several hours to get back to Father Pierre, but it seemed no time at all. She poured out her story to the waiting priest in a breathless cascade, leaving nothing out.

'What does it mean?' she demanded wildly as she finished. 'Was the dream a message? How could that young dream-maker know anything about my family?'

'You've been accepted by the Lau spirits,' said the priest calmly. 'That doesn't happen to many whites. What do *you* think your dream meant?'

'Ben Kella was standing with me on my parents' lawn,' said the nun, breathing deeply and trying to force herself to work the matter out logically. 'He saw my parents and brother behaving completely out of character. Jack even attacked me. The message was meant for Kella, I'm sure of it. The three people I love more deeply than anyone on earth were doing strange, irrational things that frightened me.' She thought for a moment. 'The implication was that someone close to Kella is going to behave in an odd way, perhaps even to harm him.' She looked to the priest for confirmation. 'Could that possibly be it? If it is, I must get a message to Ben, to tell him that he's in danger!'

'My dear,' said Father Pierre quietly, 'if the Lau gods have seen fit to warn you, assuredly they will get the same message to Sergeant Kella!'

35

KILLING GROUND

Kella lay behind a bush and watched the newly built house between the trees. Not far away he could hear the thunder of the great waterfall.

He had been at the killing ground for an hour. He had travelled from Pazabosi's village as quickly as he could. Hita would be looking for Professor Mallory as well. Kella would not put it past the old chief to tell Hita where he had put the American, just to make matters interesting.

What Pazabosi was doing had its antecedents in bush folklore. The pitting of two young warriors against each other was a staple ingredient of Kwaio legends. It would suit the old chief's sense of humour to set Kella and Hita at one another's throats, and at the same time ensure that one of the two men who had been annoying him would die in the process.

The police sergeant knew that if he was going to have any realistic chance of survival he would have to find Professor Mallory quickly and then link up with Inspector Lorrimer and his Roviana constables. If the Englishman kept to the route Kella had given him, the police party should be less than ten miles away down the track at the moment. On the other hand, if Lorrimer had decided to make his own way up into the bush he could be anywhere.

Kella studied the house again. It was the freshly constructed leaf hut he had seen on his last visit to the area. He had wondered at the time who it was being built for. It had gone up too quickly to be a family dwelling place. Many bushmen had worked hard together to erect this thatched building in such a short time. There had to be a reason for their urgency, and Kella believed that he knew what it was.

Still, it was a long shot to believe that the American academic was being kept inside the building. There were no guards, which was puzzling, and since Kella had been there no one had entered or left the long hut.

The police sergeant decided that there was only one way to find out. He got to his feet and started running through the trees as quickly as he could, zigzagging towards the door of the house.

He reached the entrance and flung it open, bursting in to the single room. He did not know what he had expected to find, but nothing had prepared him for the bizarre, writhing tableau that met his eyes.

Two naked young women and a man were squirming together in noisy ecstasy, on top of a pile of pandanus mats. A third naked woman was on all-fours to one side of the group, looking on with rapt concentration and issuing shrill cries of exhortation and encouragement to the others. In the main group, pumping brown and white limbs intermingled and then briefly separated with lascivious pleasure.

Kella relaxed, his initial amazement evaporating in sheer delight and amusement. A bald head and a long-jawed, satiated, bespectacled white face emerged momentarily from the mêlée at an impossible angle through a gap in the amalgamated, sweating bodies, and gaped up in exhausted concern at the watching police sergeant. Kella sketched an admiring salute.

'Professor Mallory, I presume?' he asked.

★　★　★

'How did you know I was here?' asked Professor Mallory.

'It was just a guess really,' Kella admitted.

Thirty minutes had passed since the police sergeant had first hurtled into the hut. Elizabeth and the two other Sikaiana women who had been conjoined so enthusiastically with the American had hurried into their clothes with many cries of dismay and outraged decency, and had flounced out of the hut. Mallory had struggled reluctantly back into his slacks and shirt and was sitting on a mat opposite Kella. Within the American, a condition of offended embarrassment seemed to be struggling with a prolonged absorbing daydream.

'I was here some days ago,' went on Kella, trying to give the American time to recover from his disquiet. 'I saw that this hut had only just been built. It had been put in an odd place among the trees. Bush people tend to stick together in small communities. A place like this, some distance from the village, was probably meant for a guest – or a prisoner. Then there was the mosquito net. Bush people don't use them. It must have been brought up especially from one of the big saltwater trading stores. You were the only whitey – white man – up here, so I assumed it was meant for you.' Kella paused. 'And then I noticed the coconuts,' he added.

'Coconuts?' repeated Mallory. He seemed too tired to make logical connections. Judging by what had been happening to the academic for the last week or so, Kella was not surprised.

'When I glanced in here that last time, a number of coconuts had been split in half and the milk collected in a bowl. That meant that at least one Sikaiana person was living here. Sikaiana and Ontong Java are the only islands in the Solomons which make their own alcoholic drinks, and the Ontong people seldom leave their island. The Sikaiana drink is a toddy fermented from coconut milk. I wondered if Pazabosi had left Elizabeth here to cook and clean for you. I hadn't realized that there were three of them and that they . . .' Kella's voice trailed off as he failed to complete the sentence.

The mention of the girl's name struck a chord with the other man. 'You've met Elizabeth?' asked Mallory, coming back, as if from a long distance.

Kella nodded. A reluctant, admiring grin creased the American professor's pale, lined face. 'You, too?' he cackled suddenly. 'With Elizabeth? Congratulations!' He frowned judiciously. 'I wouldn't like to live off the difference,' he said, 'and I'm certainly not being judgemental, but I'd say she was the best of the three. Just by a tad.'

'I wouldn't know,' said Kella stiffly, hoping to change the subject. 'I mean I only met Elizabeth briefly.'

'That one doesn't need much time, son. Only opportunity.'

'What happened exactly?' asked Kella, trying with difficulty to keep to the main thread of his interrogation. 'How did you get up here in the first place?'

'I'm writing a paper on Kwaio custom carvings,' said the American. 'I particularly wanted to see the *havu*. No white man ever has. One morning two bushmen appeared at the mission, offering to bring me up here and show me the carving.'

'They were sent by Pazabosi,' said Kella. 'He needed you as a hostage.'

'Is that right? Well, when I got as far as the custom temple behind the waterfall, Pazabosi and some of his boys were waiting there for me. They told me that the *havu* had been stolen and they had to do something about it. Scared the crap out of me, I don't mind telling you. I thought I was a gonner.'

'Pazabosi couldn't harm you. He's entered the *trochea*, the contemplative last period of his life.'

'Now you tell me! It didn't seem so reassuring at the time, that's for sure! Then the old guy presented me with a kind of ultimatum. I had to stay up here in this hut, in case he needed me, but to make life easier for me, he'd arranged for Elizabeth and the other women to keep me company.'

'Some ultimatum,' marvelled Kella.

Mallory closed his eyes in ecstatic contemplation for a moment. 'Guys who look like I do don't get many offers like that, I can tell you,' he said frankly. 'Not here, or anywhere else.'

'That would be Pazabosi's notion of irony,' said the police sergeant. 'You came up here looking for a carved representation of the sex act, and he offered you the real thing.'

'In spades,' breathed Mallory.

It would also mean that Pazabosi would not have to post guards around the house, thought Kella. He found himself liking the American for his pragmatic acceptance of his situation.

'Let me tell you, sergeant,' said Mallory, 'after the first few hours with those Sikaiana women, I decided that they would have to prise me loose with a shoe-horn ever to get me to leave.'

'I'm afraid that's why I'm here,' said Kella apologetically. 'I have to get you back to Honiara and out of the Protectorate rather quickly.'

Mallory shook his head resolutely. 'No way,' he affirmed. 'Mrs Mallory's little boy knows when he's well off.'

'I'm afraid that if you stay here another hour, you'll probably be dead,' said Kella. In a few words he told the other man about the attempts of Hita to usurp Pazabosi as leader of the Kwaio people.

'At this moment Hita's out to make a name for himself by killing the pair of us,' he finished.

'Shit,' mumbled Professor Mallory. 'I knew it was too good to last.'

'Stay here for the moment,' Kella told him, standing up. 'I'll just go and take a look round outside before we leave.'

Elizabeth was waiting for him outside the hut. Complicitly she sidled up to the sergeant, murmuring endearments. Kella regarded the extroverted girl warily.

'Are you really a schoolteacher?' he asked.

'Trained and certificated, Sergeant Kella,' she confirmed. She grinned. 'Mind you, that doesn't mean I can't do other things too.'

'Just tell me one thing,' begged Kella, trying to hold her off. 'Why did you encourage me to spend the night with you the last time I came to the village? Was that Pazabosi's idea to distract me?'

Elizabeth's limpid eyes widened at the mere suggestion. 'Certainly not,' she said with hauteur. 'Pazabosi knows nothing about you and me.'

'Then why did you do it?' asked the bewildered Kella.

The girl snuggled up against him. 'Can't you guess?' she asked softly. 'I fancy you, Ben Kella.'

Kella blinked, flattered and alarmed. Elizabeth threw her golden arms about his neck and tried to drag him in the direction of the trees. Before they could get started, another of the Sikaiana women hurried towards them and addressed Elizabeth urgently in her own dialect.

'What is it?' demanded Kella, disengaging himself with considerable reluctance.

Elizabeth looked concerned. 'There is a war party coming through the bush towards us,' she translated.

Kella had shepherded Mallory and the three frightened women as far as the killing ground before Hita caught up with them. The three bushmen came out of the trees across the plateau at a brisk trot. Kella pointed to the bush track.

'Follow that path,' he shouted to the others. 'Keep going down towards the coast. If you're lucky you'll meet a police detachment coming up.'

'What are you going to do?' asked the dishevelled Mallory.

His eyes behind the thick lenses of his spectacles were worried and unfocused.

'Never mind me! Just get the girls away from here.'

Kella whirled round to face the three bushmen. They were advancing across the bluff in a tight bunch, hoisting their spears speculatively.

Kella was not expecting anything subtle from his attackers. Hita was not a reflective man. The young warrior could have succeeded Pazabosi merely by waiting a short time for the elderly chief to die. Instead, he had insisted on challenging the old man. Any attack from the bush warrior now was likely to come from the front, in a sudden flurry of action.

One of the warriors outstripped his two companions and raced towards Kella. Drawing back his arm, the bushman hurled his spear with whiplash force. Instinctively Kella ducked. The weapon screamed through the air past his head and embedded itself quivering in the ground a few yards away.

Propelled by his own velocity the bushman continued on his run towards the police sergeant. Like his companions he was smaller and lighter than Kella. The sergeant braced himself and drove his right fist into the running man's face. The warrior's nose exploded in a spray of blood and his head jerked back sharply.

Kella stepped forward, bent his knees and punched the bushman in the kidneys with a scything left hook. The warrior doubled up. Kella seized him by the shoulders, straightened the man up and drove the top of his head with sickening force into the bushman's already blood-soaked face. The warrior crumpled to the ground and lay still. Kella scrabbled for the man's spear and held it before him as he faced Hita and the remaining bushman.

The two men had fanned out and were approaching Kella cautiously, making threatening circular motions and darts with their short spears. They knew that if they threw and missed, the burly police sergeant would then have an advantage over them. Hita snarled something to his companion. The two men ran with desperate courage at Kella.

The sergeant retreated to the edge of the cliff, the waterfall thundering just behind him. This would cut down the bushmen's angles of attack, but it certainly limited his scope for retreat.

Out of the corner of his eye Kella saw that Mallory and the three Sikaiana women were huddled together under the trees at the edge of the plateau. Again he shouted to them to run. Then the bush warriors were upon him, jabbing fiercely with their spears.

As the bushmen closed in on him, Kella launched himself forward in a rugby tackle on Hita's companion. Still clutching his spear in his right hand, he wrapped both arms around his adversary's scrawny thigh, pulling the man round and to the ground, so that he lay between Kella and the hovering and disconcerted Hita.

At the same time, with his left hand Kella grabbed the bushman's unprotected testicles. He pulled and twisted them viciously. The warrior screamed in agony. Kella released his grip on the man's thigh. In the same movement the sergeant rolled away and dragged the point of his spear across the tendons at the back of his fallen adversary's knee, severing several of them. The bushman yelled again and writhed helplessly on the ground.

Undeterred, Hita leapt over the fallen bushman to reach Kella. The police sergeant tried to scramble to his feet. He slipped on the wet grass and toppled backwards on the edge of the cliff. Hita's eyes glistened with triumph. The young warrior raised his spear to bring it down on Kella. Instinctively the sergeant shielded his face with his forearm and tried to brace himself against the fatal thrust that would surely follow.

He was suddenly aware of the pounding of running feet. Kella looked up. Behind Hita, the scrawny, middle-aged form of Professor Mallory was running clumsily but with enormous determination across the bluff towards them both, gathering momentum as he approached. The sun glistened on his spectacles.

Distracted, Hita snarled and turned to face his latest attacker, adjusting the grip on his spear to deal with the American. Kella lashed out with both feet, catching the bush warrior on the shins, causing him to stagger and lose his balance for a moment.

At the same moment Mallory's bony shoulder thudded with full force into Hita's body. The bushman staggered back several paces, waved his arms desperately in an effort to regain his balance, and then plunged screaming over the edge of the cliff. The cascading force of the waterfall enveloped Hita's body and drove it mercilessly down on to the rocks far below. The falling, broken body bounced several times on different ledges and then spiralled helplessly to the river beneath.

Awkwardly Professor Mallory teetered on the edge of the cliff. Kella forced himself to his feet and dragged the American back. Then both men collapsed panting in a heap on the grass.

Mallory was the first to recover. He climbed slowly to his feet and settled his spectacles on his nose with one trembling finger. He regarded the great waterfall with myopic awe.

'I've never done anything brave on purpose before,' he said wonderingly.

Kella looked at the three voluptuous Sikaiana women who were hurrying towards them, audibly marvelling at the American's prowess.

'Life must have been full of new experiences for you lately,' he observed. He wondered what had prompted the American into his unexpected display of resource and courage. Perhaps he had guessed what would have happened to him and the three women if Hita had triumphed.

Thirty or forty armed bushmen hurried agitatedly out of the trees in their direction. Kella stifled a groan. Then he caught a glimpse of Pazabosi. The paramount chief surveyed the scene. The bushman Kella had knocked unconscious was standing, tenderly feeling his swollen, broken nose. The man with the shattered tendons was being supported unsympathetically by two other bushmen. Pazabosi questioned the second man briefly before allowing him to be helped away into the trees. Then the old chief approached Kella unhurriedly.

'I hear that Hita is dead,' he said.

'It's a real shame,' said Kella. 'You don't have a rival any more, but it had nothing to do with you. You're smelling of roses, old man.'

Pazabosi pretended not to hear him. 'I think I can stop the others from attacking you for about an hour,' he said. 'But you would all do well to get down to the coast and join the police patrol which I hear is coming this way, before any of Hita's *wantoks* start after you.'

'We're on our way,' Kella assured him. He hesitated. There was still one aspect of the case that puzzled him. Because he had rid the old chief of the renegade Hita, Pazabosi now owed him a big favour. Perhaps he could persuade the old man to tell him what he really wanted to know.

'Before I go, there's something I want to ask you,' he said.

36

SERVICE MESSAGE

'Cain killed Abel because he was jealous of his brother, and he was cast out by his people,' said Sister Conchita. She glanced at her script. Through the glass window of the radio studio she could see the Melanesian programme assistant in the studio next door torpidly manipulating the control panel.

'Cain was so jealous of his brother that he murdered him,' went on the nun reading into the microphone, 'and as a result he was banished by his people. But perhaps Abel should have been more alert. There could be nothing worse than being betrayed and attacked by a brother. However, as Christians we should also be aware of the feelings of others. We should always ask ourselves, "Did I pay enough attention to my brother? Did I really know him? Could I have stopped him before it was too late?" Thank you! God bless you and goodnight.'

The programme assistant gave her the thumbs-up sign. Sister Conchita stood and walked through to the solitary control room of the Solomon Islands Broadcasting Service. As she entered the room the programme assistant removed a spool of recording tape from a console and scrawled a title on it with a marking pen.

'Will that be broadcast tomorrow night?' asked Sister Conchita.

'Yes, sister, at 21.55, just after the record requests programme.'

'Good.' She handed the technician a scrap of paper. 'I would like this service message broadcast as well. Could you see that it goes out tonight and tomorrow night, please.'

The programme assistant looked at the message. 'Is this right?' he asked, puzzled.

'It couldn't be more right,' the sister assured him. 'It's also very important. Will you send it out before my talk?'

'Sure,' shrugged the islander. 'Consider it done.'

Sister Conchita thanked him. Father Ignatius had looked suspicious when she had asked his permission to write and deliver the five-minute religious broadcast that the different churches took turns to broadcast every night. He had even insisted on reading her script in advance, but, finding nothing apparently offensive in its content, had dubiously given her the go-ahead.

The nun hoped that Ben Kella would hear the programme, and that if he did the content would start him thinking. Sister Conchita had not been able to forget her confused experience in the dream-maker's cave. She was convinced that she had been intended to pass on a warning to Kella to be aware of the actions of a brother.

She realized the risk she was taking. If the bishop were to find out that she had used a religious broadcast to pass on her experience at the hands of a pagan dream-maker, Sister Conchita knew that she would be shipped out of the Solomons and perhaps out of the Church, which was something that would break her heart.

Outside the SIBS building in the bright morning sunlight she saw Chief Superintendent Grice marching briskly past on his way to the Guadalcanal Club, presumably for one of his notorious liquid lunches. The usually reticent Kella had mentioned his periodic run-ins with his choleric superior. But Kella was far away on Malaita; it was time someone else kept the police officer on his toes.

'Good morning, chief superintendent,' she said innocently. 'I just want to tell you what a great job you guys are doing.'

'Really? Thank you,' bumbled the gratified police officer.

'Sure thing!' confirmed the young nun. 'It's hard to select any one particular guy, but I've got to tell you, that Sergeant Kella, he's something else again. Everyone says so!'

'Do you think so?' asked Grice, disconcerted.

'Oh, yes, sir, no doubt about it. He's the pick of a fantastic bunch. One of Honiara's finest! Good afternoon, Chief Superintendent Grice.'

Sister Conchita sailed graciously past the bemused officer. If nothing else, she thought hopefully, she must have befuddled Kella's principal antagonist in the capital even more than usual, and softened him up for Kella's eventual return to Guadalcanal.

37

ONE SIMPLE AMBUSH

'There's a message for you,' Inspector Lorrimer informed Kella.

Kella finished storying with the three Roviana policemen around their cooking fire and reluctantly got to his feet. It was mid-evening on the Ruvabi mission compound. The police patrol had arrived there from the mountains that morning. A truck had been waiting at the Sulufou road-head to take Professor Mallory, nine of the constables and the three Sikaiana women straight to Auki.

Lorrimer and Mallory were booked on a chartered flight to Honiara, the capital. The constables would follow by ship. Kella had arranged for Elizabeth and the two other women to wait at the Catholic mission in Auki until the next trading boat left for Sikaiana to take them home.

The truck was due back sometime in the next hour. Kella, Lorrimer and the three policemen had stayed on to clear things up. Reaction after the events on the killing ground had set in. Mallory had hardly stopped trembling, even when wrapped in blankets after encountering a relieved Lorrimer and his patrol on the bush track. Elizabeth had departed from Kella with a great deal of pouting reluctance, and even a show of tears.

'What sort of a message?' he asked Lorrimer.

'You're not going to believe this.'

'Try me,' said Kella patiently.

'There was a service message on the SIBS tonight. It was for you from Sister Conchita. She wants you to listen to her religious broadcast tonight.'

'Are you sure?'

'There's no doubt about it, old boy. It's due on now. I brought this across for you.'

Carefully he placed his portable radio on the ground between them and tuned it in. Slim Dusty was singing 'A Pub With No Beer'. The final nasal strains died away and the announcer introduced Sister Conchita's talk. Lorrimer and Kella listened in silence. When the broadcast had finished Lorrimer switched the set off.

'Wow!' he said. 'What was that all about?'

'Obviously she was trying to tell me something,' said Kella.

'But what? It was just a story about two brothers.'

'Two brothers who fell out,' Kella reminded him. 'The sister was warning me to beware of a brother.'

'Which one? You've got four or five, mate.'

'Somehow I don't think she meant any of them. Perhaps she didn't know herself. She just had some sort of premonition she was trying to pass on to me.'

'Who then?' Suddenly Lorrimer looked alarmed. 'Oh my God!' he exclaimed. 'What was the name of the big fellow who helped you push the truck across the ford a few days ago?'

'Brother John,' said Kella.

The two policemen looked at one another. 'Could it be him?' asked Lorrimer. 'Maybe Sister Conchita heard something, or guessed it, and sent you a coded message to warn you.'

'It won't be John,' said Kella decisively.

'I'm not so sure,' said Lorrimer, turning away. 'I'm going to send an emergency message to Honiara HQ over the mission transmitter. The duty officer there can start inquiries first thing

265

tomorrow morning and find out just where Brother John has been on Malaita over the last couple of weeks.'

The inspector hurried away. Kella thought about the huge Melanesian mission man but dismissed his suspicions. He knew what he had to do, but Brother John would not be involved.

The schoolboys were eating their evening meal noisily in the mess hut as he walked across to the house of Solomon Bulko. The mission school headmaster was sitting reading a hardback copy of *The Naked and the Dead* when Kella entered. He looked up and nodded, marking his place in the book with a leaf. A country and western record was playing on a battery-operated player.

'You know,' Bulko said, indicating the book, 'I find it very hard to identify with the Solomon Islanders in this story, when we only ever appear in the distance as terrified extras.'

'You should try Jack London's *The Cruise of the Snark*,' Kella told him. 'We're all savage headhunters in that one.'

Bulko took the record off the player. 'Charlie Pride,' he said, holding up the disc approvingly. 'A black man who made it at Nashville. There's hope for us all. I'll get to sing at the Grand Old Opry yet.'

'Don't hold your breath,' said Kella.

'Maybe not. Anyway, I was wondering when you were going to get around to seeing your old mucker. I'll open a few tins and we'll have something to eat,' said Bulko, bustling around the over-furnished room. 'Then you can watch the film in the compound with us afterwards. It's *Love Me or Leave Me* tonight. Jimmy Cagney's a bit past his sell-by date, but Doris Day's all right in it.' He looked at Kella. 'You're very quiet. Are you all right?'

'I know,' said Kella.

Bulko looked inquiringly at him. 'Of course you know,' he said calmly. 'It's your business to know. You're the bloody *aofia*. You're supposed to know everything. What particularly do you know tonight, mate?'

Kella sat down. 'The lot,' he answered wearily. 'You've been organizing the smuggling of custom artifacts out of the Solomons, helped by Mendana Gau. Oh yes, and you tried to kill Sister Conchita in the mangrove swamp.'

'Oh, come on,' expostulated the headmaster, sitting down abruptly with an unconvincing laugh. 'Are you trying to wind me up? What are you on about, Ben? This is me, remember? Your old mucker.'

'I heard that someone from the school had been up by the treehouse where Gau stored the surplus carvings waiting to be brought down to the mission. That same person was also seen at the killing ground by the custom temple,' said Kella.

'So? There are a lot of people at this school, sunshine. Seen one, seen 'em all, especially from a distance.'

'Exactly,' said Kella. 'I assumed that they meant Peter Oro, because he was killed in Kwaio country. But the teachers wear the same uniform as the students here at Ruvabi. It wasn't Peter Oro who'd been up there. It was you. Pazabosi told me so yesterday. I did him a favour by getting rid of one of his rivals. He figured he owed me one. I asked him what Peter Oro had been doing, collecting artifacts from the bush villages. That was something I hadn't been able to work out.'

'You're slipping,' said Solomon Bulko spitefully, standing up again.

'Pazabosi told me that the boy had nothing to do with it. It wasn't Peter Oro who was buying the carvings and who stole the *havu* from the waterfall temple. It was you. Several people saw you there. They never imagined that their *havu* would be in any danger from the school headmaster.'

'A good reputation is worth more than gold,' said Bulko.

'You sometimes go up into the bush area to see if there are any candidates from bush schools for a place at Ruvabi, so you weren't an uncommon sight there.'

'If you only knew the agony I underwent climbing the side of that bloody mountain,' said Bulko unemotionally. 'Is that all? It seems a bit flimsy on the evidence side to me, Ben.'

'Don't worry about evidence,' Kella assured him. 'When Mendana Gau hears that I've arrested you, he'll sing like a mynah bird to shift most of the blame in your direction.'

'Gau,' said Bulko wryly, deflated. 'I needed him because he had a right to come and go in the bush on trading expeditions. Believe me, he wouldn't have been my first choice for a partner.'

'Is that why you tried to have him killed, too?' asked Kella. The headmaster looked at him inquiringly. Kella went on. 'I don't think you told Gau that you'd stolen the *havu*. You hoped that when he went up to make the next routine collection of carvings, he would be killed by the bushmen looking for vengeance. That would have got rid of a potential witness and left you in sole charge of the racket.'

'Bloody bushmen,' said Bulko with rancour. 'With all the practice they've had over the years, you'd think they'd be able to organize one simple ambush.'

'How did you expect to get away with it?' Kella asked. 'Sooner or later the Kwaio people would have broken into the school and chopped you down, like they did Gau.'

'I've put in for a transfer to a school on Guadalcanal,' said Bulko. 'It's due to come through next month. I would have been safe over there, if you hadn't interfered.'

'It was the arrival of Sister Conchita that prompted you to steal the *havu*, wasn't it?' asked Kella.

A flicker of reluctant appreciation crossed the headmaster's eyes. 'How do you make that out?' he asked.

'It was something the sister told me. She mentioned that she'd studied island religions in her training. Carvings are an important part of Melanesian faiths. You were afraid that she would notice that some of the artifacts in the boxes of carvings made by the students to be sold in Honiara were genuine relics.'

'Do you reckon?'

'Oh yes. I almost noticed it myself, and I wasn't in the mission house long. I saw that some of the carvings in the open crates looked black and ancient. I assumed that the students had used boot blacking to make them look older, but they were the real thing. Father Pierre's eyesight was too bad for him to notice such things, but you knew that Sister Conchita would discover the truth before long.'

'I knew I didn't have much time left before she found out,' nodded the headmaster. 'I wanted to make one last big haul before I transferred out. So I went up to the killing ground and stole the *havu*. As you said, the local people were accustomed to seeing me inspecting the handful of mission schools up there.'

'Did you have to try to kill Sister Conchita?' asked Kella astringently.

Bulko shrugged. 'I saw her talking to you down by the river. I didn't know what she might be telling you. I couldn't take a chance, so I shot at you and then followed you into the mangrove swamp. I should have known that I didn't stand a chance against you there.'

'And I thought I knew you,' said Kella, shaking his head. Suddenly he understood the message that Sister Conchita had been struggling to get through to him, probably not appreciating its true significance. 'You were like a brother to me, Sol.'

'Who knows anybody?' asked Bulko. 'I get paid peanuts for running this school for the mission. I'm patronized by the expats and treated as a traitor by my own people. What did I do that was so bad? I bought a few old carvings from bushmen who didn't want or appreciate them, and I sold them to collectors who did both.'

'And you tried to kill a harmless nun. I've got to arrest you for that, Sol.'

'Come on,' wheedled Bulko, extending his hands in a conciliatory gesture. 'What good will that do? Let me resign and go back to my district. I promise I'll keep out of your way.'

'Sorry, I can't do that.'

'For God's sake why not?' exploded Bulko. 'All I've done is cheat whitey. Who gives a shit?'

'You're missing the point,' said Kella. 'When you tried to murder Sister Conchita, she was under my protection. I can't let that go.'

'So it all comes down to bloody custom again, does it?'

'Yes,' said Kella. 'It usually does.'

The three Roviana policemen were waiting for them outside the leaf house. Some of the staff and students had been alerted by their presence. Quite a large, silent crowd had gathered as the policemen escorted the headmaster away. Bulko stared straight ahead, not giving his school a backward look. He was suddenly unknown to Kella, as if a stranger was occupying the Western District man's substantial body.

'The truck will be waiting at the road-head,' Kella informed the departing officers.

He watched the three uniformed men take his friend down the track beneath the trees towards the river. A deep sense of loneliness engulfed Kella. It was as if he was trying to remember a song he had once loved, but neither the words nor the music would come back into his head.

Then he picked up his pack and started to walk after the others.

38

GRADUATION CEREMONY

The female students of Nazareth College outside Honiara were wearing grass skirts, *leis* of brilliant hibiscus flowers, and anklets formed from clusters of nuts. They were performing a Fijian cane-cutting dance taught to them by a sister from Suva.

Kella walked away from the crowd of onlookers and entered the empty bamboo church. Most of the Catholic expatriates in the capital had been invited to the graduation ceremony and the blessing of the college buildings. Kella could see at least one of the British chief inspectors of police, in his dress uniform of white jacket, trimmed with gold braid, black trousers with gold stripes, and white gloves.

Sitting in the cool calm of the church, Kella wondered who could have invited a lapsed Catholic like himself to the ceremony. Already this afternoon he had seen Father Pierre in the distance, and he knew that Sister Conchita had been teaching the students here occasionally during her enforced stay in the capital. He had not spoken to either of them since his return from Malaita several days before.

He had made his report to Chief Superintendent Grice in his office on the day of his return. Inspector Lorrimer, hawk-like and inscrutable, had also been present.

'How's Professor Mallory?' asked Kella, before either of the white men could say anything.

'He flew out an hour ago,' said Chief Superintendent Grice, looking pleased, but as usual bewildered by events. 'He seemed a bit tired and disorientated. But that's only natural considering the ordeal he's been through.'

'Quite so, sir,' said Kella. On their way down from the killing ground he had agreed with Mallory that no point would be gained by including details of the activities of the three Sikaiana women in any official report on the American, chastened as he was and soon to be reunited disenchantedly with his wife.

That would not prevent the saga spreading rapidly over the bush telegraph, but it would be a long time before any of the expats got to hear of it. By then, the tale would have grown so embellished in the repeating that it would have entered Malaitan folklore, and no one would ever be certain exactly what had happened in the cabin up by the waterfall. All of which suited Kella very well.

'I think it's marvellous what that man did,' harrumphed Grice. 'The way he came to your assistance and pushed Hita over the ledge, why, the professor deserves a medal.'

'Somehow, Chief Superintendent, I think that Professor Mallory regards himself as already being well rewarded,' answered Kella.

Grice, accustomed to years of snide but inexplicable remarks from subordinates, grunted suspiciously. Kella managed to keep a straight face. He did not dare look at Inspector Lorrimer.

'I've read your report,' said Grice, indicating the pages typed up by a fastidious secretary from the sergeant's waterlogged, sweat-stained and almost indecipherable notes.

'Extraordinary story,' continued Grice, regarding Kella with new respect. 'How long had this headmaster Bulko been smuggling custom carvings out of the Protectorate?'

'For quite some time, I fancy,' said Kella. 'He had help from Mendana Gau of course, and we suspect that John Cho has been fencing the items here in Honiara and arranging their departure overseas.'

That would explain why Cho had been so eager to recruit him on that night in his office, Kella thought. The Chinaman had been alarmed by his investigations on Malaita and had sought to deflect him from them. His declining of Cho's offer had also probably led to Cho sending so many islanders after the sergeant to try to kill him on the beach by the wharf.

'And Bulko's desperate effort to steal the *havu* from the waterfall triggered everything off?' asked Grice. 'The killing of Senda Iabuli by his people, Professor Mallory's kidnapping, Peter Oro and Gau being hacked down by Hita, Pazabosi leaving his area to put the bones curse on you, to try to stop your investigation.'

'Just about,' confirmed Kella. Actually, many things had swum together in a pattern because different spirits had been out of harmony at the time, but there was no point telling Grice that.

'Solomon Bulko got greedy,' he said. Kella thought of the contents of the headmaster's leaf house, the battery-powered lamp and record player, the collection of films, the basketware furniture, the expensive stove. All these possessions on a mission school headmaster's salary should have alerted him long ago, but he had always expected Bulko to live well. It was all a part of the man's expansive ambience. Kella had allowed his friendship with the witty and happy-go-lucky headteacher to blind him to the obvious, until it was almost too late.

'When Bulko sent the boxes of carvings to Honiara,' Lorrimer told Grice, 'he bribed someone at the Customs station to extract the genuine artifacts from the boxes and take them to John Cho. It was a nice little scam. They might have carried on almost indefinitely, but then Sister Conchita turned up, who could spot genuine carvings from those made at the mission. Bulko tried to get rid of her.' The inspector glanced at Kella. 'And that aroused the ire of our friend and colleague here,' he concluded.

'Unfortunately, it never occurred to me that it was Bulko who was trying to kill us in the swamp that night,' said Kella. 'I couldn't see who it was in the dark. It was obvious that our attacker couldn't move too easily, so at first I assumed that it was Mendana Gau, who's in pretty poor condition.' The police sergeant hesitated. 'Or, I thought it could have been John Deacon,' he concluded. 'He's got a gammy leg.'

'The plantation manager?' Grice was scandalized. 'How could he have been involved?'

'He exports seashells without a licence,' said Kella. 'It would only be a short step from that to buying carvings and smuggling them out. But the man who was chasing us was a poor shot, so that ruled out Deacon.'

'I should think so,' snapped Grice. 'He's a white man.' He noticed that Lorrimer and Kella were looking at him. He flushed slightly. 'Go on,' he ordered. 'Can you prove that it was Bulko who attacked you and Sister Conchita that night?'

'I managed to inflict a pretty severe cut on the leg of the man who shot at us,' said Kella. 'Bulko has a nasty gash in the same place. I noticed that on the couple of occasions I visited his school afterwards, Bulko had stopped wearing shorts in favour of slacks or a long *lap-lap*. I should have put two and two together at the time, but I didn't. Perhaps I didn't want to. Sol was my friend.'

'Mendana Gau's evidence will convict Bulko,' said Lorrimer confidently. 'We'll find their man in the Customs Department, and he'll probably talk as well.'

'So Bulko overreached himself when he stole that *havu*,' said Chief Superintendent Grice.

'As I said, he got greedy,' said Kella. 'He was the brains behind the operation, not a thief up in the bush like Mendana Gau.

Mind you, you can see the temptation. The *havu* will fetch tens of thousands of dollars from the right collector in Australia or the USA.'

'Why on earth weren't the police sent for in the first instance?' demanded Chief Superintendent Grice indignantly. 'That's what we're here for.'

'You're forgetting, sir,' Kella reminded his superior with quiet satisfaction. 'There was no one on patrol in the high bush at the time. You had withdrawn me from Malaita in the run-up to the theft. That's why Pazabosi was able to kidnap Professor Mallory and hold him as a possible negotiating tool in case he had to confront the renegade Hita.'

In fact, thought Kella, Pazabosi had kidnapped Mallory for the same reason that he had placed a public bones *tabu* on the police sergeant. The old chief had known that his ostentatious flouting of the official law would only incense Kella and make him all the more determined to invade the high bush country to find out what was happening there. In the process, it was highly likely that the sergeant would come up against the hot-headed Hita and either arrest or kill him, thus disposing of the old chief's only rival, and allow him to enter the last days of his life in the tranquil contemplation of the *trochea*. Again, this would all be too complicated to attempt to explain to his English superiors.

'Incredible,' said Grice. 'Let me see if I've got it right. The two villagers who murdered Lofty Herman before the Japanese could find him are dead. Hita slaughtered Peter Oro as a sign for saltwater people to keep out of Kwaio country, and half-killed Mendana Gau for taking custom carvings from the area, but now Hita's dead as well. The headman ordered the custom killing of Senda Iabuli because the old man was in league with the devil. Well, we'll never be able to prove anything there.'

'That's about it, sir,' said Kella.

Grice brightened up. 'On the other hand,' he said, 'we've

broken up an artifacts smuggling racket. We've arrested Solomon Bulko and Mendana Gau for the smuggling. We've also recovered Professor Mallory unharmed. All in all, not bad work, not bad at all.'

'Thank you, sir,' said Kella humbly.

'Although,' frowned the chief superintendent, 'we can't prove that John Cho was involved in the Honiara end of the smuggling, and above all, we haven't recovered the *havu*.'

'I'm afraid not, sir.'

'So there you are,' said Grice sententiously. 'It's rounding off the details of a case which is important. Tidying matters up. Bear that in mind in future, Sergeant Kella.'

'Oh, I shall, sir,' said Kella. 'Thank you very much.' To his right Lorrimer was unable to suppress a snort of derision. 'Excuse me, sir,' the sergeant went on. 'Do you know what's going to happen to Father Pierre and Sister Conchita, now that Father Pierre is no longer a suspect?'

'The old priest was never a suspect,' said Grice quickly. 'He was just giving us the benefit of his considerable experience on Malaita. I understand that he and Sister Conchita will be returning to Ruvabi in the near future.' The chief superintendent paused for effect. 'So you'll be able to see them both when you return to Malaita,' he concluded with a flourish.

'Return?' asked Kella, his pulse quickening.

Grice waved an embarrassed hand. 'You didn't do such a bad job over there this time,' he conceded gruffly. 'I suppose there's something to be said for local knowledge. You're being put back in charge of the Auki sub-station – strictly for a probationary period, of course.'

'Of course,' said Kella contentedly. 'Thank you, sir; that's good news.'

'Incidentally,' said the chief superintendent, changing tack, 'this Sister Conchita, could she be described as eccentric?'

'Sister Conchita could be described as many things, sir,' replied Kella, his heart beginning to sink. What sort of trouble had the nun got him into this time?

'Extraordinary woman. She stopped me in the street the other day to praise you to the skies.'

'I'm sorry she bothered you,' said Kella.

'No, no, it was no problem. Bit of a surprise, that's all. Still, we need all the good public relations we can get. Well done, sergeant!'

'Thank you, sir,' said Kella.

It certainly was good news about going back to Malaita, thought Kella, still luxuriating in a warm glow as other guests, white and Melanesian, began to enter the thatched church and fill up the benches. Sister Conchita may have overdone it as usual by teasing Chief Superintendent Grice in public, but by her standards it had been a relatively minor riposte, and as such one to be thankful for.

Someone slid into place next to him. It was the rotund Sergeant Ha'a, glistening with sweat and looking unusually excited.

'That Mallory,' he said wistfully in an undertone. 'Shacked up for days with three Sikaiana women. Do you think he'll ever recover?'

'I don't think he's bothered much whether he does or not,' whispered Kella. 'Bound to have some good memories though.'

'Even if only from a wheelchair with a rug over his knees as he sips his cocoa.'

'Anyway, what are you doing here?' asked Kella. 'Do you want to talk about Sikaiana women, or are you thinking of turning Catholic?'

'I know which of those two I'd prefer,' said Ha'a promptly.

Reluctantly the plump police sergeant tore himself away from his erotic reverie and returned to business.

'We've cracked the artifacts smuggling business,' he said with an air of triumph.

'How did you manage that?' asked Kella.

'One of the sisters from the mission was down at the wharf the other day. She noticed that a box of schoolboy carvings from Ruvabi contained genuine custom carvings. She came to HQ with the news. Luckily she met me there, and I took over.'

'Was that Sister Conchita?'

'As a matter of fact it was. How did you know?'

'I guessed,' said Kella.

'Right. Anyway, there's more. I flew back from the Western District this morning. Joe Dontate has given up his job as a troubleshooter for the Cho family. He's returned to Gizo to open another trading store.'

'He told me he was going to do that,' said Kella, recalling his conversation in Chinatown with the broken-nosed bartender. 'What about it?'

'As you know, the Cho family already own stores around Gizo and Munda in the West. They're trying to give Dontate a hard time.'

'Big mistake.'

'I'll say,' chuckled Ha'a. 'Joe wants to reciprocate and provide the Chos with some grief before he squeezes them out.'

'How?'

'When the custom carvings reached Honiara, one of the Customs inspectors in Cho's pay took them out of the box from Ruvabi and and smuggled them out to Cho. From what I can make out, Cho has a network of suppliers all over Malaita – traders, planters, teachers and the rest. Dontate told me that he knows where John Cho keeps those carvings. The Chinaman hasn't had time to ship the last lot out yet, with all the fuss over

Bulko's arrest and the heat being on. The crates are in a warehouse behind the Lantern Bar.' Ha'a paused for effect. 'Dontate thinks that the *havu* is probably stashed among the loot.' Ha'a hesitated and then said tentatively, 'Seeing as it's your case, I thought you might like to lead the raid on the warehouse.'

'You do it,' said Kella, his happiness intensifying. 'I have a modicum of faith in you.'

'Up yours too,' said Ha'a equably. His loud remark caused disapproving heads to turn from the benches around them. Ha'a started to slide away. He had been gunning for the Chos for a long time. 'I've had the place staked out since noon.' A thought occurred to the fat policeman and he slid back towards Kella.

'By the way,' he muttered, 'Joe Dontate says that if it will help, he'll be willing to give evidence in court that Cho tried to bribe you and that you turned him down. Can't be bad, eh?'

'Better than a slap in the belly with a raw bonito,' agreed Kella, thinking of the beating he had undergone on the beach. He looked up. 'By the way, does Superintendent Grice know anything about your plans?'

'Of course not,' said Ha'a, looking puzzled. 'Should I have told him?'

Kella thought for a moment. Then he decided that he and the superintendent were never destined to be bosom friends anyway.

'No,' he said decisively. 'What the hell! Why should we break the habit of a lifetime?'

'Why indeed?' agreed Sergeant Ha'a. The plump policeman sketched a salute and walked away, deliberately stepping on a number of well-shod expatriate feet as he did so. Kella returned to his thoughts. If he could return the *havu* to its waterfall temple, and persuade the bush people that it had been the long-gone American Mallory who had killed Hita, he might find himself accepted in the Kwaio territory again, especially as Pazabosi should now be well disposed towards him.

Kella thought that he ought to be able to persuade the bush people that the recent events were all part of a bargain negotiated with the ghosts. That should bring at least a temporary peace to the area, especially when it became known that Solomon Bulko was going to serve a long term of imprisonment for the theft of the icon and the attempted murder of Sister Conchita.

Kella was looking forward to returning to Malaita. For one thing, there was every chance that Elizabeth would still be waiting in Auki for a rare and hopefully long-delayed trading vessel to Sikaiana. He would also have to think hard about John Deacon. Kella considered the traces of yellow powder he had discovered in Lofty Herman's hut. It must have been the residue of the gold prospected by the beachcomber from the river nearby. No islander would have entered the *tabu* hut to steal anything. Mendana Gau had fled from the threat of the Japanese long before Herman's death.

That left only Deacon. Kella had been wrong in suspecting him of trying to kill Sister Conchita, but there were too many other black marks on the plantation owner's record in the islands. Kella would have to find out exactly when the Australian had sailed from Malaita to join in fighting the Japanese on Guadalcanal in 1942. The police sergeant was prepared to bet that he had not gone until after the death of Lofty Herman.

Almost certainly, Deacon had stolen the deposits of gold stored in Herman's hut. He had then left in his vessel to harry the Japanese, having recruited Kella and Pazabosi and a few others as his crew members. After the war he must have sold the gold to pay a lump sum for the first few years' lease on the plantation.

By buying the plantation lease with anything stolen from a dead man, Deacon had breached custom law, so now all bets were off. Perhaps, thought Kella, it would be a fitting punishment to seize the land back from the Australian and at the same time please his brothers by letting them take over and work the copra when the current lease ran out at the end of the year. Kella would have to consult the spirits about the matter.

In the meantime, there was the white man's church service to enjoy, he thought, relaxing. Again, he wondered who had invited him. He hoped that it had been Sister Conchita. He did not yet know her well, but her doughty reaction to the dangers of the swamp had mightily impressed him. It saddened Kella to think that because of his slowness in solving the crimes on Malaita, Sister Conchita and Father Pierre had been forced to spend time away from their beloved mission at Ruvabi.

Perhaps it had all been for the best though, he thought optimistically. He had heard about Sister Conchita's pilgrimage up Mount Austen to meet the dream-maker. Father Pierre must have thought highly of the young nun to send her up into the high ground in an effort to start to add the Lau truth to her existing Christian beliefs. She still had a long way to go, but it would not be dull in the Solomons with the Praying Mary around, and it would certainly be interesting to observe her progress. Although, thought Kella ruefully, with the nun's apparent predilection for stirring up trouble, it would be best, whenever possible, to do so from a safe distance.

The voices of the island choir swelled. A procession entered the church from the back, led by the bishop. After a coterie of priests, Sister Conchita and other white-robed teachers followed him in a demure line, eyes cast down. As she passed his row Kella looked up at the sister. Her face was calm and contemplative, almost rigid in its concentration. Yet as she glided by her eyes flickered up for a moment in the police sergeant's direction and Kella could have sworn that the nun had winked at him.

In the same moment, Sister Conchita started to mouth something. The sergeant leant forward to catch the breathed words before they were borne lightly away.

'We're going home, Kella!' whispered Sister Conchita joyously.

Chapter One

THE JAPANESE DESTROYER *came out of the night at forty knots like
a huge shark snarling across the lagoon. It struck the small American craft
and cut it in half before disappearing into the blackness. Part of the fragile
plywood and mahogany vessel sank almost at once, with two of the thirteen-
man crew already dead. Sprays of gasoline were flung across the surface of
the water, burning intermittently.*

*The young lieutenant in command of the craft had been at the wheel
when the ramming had occurred. Fearing that the flames spreading
across the water might reach the chewed-up remnants of the vessel and
destroy them, he ordered the survivors over the side. In seconds, the
crushing wake of the already invisible destroyer had extinguished the
blaze. The eleven survivors, two of them badly hurt, hauled themselves
back on board.*

*They remained huddled on the fractured, water-slopped deck until
daybreak. As the sun edged over the horizon, the two ensigns and eight
enlisted men looked to the lieutenant for instructions.*

*'What do you want to do if the Japs come out?' he asked. 'Fight or
surrender?'*

*The remaining half of the plywood coffin began to settle in the water,
almost obscuring the inscription on its splinter shield: PT-109.*

1

Chapter Two

'THE PROBLEM IS,' said Sister Brigid, loudly enough for Sister Conchita to hear above the noise of the crowd, 'when does an inconvenience transcend into sacrilege?'

Sister Conchita smiled sweetly and resisted the temptation to batter the elderly Irish nun about the head and shoulders with one of the carvings for sale on the table by the door leading to the refectory. On display were ebony walking sticks inlaid with mother of pearl, patterned pandanus baskets, vicious-looking stone war clubs and the engraved prows of several miniature war canoes, known as *toto iso*. Sister Jean Francoise should have been in charge of the stall, but Conchita could see the French nun through the open window, her habit hitched above her scrawny ankles, paddling contentedly in one of the rock pools on the white-sand beach, ignoring the visitors eddying around her. That left only Sister Johanna, and she almost certainly would be engrossed in dismantling and reassembling a piece of domestic machinery somewhere in the building.

In the reception room of the old stone building, the visitors to the mission's first ever open day surged through the doors and out into the gardens leading down to the reef and the open blue sea beyond. Behind the house, wooded foothills swelled in green profusion until they merged into the extinct volcanic mountain in the centre of the small island. Marakosi was a beautiful enough mission station; it was a pity about the three elderly rapscallions who had

3

made up its religious complement for so many decades and who were slowly driving Sister Conchita mad.

'It's all very *modern*,' said Sister Brigid in a tone that emphasized that the word was not meant as a compliment.

'Please keep circulating,' Sister Conchita exhorted the visitors, continuing to ignore the older nun. There was hardly room to move inside the house. 'The whole mission and its grounds are open to you today.'

'And don't we know it,' said Sister Brigid loudly, to no one in particular. 'There's not room left to swing a cat.'

There was no doubt about it, thought Sister Conchita, smiling until her face hurt, she would have to fetch Sister Jean Francoise back inside. The elderly French sister might be as crazy as a coot, but at least she seemed to have some influence on Sister Brigid. Perhaps she could keep the acerbic Irish nun quiet until the guests had left. It definitely was time to clutch at straws. Brigid was a sour, withdrawn woman who spent most of her time as far as Conchita could make out standing on the reef staring out at the lagoon. Officially she was in charge of housekeeping at the mission, but the layers of dust everywhere and the dreadful food they had been eating for the last month bore witness to her lack of commitment in these areas.

'Excuse me,' said Sister Conchita brightly, pushing through the throng like a very small but extremely determined running back. There were at least sixty visitors in the room and another two or three hundred scattered about the mission building and grounds. They were mostly Solomon Islanders, bolstered by a few expatriates from the nearby tiny district centre of Gizo, all attracted by the prospect of seeing what the notorious Marakosi Mission was really like. Leavening the attendance was a group of bewildered-looking American tourists who were staying at the government

rest-house over at Munda, a nearby island. The Solomons consisted of a string of hundreds of beautiful and remote tropical
islands, five hundred miles east of Papua New Guinea and a thousand miles north-east of Australia. The islands were difficult to
reach, and the tourist trade was in its infancy.

There was a human logjam at the door leading to the small in-
house chapel used by the sisters for their private devotions. A bulky
female American tourist in shorts stretched dangerously across her
thighs had stopped in the open doorway and was brandishing a
carved model of a turtle above her head.

'Where do I pay for this?' she demanded.

'We must all pay for our transgressions eventually,' said Sister
Brigid coldly before Sister Conchita could reply, her voice rising
and falling like a dagger plunging with deadly accuracy into a body.
'How and when lies in the hands of the Almighty.'

Not if I get to you first, Sister Conchita promised herself
vengefully, squeezing past and emerging from the front door of the
two-storey mission house on to the stone terrace leading to the
beach and the calm lagoon beyond. Blocks of coral jutting out
into the sea broke the force of the waves thundering against them
in the distance beyond the reef and provided a safe anchorage for
smaller vessels. She stopped outside, luxuriating in the sudden
peace, although even here her mind was registering automatically
the improvements needed. The ancient and cracked mission bell
used to regulate the nuns' day with its strident summonses to
matins, lauds, vespers and compline was suspended from a
crossbar between two wooden posts that needed strengthening. It
was tolled from the first sunrise Mass, and then regularly through
the day to summon the nuns to meals and work sessions, ending
with evening prayers.

Those visitors who had escaped from the heat of the house

were scattered across the sand. The flower beds around the mission were overgrown and unkempt. A vegetable patch had surrendered almost completely to rough grass. Chickens and pigs wandered unchecked around the fringes of the crowd. A few dispirited yams struggled through the baked earth. It would not have been difficult to rotate the crops, with sweet potatoes following cabbage, but no one had made any effort to do so.

Conchita could not imagine why so many visitors had turned up. It might not be much, she thought, but the open day was probably the most interesting thing that had happened at the mission for generations.

There was so much to do, and it looked as if she was going to have to do most of it herself during her stay, she agonized, heading for Sister Jean Francoise, who was still paddling happily, oblivious to the strangers all around her. Like the other two nuns on the station, she would be well into her seventies now, small and bird-like in her movements, her face lined and weathered brown by the sun, but still possessing traces of the pretty and vivacious country girl she must once have been before she came to the Solomons.

'Sister Jean Francoise,' coaxed Conchita. 'We really do need your help in the mission. Do you think you could possibly spare us an hour or so?'

The French nun looked up from contemplating the smooth surface of the rock pool. She smiled beatifically, radiating an all-pervading charm.

'In the mission?' she asked with only a faint trace of an accent. 'But I am the laundry and garden sister. I seldom enter the mission except to eat, pray and sleep.' She paused, and then giggled. 'Almost literally I have been put out to pasture.'

'Even so, it is our first open day. There are so many people here. We could do with your help.'

'Open day?' Sister Jean Francoise looked about her vaguely, as if seeing the visitors for the first time. 'Oh yes, I remember something about that. An effort to modernize us, I believe. Throwing the mission open to the public. I don't understand. It is most unlike Father Karl to approve of such a thing. He is a very private man.'

'I'm afraid that Father Karl is dead,' said Sister Conchita.

An expression of sadness passed over the elderly nun's face. 'Oh yes.' She nodded. 'Now I remember. The poor man was ill for so long. You know, he got quite senile towards the end. It must be very sad, when your mind goes.' She started hopping around the pool again, sending up tiny splashes of water. 'I believe they're sending a sister from Honiara to run the mission until a new priest is appointed, some American girl with a strange name. I wonder when she will arrive.'

'I'm the new sister in charge,' said Conchita. 'I'm Sister Conchita. I've been here a few weeks now. That's why—'

'What an unusual name,' mused Sister Jean Francoise. 'Do you perhaps have Mexican antecedents? Of course, that would be nothing to be ashamed of. Perhaps you could teach the children at the school La Danza del Venado. That's where they have to imitate deer, you know.'

'I'm afraid I don't dance. As for my name, I thought originally that I was going to be sent to a mission in South America after I had finished my training,' said Conchita automatically. She had given this explanation many times since her arrival in the Solomon Islands. 'So I picked what I thought would be an appropriate name for the region.'

'And then they sent you here instead,' said Sister Jean Francoise, placing a damp, sympathetic hand on the other nun's arm. 'I really don't envy you, my dear. You're so young and we've all been here so long. I imagine that the more senior members of the staff in

Honiara prudently turned down the chance to reform us and left us to your best efforts. I'm afraid we've all got rather set in our ways at Marakosi.'

You can say that again, thought Conchita, trying to be philosophical and forget the litany of slights, insults and outright insubordination that had already been her lot at the hands of her new colleagues, ever since the mission vessel had delivered her at the island.

'So, if you don't mind, Sister,' she said, indicating the mission building.

'If I don't mind what?' asked Sister Jean Francoise, wriggling her toes sybaritically in the warm water. She looked across at a school of dolphins playing out in the lagoon.

With an effort, Sister Conchita forced herself to be patient. 'I'd like you to help us inside.'

'Why, certainly,' said Sister Jean Francoise, raising an eyebrow in surprise and stepping out of the pool, slipping her feet into an ancient pair of flip-flops. 'You only had to ask.'

The French nun started to walk towards the building. A thought seemed to strike her and she looked back. 'By the way, who are you, my dear?' she asked vaguely.

'I've told you, I'm Sister Conchita.'

'Ah.' A twinkle appeared in the nun's eye. Suddenly she seemed neither aged nor abstracted. 'I expect you really want me in the mission to keep Sister Brigid under control. She can be something of a trial, I agree, and she doesn't usually take to strangers because she's so shy. She's Irish, you know, and occasionally outspoken. She has the heart of a lion, though. During the war she guided the crew of a crashed American aircraft for three days through the Japanese-occupied territory to safety. It was so sad what happened to her after that. She hasn't left Marakosi for ages. None of us have, I suppose.

We must be adding a whole new meaning to the term "enclosed society".'

Sister Jean Francoise waved and walked away, nodding affably to the visitors she passed. Exasperated, Sister Conchita wondered how much of the Frenchwoman's apparent senility was an act. She prepared to follow the other nun. There was so much to do that afternoon. There were refreshments to prepare and serve to the visitors, prescriptions to be made up and bandages cut in the dispensary, plans for a proposed new boarding school to be put before the other nuns, the kiln used for melting coral into limestone for walls to be serviced, and above all the eccentric and unpredictable sisters to be supervised in their idiosyncratic endeavours.

In spite of her resolve, Sister Conchita felt very tired. Impulsively she turned and entered the mission church, a large, sprawling building with a sloping red tin roof and thin white stone walls. If she were to take her problems to the Lord for a few minutes it would help.

It was dark and cool inside. In front of the altar table were rows of wooden benches placed on an earthen floor packed hard by the feet of generations and covered with woven mats and sand. A large upturned shell served as a font. A metal candle-snuffer leant against it. A hand-carved mahogany cross hung from one of the walls. Gratefully Conchita began to yield to the ambience of calm, something in short supply since she had arrived on the island.

She saw with a start that someone else was already inside the building. He was a white man of about forty, plump and dishevelled, in white shorts and a floral shirt. He was well below average height, resembling an aggressive jockey who had ridden too many losing horses. He was kneeling in front of the altar rail, one arm extended to rest on the carved wooden cross in an attitude of supplication. Instinctively Sister Conchita turned to leave him alone, but the man heard her and scrambled clumsily to his feet.

'Pardon me,' he said in a New York accent. 'I was just resting. It's so hot outside.'

'For a moment,' smiled Sister Conchita, embarrassed at intruding on what obviously had been a private moment, 'I thought you might be claiming sanctuary.'

'Is that what it looked like?' said the man vaguely. He began to move away from the altar rail. He did not come up to Sister Conchita's shoulder. 'A lot of people would like the chance of that in their lives, I suppose. To find a safe place, set aside from normal existence, especially if someone's looking for you.'

'Certainly, if that is what you seek.' Conchita was surprised. The man looked more like a miniature hoodlum than a philosopher. She really must stop making snap judgements. 'However,' she went on, trying to marshal her thoughts, 'some claim that sanctuary is in fact the spot where heaven and earth meet. In strictly legal terms, of course, the concept of using a church as a place to claim safety was done away with in the seventeenth century.'

'That's a shame,' said the man. 'You can never find a refuge when you need one.'

'Of course,' said Conchita, 'it must be remembered that the guilty have never been protected merely by the presence of the sacred. A degree of repentance also has to be involved.'

'Oh, that old thing,' said the man. 'I'm Ed Blamire, by the way. I'm with the tour party.'

'Sister Conchita,' said the nun, taking the small man's extended hand. She hesitated, anxious to get back to her duties in the house but aware that somehow the visitor to the mission needed her. 'What do you do for a living, Mr Blamire?' she asked politely.

'Oh, I've done a lot of things in my time,' said the tourist.

'Tinker, tailor, candlestick-maker, security, pilot, tree-hugger, I even dived for pearls off Hawaii for a time.'

'Very interesting,' said Conchita. 'However, at the moment I feel that you are looking for something. Can I help?'

For a moment she thought the tourist was going to say something of importance to her. Then he shook his head and turned away.

'One thing I haven't been is a good Catholic,' he said.

'Welcome to the club,' said Sister Conchita.

'I remember one or two things though,' said the man. '*The letter kills but the spirit gives life*, is that right?'

'The Second Book of Corinthians,' said the nun. 'Very well, Mr Blamire, I shall be here at the mission if you would care to talk to me. Good afternoon.'

As she headed for the side door of the church, Blamire had turned back and was standing in front of the altar again, his shoulders slumped. Sister Conchita knelt in the aisle and prayed quickly for the other sisters at the mission, for herself that she might be fit for her new task, and for the tourist at the altar who seemed lost and troubled.

She emerged from the church to an area of the beach roped off from the rest of the mission grounds and hidden from sight of most of the visitors by the church building. A huge pile of coconut husks had been assembled to a height of ten feet above the ground. This was Sister Conchita's brainchild. She had been preparing it for most of the month since she had arrived at Marakosi, ever since she had learned that it had been a mission tradition dating back to before the war that ships visiting the station would be greeted by a blazing pyre of husks set off by the nuns.

A wooden torch soaked in oil and a box of matches lay on the ground ready for the ceremony. Sister Conchita intended to wait until dusk, just before the open day was due to end, and then ignite the bonfire to bid farewell to the departing guests. She checked that everything was in place and went back round the side of the church to join the crowd.

She noticed with satisfaction that the other attractions she had organized for the day seemed to be drawing plenty of attention. Among the outer fringe of trees, Malaitan labourers from the local logging camp, supervised by a white overseer, were felling a kapok tree with a two-man power saw, while others were stripping the branches from several felled trees with economical blows from their bush knives. On a marked-out course on the sand, islanders were racing one another over a sixty-yard distance carrying heavy bags of copra on their shoulders.

Out in the lagoon, a dozen large canoes provided the incongruous sight of members of a brass band lustily playing 'Abide With Me' on their highly polished cornets, trumpets, tubas and trombones. This was the self-styled Silver Band of the Christian Fellowship Church, a recent breakaway denomination from the United Methodist Church of the Solomons. Its members had built a village called Paradise on the nearby island of New Georgia. The leader of the new church, the Holy Mama, who claimed to be the fourth member of the Trinity, was sitting approvingly in one of the canoes of the flotilla, waving his arms decorously in time to the music. He was an elderly islander wearing a long white robe and a shell-decorated turban. Sister Brigid and the other nuns had objected to his presence because he was reputed to have designated a dozen of the most attractive girls from his island as his personal angels. The more pragmatic Sister Conchita had felt, as the moment drew near, that her cherished open day threatened to be so lacking in entertainment that she was willing to overlook any teething troubles experienced by the CFC and the personal peccadilloes of its founder, as long as its instrumentalists could provide a selection of rousing hymns played roughly in tune.

On her way back to the mission house, Sister Conchita could not put the man in the floral shirt out of her mind. Had she ignored a cry for help? Mr Blamire had denied the fact, but perhaps she should have been more sensitive to his needs, whatever they might have been. It seemed to her that the plump man in the church had been very frightened.

By the time she arrived back inside, Sister Johanna had appeared from the recesses of the house. Tall and angular, with a face apparently consisting of little but straight planes, the German nun had a forbidding appearance. Her hands were deeply engrained with dirt and oil, brought about by years of toil as the mission's mechanical genius. There were several smudges on her face. She greeted Conchita with a chilly nod.

'So many people,' she said gutturally. 'One would almost suppose that your plan had been a success, Sister Conchita.'

Sister Brigid snorted. 'Nonsense! It's all an irrelevance. What are we to expect next? Swings and roundabouts? This used to be a working mission.'

'Not for some years, as I understand it,' said Conchita, before she could stop herself. She was at once aware from the severe expressions on the faces of the other sisters that she had made yet another error. 'I believe that you have been more of a contemplative order lately,' she said in an effort to redress the balance. 'I have never served in a cloistered mission before.'

'How long have you been in the Solomon Islands now?' asked Sister Brigid after a chilly pause.

'Six months.'

'You are surely very young to have been appointed to a position of authority,' said Sister Johanna. 'Even over us.'

The other nuns laughed. Conchita resolved that they would not trample her underfoot again that afternoon.

'As it happens, I'm twenty-six,' she said, 'but I feel that I'm growing older by the minute, Sister.'

'Twenty-six,' said Sister Johanna. 'I have habits older than that.'

Sister Brigid cackled. It was strange, thought Conchita, how protective the other two nuns seemed of her, and how quick they were to come to the defence of such an apparently graceless and unpleasant woman.

'You mustn't tease the child,' said Sister Jean Francoise vaguely. 'I'm sure she means well. She's new, that's all.'

From out in the grounds there came a sudden crackling noise. This was followed almost at once by a muffled roar, and then by screams of terror from the visitors on the beach.

The sisters looked askance at each other. Conchita was the first to guess what was happening.

'Someone's set fire to the bonfire too soon!' she said.

She turned and led the other nuns out of the house and down past the church to the roped-off area containing her laboriously prepared bonfire. Most of the other visitors were hurrying in the same direction, gathering by the ropes. The heat from the fire was almost unbearable. Thick clouds of smoke obscured the pile of coconut husks. A sudden swirling breeze parted the smoke, revealing the fact that the husks were now blazing.

One of the female tourists screamed and pointed at the side of the pyre. The other visitors took up her cry. Sprawling across the side of the blaze, almost in an upright position, was the body of a white man in a floral shirt. His eyes were open and he was staring sightlessly at the crowd. Two courageous islanders charged forward and dragged the smouldering body free of the husks. They hurled the man to the ground and beat out the flames with several of the empty sacks in which the coconuts had been collected.

Conchita forced herself to go forward. The islanders stood aside, shaking their heads dolefully. The nun knelt at the side of the man. Enough remained of his charred face and body to enable her to recognize that it was the tourist Ed Blamire, and that he was dead.

'Take him up to the hospital,' she whispered to the islanders, although she knew that it was too late to do anything for him. The two men took Blamire's body by the shoulders and legs and carried him through the now silent and awe-struck crowd.

'Ladies and gentlemen,' said Conchita, rising and facing the visitors. 'There has been a dreadful accident. I'm afraid that the open day must end at once. Will you please leave as quickly as possible?'

The crowd began to disperse in small shocked knots. Conchita saw that the other three nuns were accompanying the body back to the mission house. She hesitated, and entered the church through the side door to say a prayer for the dead tourist. Inside, the place was a shambles. The altar table had been knocked over, the crucifix had been torn from the wall, the shell font had been smashed and several benches had been overturned. Sister Conchita surveyed the carnage.

'Sanctuary!' she muttered to herself in horror.

OTHER TITLES IN THE SOHO CRIME SERIES